Hope: A Tragedy

Hope: A Tragedy

Shalom Auslander

W F HOWES LTD

This large print edition published in 2012 by
W F Howes Ltd
Unit 4, Rearsby Business Park, Gaddesby Lane,
Rearsby, Leicester LE7 4YH

1 3 5 7 9 10 8 6 4 2

First published in the United Kingdom in 2012
by Picador

A CIP catalogue record for this book is available
from the British Library

ISBN 978 1 47120 589 7

Typeset by Palimpsest Book Production Limited,
Falkirk, Stirlingshire
Printed and bound in Great Britain
by MPG Books Ltd, Bodmin, Cornwall

MIX
Paper from
responsible sources
FSC® C018575
www.fsc.org

We were liberated from death,
from the fear of death;
but the fear of life started.

H. Rosensaft, Yesterday: My Story

Hide in the sky,
hide in the sky,
who wants to come with me
and hide in the sky?

Serj Tankian

CHAPTER 1

It's funny: It isn't the fire that kills you, it's the smoke.

There you are, pounding on the windows, climbing higher and higher through your burning home, trying to get away, to get out, hoping that if you can just avoid the flames, perhaps you'll survive the fire, but all the time you're suffocating slowly, your lungs filling with smoke. There you are, waiting for the horrors to come from some *there*, from some *other*, from without, and all the while you're dying, bit by airless bit, from within.

You buy a handgun – for protection, you say – and drop dead that night from a heart attack.

You put locks on your doors. You put bars on your windows. You put gates around your house. The doctor phones: It's cancer, he says.

Swimming frantically up to the surface to escape from a menacing shark, you get the bends and drown.

You resolve, one sunny New Year's Day, to get back into shape. This is the year, you insist. A new beginning. A new start. A stronger you, a tougher you. At the health club the following morning, just as you're beginning your third set of bench presses, your muscles cramp and the barbell collapses onto your neck, crushing your windpipe. You can't cry out. Your face turns blue. Your arms go limp. There, on a poster on the wall beside you, are the last words you see before your eyes close and darkness envelopes you for eternity:

Feel the Burn.

It's funny.

CHAPTER 2

Solomon Kugel was lying in bed, thinking about suffocating to death in a house fire, because he was an optimist. This was according to his trusted guide and adviser, Professor Jove. So desperate was Kugel for things to turn out for the best, proclaimed Professor Jove, that he couldn't stop worrying about the worst. Hope, said Professor Jove, was Solomon Kugel's greatest failing.

Kugel was trying to change. It wouldn't be easy. He hoped that he could.

Kugel stared silently at the ceiling above his bed and listened.

He heard something.

He was certain of it.

Up there.

In the attic.

What is that? he wondered.

A scratching?

A rapping?

A tap-tap-tapping.

The other reason Solomon Kugel was lying in bed, thinking about suffocating to death in a house

3

fire, was that someone was burning down farmhouses, just like the one he and his wife had recently purchased. The arson began soon after the Kugels moved in; three farmhouses had been torched in the six weeks since. The Stockton chief of police vowed he would catch whoever was responsible. Kugel was hopeful that he would, but hadn't slept since the first farmhouse lit up and burned down.

There it was again.

That sound.

Maybe it was mice.

It was probably mice.

There are a hundred farms around here, jackass. Why would he target you? It's *farm* country.

You're frightening yourself.

You're torturing yourself.

It's narcissistic.

It's delusions of grandeur.

It's optimism.

It's mice.

Didn't sound like mice, though.

Kugel thought frequently about death and even more frequently about dying. Was this, too, he wondered, because he was an optimist? Precisely, Professor Jove had declared. Kugel loved life, observed Professor Jove, and so he expected far too much of it; hell-bent on life, he was terrified that someone would cause, by violence or accident, his untimely death. Kugel, in his own defense, pointed out that he didn't think anyone was actually trying to kill him, he simply thought it well

4

within the realm of possibility that somebody, unbeknownst to him and for reasons yet to be revealed, might be; there is a line, he argued, thin as it may be, between paranoia and pragmatism.

Kugel's mother, for her part, worried less about death than she did about life. Her own life, sadly, had gone too well, too smoothly; above average in comfort and security, below average in suffering and pain; better than anyone had a right to expect and callously lasting far longer than anyone could rightly demand. Alive, and happy, she cried.

Kugel thought specifically about the experience of dying. He thought about the pain, about the fear. Most of all, he thought about what he would say at the final moment; his *ultima verba*; his last words. They should be wise, he decided, which is not to say morose or obtuse; simply that they should mean something, amount to something. They should reveal, illuminate. He didn't want to be caught by surprise, speechless, gasping, not knowing at the very last moment what to say.

No, wait, I *oof*.

I haven't really given it much *splat*.

If I could just *ka-blammo*.

We are all mankind a story, collectively and individually, and Kugel didn't want his individual story to end in an ellipsis. A period, sure, if you're lucky. An exclamation mark, okay. A question mark, probably; that seemed the punctuation all stories, collectively and individually, should end with after all.

Not an ellipsis, though.

Anything but an ellipsis.

Don't end it like this, said Pancho Villa, at a loss for words after being shot nine times in the chest and head. Tell them, he said before dying, I said something.

Kugel kept a small notebook and pen with him at all times for just these thoughts; now and then, when a fitting last sentiment or final set of words occurred to him, he would quickly write them down. Over the years he had filled many such notebooks but had yet to arrive at the precise right notion. The difference between the right word and the wrong word, said Mark Twain, is the difference between lightning and the lightning bug.

Twain's last words, to his daughter, were: If we meet . . .

Then he died.

So timing's important, too.

Kugel hoped, when the time came, that whatever he said would someday be re-said; would be heard and retold, for however many generations remained before The End. He hoped it would be something his beloved son, Jonah, could remember; something the boy could look to in times of trouble long after his father had passed, and find within those few carefully chosen words some light, some guidance, some wisdom (assuming, of course, that Jonah didn't predecease him, or that they didn't die together, father and son, in some tragic accident; were that to be the case, Kugel knew exactly what he would say to Jonah as the plane, for example, was plunging toward earth: he would say, I'm sorry. I'm sorry, but at least it's over. Or something to that effect: Well, son, that was the rough part. The living's over. After this, kid, it's all gravy . . .).

This, ultimately, is what Kugel hoped: that his last words would somehow make all this amount to something, all this . . . this life, this effort, this toil and time and terror. This unintentioned, unrelenting existence. That it wasn't just a stage, that we weren't merely players. Kugel could never believe in God, but he could never not believe in him, either; there should be a God, felt Kugel, even if there probably wasn't.

According to Luke, author of the Gospel of the same name, Jesus, dying on the cross, said this: Father, into thy hands I commend my spirit.

Eh.

A little obvious. A little self-congratulatory. A little smug. Where else was your spirit going to go but to God? The moment before you meet your Maker is probably not the best time to be acting like you're doing Him some big favor by commending Him your soul.

Kugel was approaching forty, and though he hadn't yet decided for certain what he wanted his last words to be, he had long known for certain what he didn't want them to be: he didn't want them to be begging. More than anything, he didn't

7

want to beg. No pleases. Or nos. Or waits. Or please, nos; or no, waits; or wait, pleases. Or no, no, nos. Or please, please, pleases. Or wait, wait, waits.

Please don't hurt me, Louis XV's mistress begged her executioner as he led her to the guillotine.

He hurt her.

Let's cool it, brothers, said Malcolm X to his assassins.

They shot him sixteen times.

Perhaps they had cooled it, thought Kugel. Perhaps they'd been planning on shooting him twenty times. It behooves the victim, in these matters, to be specific.

Kugel's dread of begging was due to neither a sense of pride nor a surfeit of courage; he simply hoped that he wouldn't be in a situation where begging might help. You can't beg old age. You can't beg cancer. He could live with those deaths. You can't beg a car not to hit you, a piano not to fall on your head. You can only beg people. Any situation where begging might be of some assistance had to be one in which your life was in the hands of another human being, a woefully precarious place for your life to be in. Kugel was determined not to die at the hands of another, if only to disprove his mother, who insisted that her last words, and her son's last words, and her son's son's last words, whatever they might be, would be said in a gas chamber.

8

Or in an oven.

Or at the bottom of a mass grave.

Or at the top of a mass grave.

There it was again. That tapping sound.

Placement in the mass grave mattered, Kugel supposed, only if you were still alive; if they shot you somehow in the leg or arm, and your wounds weren't fatal. In that case, it would be a far, far better thing to be at the bottom of the mass grave, where the weight of the corpses piled above would crush you to death and end your life quickly, mercifully, rather than dying slowly and painfully at the top of the corpse pile, perhaps even being alive when they buried you.

Tap. Tap-tap-tap.

He was sure of it.

In the attic.

Unless they shot into the corpse pile a second time. Then, of course, top of the corpse pile might be better.

This is what Samuel Beckett's father said right before he died: What a morning.

A bit of irony, thought Kugel. A smile. The laugh that laughs at that which is unhappy.

Or dropping dead.

He might use that:

What a day.

Looks like rain, suckers.

Kugel wondered what his own father's last words were, or if he had last words, or if he was dead or if he was alive.

Mistakes were made?

Kugel had a theory. Kugel was certain that whatever last *words* a person chose to utter in his final moments, everyone shared the same final *thought*, and this was it: the bewildered, dumbfounded statement of his own disappointing cause of death.

Shark?

Train? Really? I get hit by a *train*?

Malaria? Fuck off. *Malaria?*

Regardless of what was *spoken*, this and only this was a human's last *thought*, the last pure cognition that passed through a human being's mind, every human being's mind, before that mind ceased to function evermore. Not *Shema yisroel adonai elohainu adonai echad*. Not Forgive me, Father, for I have sinned. Only the ludicrous, laughable cause of its own unfathomable demise.

Cancer?

Tuberculosis?

Benito Mussolini's last words, as he faced his executioner were these:

Shoot me in the chest!

His last *thought*, though, Kugel was certain, was this:

Shot in the chest?

There it was again – that sound.

A scurrying of sorts. A sliding.

Kugel sat up.

It was something.

There was something up there.

No death, after all, does any life any justice. Our

10

endings are always a letdown, an insult, a surprise, dumber than we thought and less than we'd hoped for.

Crucifixion? thought Jesus. Get out.

Hemlock? thought Socrates.

Wrapped in a Torah scroll and burned alive? thought Rabbi Akiva. You have got to be shitting me.

That sound again.

What did an arsonist sound like, anyway?

Kugel listened.

Beside him, he could hear his Brianna, his Bree, his hero, his love, deep in her wonderful Prozacian slumber. He could hear Jonah, across the hall, bedsprings creaking as he shifted in his own deep sleep. Tylenolian.

It's a tough place to get some sleep.

Earth, that is.

Of course they didn't always shoot a second time into the mass graves. That's life for you: a colossal inescapable corpse pile – and no second shooting.

Kugel crept quietly from the bed and knelt on the floor beside the heating vent at the side of his nightstand. The wooden floor was hard against his knees, but he put his hands on either side of the vent, bent over, and pressed his ear against the cold metal register.

Through the vent, he could hear the tenant moving about in his bedroom downstairs (he'd moved in two weeks before, and Kugel still couldn't recall his name; it was Isaac, or Ishmael, or Esau – something biblical); he could hear the buzz of applause and laughter coming from the tenant's TV, which the tenant left on all night long. Below that he could hear Mother, in her bedroom beside the tenant's, moaning in agony and pain. Mother was alive if she sounded like she was dying; if she sounded like she was peacefully sleeping, then she was probably dead.

And he could definitely hear tapping.

Upstairs.

In the attic.

A ticking?

A tapping.

As if some mouse were gently crapping, crapping on his attic floor.

Like little mouse feet.

Like typing, almost.

Marsupial Proust, he joked. Jules Vermin. Franz Krapper.

It was probably just mice.

Quietly, so as not to wake Bree, Kugel stood, pulled on his robe, took the tall metal flashlight from beside his bed, tiptoed as best he could across the old, creaky floorboards, and stepped out into the coolness of the dark hallway.

Would an arsonist start a fire in the attic?

Don't they start them outside? Around the foundation?

It's not an arsonist.

You're being ridiculous.

He grabbed the rope that hung from the attic

door, and pulled it slowly toward him, hoping not to find an arsonist, hoping to find a mouse, hoping, at the very least, to find some mouse droppings; if he found mouse droppings he would know it had been a mouse making the noise, and then perhaps he could at last get some sleep.

Such is life, he thought as he unfolded the wooden attic stairs: you get to a point, one day, where you are hoping to find crap; where the best possible outcome of all possible outcomes would be the discovery, praise Jesus, of a pile of shit.

Kugel climbed the creaky stairs as quietly as he could.

Maybe it was a mouse.

He reached the top of the stairs. The attic felt hot, hotter than the rest of the house. The tapping suddenly ceased.

Hello? whispered Kugel.

Probably just a mouse.

Hello?

And, hearing no reply, Kugel crawled into the dank, damnable darkness above.

CHAPTER 3

T he rural village of Stockton, population twenty-four hundred, was famous for nothing. No one famous had lived there, no famous battles had been waged there, no famous movements arose there, no famous concerts had been held there. A popular local bumper sticker read: Nobody Slept Here. Birthplace of Nothing, read another. Recently, a local artist had placed mock historical markers around town; On This Spot, read one, the Framers of the Constitution of the United States of America Never Met. This Is Not the Place, read another, Where George Washington Battled the British; That Place Is Elsewhere.

Stockton's non-history was a matter of pride for the townspeople, and had, of late, begun to attract many former city dwellers, urban professional families, and young couples looking for a home unburdened by the past, unencumbered by history.

Like many other newcomers, the Kugels had chosen Stockton because history had not. They purchased an old wooden farmhouse where no Founding Fathers had spent their childhood, on twenty pristine acres of land the Lord never promised to anyone, overlooking a rolling, non-famous valley where nobody had ever done anything of much consequence to anyone. The Kugels wanted a new start, for each other, for themselves, for Jonah. After the past year, they all needed one.

Three years before, when Jonah was born, the midwife took him, wrapped him in a blanket, and handed him to Kugel. Kugel held the child in his arms, looked down into his big blue eyes, and whispered:

I'm sorry.

Lovely, Bree had said.

Jonah was beautiful and innocent and pure, so Kugel felt terrible guilt for bringing him into this world. To father a child was a horribly selfish act, a felony, in fact – everyone here in this world is a kidnap victim from some better place, or from no place at all, and Jonah had been dragged here, by Kugel and Bree, against his will, without provocation, without consent, without any good goddamned reason whatsoever beyond their own selfish desires.

Kugel looked down at the tiny person in his arms, pink and cold and furious, and shook his head.

He oughta sue, said Kugel.

It's a joyous moment for us all, said Bree. I'll tell him about it when he grows up.

If, said Kugel. *If* he grows up.

And then, last year, they'd almost lost him.

15

Jonah had always been a sickly child; he was spiritually gorgeous and physically a mess. Kind and generous and giving, and sneezing and coughing and diarrheic. He was fair, like Bree, and slight, like Kugel. Kugel gave him multivitamins, extra C, chewable zinc, probiotics, antibiotics, and something called Liquid Garden, a vile powdered nutritional drink, every glass of which was a killing field filled with the tortured remains of thirty vegetables and 'over seventeen fruits' (the lack of manufacturer's specificity on this issue made Kugel concerned about giving it to Jonah – they should know exactly how many fruits, shouldn't they? – but not as much as the idea of Jonah's dying of malnutrition if he didn't give it to him).

Bree was not as hopeful as Kugel that these pricey pills and costly concoctions would have much positive effect.

This child, she said, is going to have the most expensive pee in the Northeast.

Despite all Kugel's precautions, though, last winter, Jonah became terribly ill. One cold December night, there being no other symptoms besides a slight cough, Jonah's temperature suddenly spiked. As it was not uncommon for Jonah to be ill, or for his temperature to spike, Kugel and Bree didn't take too much notice, but over the next two days, Jonah's lungs quietly filled with fluid, he lost weight, and finally, after being rushed through the night to the nearest hospital,

16

he was placed in an isolation unit for almost three weeks.

Do you see now? Kugel had said to Bree.

Do *I* see?

Do you?

Do *you*?

Do *I*?

There had never been a conclusive diagnosis. It was probably, they were told, just a bug, but bugs these days were getting stronger, becoming more resistant. A cold today, said the nurse, is like flu ten years ago; a flu today is like pneumonia twenty years ago.

What's pneumonia today like? Kugel asked.

Like that, she said, pointing to Jonah in his bed, an oxygen mask strapped to his face, monitors monitoring, beepers beeping, tubes running from the tubes running from his skeletal arms.

We almost lost you there, little buddy, Kugel whispered to Jonah the morning of their discharge, gently smoothing the boy's hair with his hand. We almost lost you.

Lost me where? Jonah had asked Kugel.

It means you almost died, Bree had answered. It's an expression.

Jonah was focused on the television, where SpongeBob was doing his best to pacify a furious Squidward. At last the nurse brought their papers and Bree turned off the TV.

I'd rather be dead than lost, Jonah said to Bree.

Why? asked Bree.

Because if I'm dead I won't know it.

Well you're neither, said Bree. Let's get out of here.

The experience had taken its toll on their marriage. Kugel sensed that something bad had grown between himself and Bree, or, worse, that something good between them had diminished. He was upset with himself: Why hadn't he pressed the pediatrician more? Why hadn't he taken Jonah to the hospital sooner? Why hadn't he trusted his instincts? And he was upset with her, too – why couldn't she see how sick Jonah was? Where were her maternal instincts? Why didn't she get him immunized sooner (against what? against everything, goddamn it)? – and he suspected she felt the same about him, that they were mutually disappointed in the other's inability to save their child, to protect him, to keep the monsters from the house. The ark of their marriage, charged with delivering Jonah from the tumultuous storm of life, had been shown to be rickety, ramshackle, rheumatic; it had been nearly sunk by the tiniest of bugs. And so they decided to move, to flee. The city seemed filled with danger and disease, and every room of their apartment carried a memory of some disagreement, some argument between them, or, worse, some memory of Jonah's illness – the couch upon which he lay unmoving, the blanket they had wrapped him in as they dashed to the hospital. Early that spring, a friend told them about Stockton. They visited, stayed for a while and, one fine spring morning, met with a real estate agent named Eve, who showed them a farmhouse for sale just five miles out of town. Kugel hoped the country would be safer; Bree hoped it would simply calm her husband's nerves. Both hoped it would give them all a fresh start.

It was a small but charming farmhouse, built in the mid-1800s. It had originally sat on a plot of land over two hundred acres in size, but in recent years parcels of the land had been sold off to builders and developers. Still, the farmhouse came with twenty proud acres of dense woodland, and was in excellent structural condition for a home its age. A few minor upgrades had been done about twenty years earlier – the most significant of which were the installation of a modern forced-air heating system and the addition of four dormer windows to the attic – but it was otherwise original, from its period silver doorknobs to its period oak trim. Out front, two large bluestone slabs led up to a charming veranda with wide plank floors, turned columns, and a small metal chime that was never without a soft breeze to encourage its gentle song. There were two original stone fireplaces, one in the living room and one in what was now one of the two downstairs bedrooms; both of the hearths had been sealed when the forced-air system was put in, but they were charming, despite their lack of utility. There were two bedrooms upstairs, as well as the two downstairs; originally, the southern half of the downstairs had been a dining room, but as part of the remodel it was converted into two small bedrooms, which the Kugels decided could be rented out to help cover the mortgage; once they settled in, Bree could use the attic as her writing studio; it wasn't clean, she remarked, but it was reasonably well lit. Best of all, Eve informed them, Mr Messerschmidt, the elderly owner who lived there with his middle-aged son, was asking far below market value.

Why? asked Kugel. Is there something wrong with it?

Of course there's something wrong with it, Eve had said. I'll tell you what's wrong with it, Mr Kugel: The stairs creak when you step on them. There are flies in the summer and mice in the winter. Some of the windows stick, some don't open at all, and there's a funky smell in the spring that gets replaced by an even funkier smell in the fall. It's old, Mr Kugel, that's what's wrong with it, just like I'm old, and you are going to become old. It's imperfect in a world that demands perfection, its flaw is that it has flaws. Full disclosure, Mr Kugel: it's real. You want fake, I can show you fake. I've got a fake version of this farmhouse five miles up the road, costs ten times as much. The stairs are new, the windows are double-glazed, and the natural swimming hole was drained, dried, dug up, and turned into an unnatural swimming pool – heated, chlorinated, backwashed, and skimmed. The soil in the backyard was trucked in from up north, the grass came in great green rolls on the back of a flatbed truck from down south. There's a patio made of concrete that was made to look like stone, a deck made of plastic that's made to look like wood. There's a chef's kitchen that's never used because the couple that built it never cooked. It's insulated so well that you won't know if it's winter or summer without looking out the window, which you wouldn't do because it's precisely what's outside that window that the house is insulated from: reality. Fake's going to cost you these days, Mr Kugel. Reality's on the block for cheap.

Kugel looked to Bree, squeezed her hand and smiled.

What about that smell? asked Bree.

What smell? asked Eve.

You don't smell something? asked Bree.

Kugel sniffed.

I smell something, said Kugel.

It smells, said Bree, like something died.

Eve smiled.

That, said Eve, is the smell of honesty, Mrs Kugel. That's the smell of someone not trying to pull the wool over your eyes. That's what truth smells like, folks, which is why you don't recognize it. Suck it up, Mrs Kugel, fill your lungs. The way the world out there is going, this may be the last time you smell it.

Mm-hmm, said Bree.

Kugel looked to Bree, squeezed her hand again, and smiled. They moved in four weeks later. Kugel's elderly mother joined them soon after.

You're kidding, said Bree.

She's dying, said Kugel.

We can't afford it, said Bree, vacillating between shock and rage. We need that rent to make the mortgage. What's the point of moving to a place with no past if you're going to bring your mother along?

They've given her two weeks, said Kugel.

But that, they both knew, had been well over six months before.

CHAPTER 4

I t was hot in the attic when Kugel climbed up into it, stiflingly so.

Kugel didn't like attics, he never had. The roofing nails overhead like fangs, waiting to sink into his skull; the cardboard boxes and plastic crates and leather trunks – tombs, sarcophagi – full of ghosts and regret and longing and loss; worse yet was the implication in all this emotional hoarding that the past was preferable to the present, that what came before bests whatever comes next, so clutch it to your chests in mourning and dread as you head into the unknowable but probably lousy future. Old hats, misshapen sweaters (always too small now, never too big), outdated electronics that seemed so impressive at the time and now seem so feeble and useless (was that the best we could do?), gift wrap for gifts never given, dirty magazines that outlived the dirty men who bought them, photos of people whose names one can no longer recall, letters from the long-since dead, stray keys to locks long since forgotten, locks whose keys were long since lost, things once deemed so important they required protection now no longer even remembered.

Kugel was a chucker.

Kugel chucked.

Mother was a hoarder.

She kept everything.

Ever since the war, she said with a sigh as she packed for the move to Kugel's new home, putting yet another torn, fading scrap of paper into yet another straining, overfilled box.

Most of Kugel's boxes were filled with books. Science, philosophy, art, literature; the philosophy of science, the science of literature, the art of philosophy, the science of art, books about other books and the books about those books about other books; Gogol on Pushkin, Nabokov on Gogol, Wilson on Nabokov on Gogol. Joyce on *The Odyssey*, Beckett on Joyce, everyone on Beckett. Kugel had grown weary of them, ashamed of them, in fact – of the hope he had placed in them, of the answers he had sought from them – but he still couldn't bring himself to throw them away, like old medicine bottles full of remedies that never worked but that you didn't dare throw away on the off chance they would someday do what they promised, that you'd be stricken by chance with the one disease only they could cure, two weeks after they'd been pulled off the market. Kugel had taken a week's leave from work after moving in, and spent his days heaving box after box up into the attic when he would have rather thrown them all in the trash. They say you can't take it with you, but good luck trying to leave it behind.

Something reeked. Kugel winced, held his breath.

The stench in the house had gotten worse since Eve first showed it to them. Immediately after signing the mortgage, and before even phoning the movers, Kugel had spent thousands of dollars on a professional vent cleaning service, but the putrid smell returned almost immediately after they settled in. Up here in the attic, noticed Kugel, it smelled worse than it did downstairs. Like sewage. Like rot.

God, he hated attics.

He tugged on the white string that hung from the overhead bulb.

Hello? he whispered as the light came on.

Mother must have been up here at some point, or Bree, perhaps, anxious to get her office going, because the boxes he had so haphazardly tossed up here weeks before now lined three sides of the attic in neat, uniform walls, four boxes high, and in some places five. The walls were arranged in a wide square U shape, the base of which stood against the southern wall, the two legs traveling half the length of the western and eastern sides of the attic, respectively, and blocking two of the four dormer windows, leaving just one window clear on either side of the attic. An old chair, a pair of old end tables, and a rolled-up carpet were carefully stacked at the far end of the attic, where a head-less sewing mannequin stood silent guard against possible intruders.

Kugel – begin-againer, starterer-anew – got down on his hands and knees in his attic and began looking, hopefully, for shit. He wasn't about to start crawling around behind those walls of boxes, but he checked along the base of the two dormer windows, and along the northern gable side of the house, too. He found a few stray drop-pings here and there, but they were old.

He wiped his hands and sat back on his heels.

There's life for you, Kugel thought. Shit every-where until you need some; then there is none.

Last words?

Not bad.

He'd have to remember to write those down once he got back to bed.

Kugel wiped his brow. The oppressive heat and suffocating stench were making him dizzy.

Kugel stood, as best he could, to leave, but as he did, noticed an orange extension cord running off the secondary outlet in the overhead light fixture. He followed it along the rafter to which it had been tacked, down to where it departed the roof and dropped to the end of the westernmost wall of boxes, where it met up with a dangerously overloaded power strip lying on the attic floor; each port of the strip had a double outlet expander, some had triples, and each of those expanders were fully loaded themselves, spilling over in an entrail-like mess of yellow, black, and orange cords that snaked around behind the wall of boxes. Electrical systems in old houses were notoriously dangerous, and even a small spark in a house built as this one was, of dry, century-old wood, could very quickly become an inferno.

Won't need an arsonist with this going on, muttered Kugel.

Kugel went to the wall of boxes and, from the top of the center stack, pulled away a cardboard box labeled Jonah-Clothes-Winter, and another, beneath it, marked Photos/Mother/1 of 6. He leaned over and looked behind the wall – and suddenly felt as if the blood had drained from his body, as if it had run out through holes bored through the soles of his feet; his whole body felt leaden, stiff, nailed into place. He wanted to scream but found that he couldn't breathe.

At last he forced himself backward, falling to the floor as he did. He fumbled for his flashlight, scrambled to his feet, and stepped cautiously toward the wall; hands shaking, heart pounding, he aimed the beam of light into the darkness behind.

No, he hadn't imagined it.

He hoped he had, but he hadn't.

There, on the floor behind the boxes, lay the huddled blanket-wrapped body of an elderly woman. He tapped the flashlight against the rafter overhead, trying to rouse her.

Hey, he whispered.

Nothing.

He stood on his toes, leaned farther over the wall. She stank like decay, like death. Was she dead?

Hey, he said.

Was she dead? Who was she? Was she the arsonist? Was she dead? How was he going to get a dead body out of here without Jonah knowing?

Keeping the light on her with one hand, Kugel pulled down another couple of boxes from the wall with the other, and though the boxes dropped heavily to the attic floor, she didn't stir. She was on her side, curled in a fetal position on top of a small mound of worn quilts and tattered blankets. Her face was buried in her arms, but Kugel could see her sparse, unkempt silver hair, the blue fallen veins of her lower arms, the gnarled bones of her withered, skeletal hands.

The more boxes Kugel cleared away from the wall, the worse the woman's stench became, and Kugel had to fight the urge to turn his head; the smell seemed to engulf him, to pass right through him, foul and putrid, and he gagged. He covered his nose and mouth with his free hand, but the thought of breathing her in, of drawing her within him, caused him to gag again.

He stepped back, swinging the beam of light around the attic, hoping to find a quilt or a tarp; perhaps he could wrap her body in it and drag it down the stairs without waking up Jonah, perhaps it would reduce the smell.

And then what, genius? Leave her in your car? You're going to leave a dead body in your car?

He had no idea how much time had passed since he'd first left his bed. An hour? More? He returned to the wall, leaning over even farther this time, his heart pounding so furiously that he wondered if Bree could hear it downstairs; a bead of sweat ran down his forehead, another streaked down his neck as he stretched out his arm toward the old woman and reached out with his flashlight, slowly, slowly, until at last, with its end, he nudged her shoulder.

Nothing.

He nudged her again.

Dead. She was dead.

Okay, that was better than alive.

Or maybe it was worse.

He reached out one more time, but just as he did, that ancient bony hand, as if rising unbidden from the grave, swatted angrily at the end of the flashlight.

Jesus Christ, Kugel hissed, darting back from the boxes and raising the flashlight overhead as if to strike.

Jesus fucking Christ, he said.

The old woman coughed – a sickly, terrible cough – and pulled the tattered blanket over her exposed shoulder.

Close, she muttered.

Her voice was raspy and dry, and she coughed again as she pushed herself up onto her hip.

You're alive, said Kugel.

She wiped the spittle from her lips.

I won't tell if you won't, she replied.

Who are you? Kugel asked, aiming the light at her face. What do you want? Are you the arsonist? How long have you been here? Do you need help? Should I call an ambulance? Are you the arsonist? Are you okay? Who are you?

She coughed again, and cleared her throat.

I'm Anne Frank, she grumbled.

She's mad, thought Kugel. She's alive, yes, I suppose that's a relief, alive is better than dead, it must be better than dead, and yet she's very obviously mad. Should I run? Should I lock the attic door? How could I lock the attic door? I could get a long two-by-four; I could jam it underneath, between the hallway floor and the attic door, yes, so she couldn't open it, so she couldn't get out. Who says she wants to get out? Where am I going to get a two-by-four? The barn? The cellar? I should have a two-by-four, a man should have a two-by-four in the house, he should, a man should, a man would.

She turned her back to him, shielding her eyes from the light and shuffling farther back into the dark eaves, but before she disappeared he could see that she was hideous, horribly disfigured, and terribly old – Kugel thought he'd never seen anyone so old – the white of her right eye yellowed with age, the left eye clouded with cataracts, dead, unseeing. Her skin, sallow and gray, was thin,

30

almost transparent; the hair on her head, what there was of it, was sparse in some places, bare in others. Her shoulders hunched up around her ears, and a massive hump on her back forced her skull forward so that she faced the ground, head bowed, even when looking straight ahead.

What are you doing here? Kugel whispered, his terror beginning to give way to anger. What do you want?

I want you, she croaked, to turn off that goddamned light.

Who are you? he quickly replied, pointing the flashlight at her. How did you get in here?

She scurried farther back into the eaves, holding up a hand, trying to get away from the harsh beam of light.

I told you, she growled. I'm Anne Frank. Now, turn off that goddamned light.

Fear is not an end state; it is a precursor, a catalyst, it becomes something – occasionally submission, more often violence or rage. Kugel yanked another box from the wall and threw it to the floor with a crash, then another box followed, and another after that.

Who are you? he asked, his voice rising as he tore down the wall of boxes, forgetting Bree and Jonah and Mother downstairs. What are you doing here? Who let you in? How did you get into my house?

By the time he finished, half a dozen boxes lay strewn about, upended, their contents spilled across the floor. Kugel, breathing heavily, flashed the light at her again.

Who are you? he demanded.

He wanted to see fear, he wanted to watch her cower; instead, with an insouciant air of annoyance and bother, the old woman pulled her cardigan around herself with one hand and fixed her hair with the other.

Oh, she said with a derisive sigh, how I do adore meeting the homeowners.

Kugel tore another box down from the wall. Old textbooks spilled out, postcards, a badge of some childhood honor. Four more boxes followed the first to the floor, and when it was over, Kugel had revealed, behind the remaining boxes and to the left of her bed, what seemed like a small table – a two-foot-long scrap of splintered floorboard lay across a pair of Bree's old shoeboxes – on top of which sat a small lamp, a laptop computer, and a small laser printer.

He aimed the flashlight at the makeshift office.

What the hell? he said softly, reaching out toward the pile of neatly stacked papers sitting facedown beside the printer.

The old lady moved very quickly, though, much more quickly than he would have guessed she could, and shouted No! as she slammed down her hand on top of the papers.

Kugel reared back.

You can read it, she growled, when I'm done.

Kugel looked at her, trying to decide if she was

real or if this was something else, a dream, a nightmare, maybe a hallucination. He hadn't slept well in a while. The stench, though, convinced him it was real.

I'm calling the police, he said.

He snapped off his flashlight and backed toward the stairs, afraid to turn away from her. She waved in annoyance again, shuffled forward out of the eaves, settled in front of the computer and, as if nothing at all out of the ordinary had occurred, began to type.

That was the sound. The tapping of the keyboard. He'd been hearing it for days.

Kugel stopped at the head of the attic stairs.

And let me tell you something else, he said.

She continued to type, paying him no attention.

I don't know who you are, he said, or how you got up here. But I'll tell you what I do know: I know Anne Frank died in Auschwitz. And I know that she died along with many others, some of whom were my relatives. And I know that making light of that, by claiming to be Anne Frank, not only is not funny and abhorrent but it also insults the memory of millions of victims of Nazi brutality.

The old woman stopped typing and turned to him, fixing that hideous yellow eye upon his.

It was Bergen-Belsen, jackass, she said.

Kugel continued to glare at her, even as he felt a flush of shame color his face. He turned and began climbing down the stairs.

33

And as for the relatives you lost in the Holocaust? she continued.

Kugel stopped and looked at her, and when he did, she yanked up her shirtsleeve, revealing the fading blue-black concentration camp numbers tattooed on the inside of her pale forearm.

Blow me, said Anne Frank.

CHAPTER 5

You expect certain things when you move to the country. You just do. You expect these things because you've seen the films, you've watched the TV episodes. You expect dishonest carpenters and creepy locals. You expect deer eating your petunias and raccoons toppling your garbage. You expect poison ivy and power outages and colorful neighbors and mice.

You don't expect arson.

And you sure as hell don't expect Anne Frank.

Kugel sat on the edge of his bed, staring down at the telephone in his hand. Behind him, Bree snored softly in her blissful, oblivious slumber.

The numbers on her arm.

They were a problem.

A big fucking problem.

If she didn't have numbers on her arm, he would have phoned the police immediately. Maybe not immediately – he would wait until morning for Bree to take Jonah to day care, no need to frighten the child – and then, when they had gone, phone the police without delay. But she had numbers, didn't she, he had seen them, those damned numbers, and the numbers meant that Anne Frank or not, consumed by madness or not, half-dead or not, rotting like a hundred-year-old corpse or not, the old woman was a goddamned Holocaust survivor.

Which was a problem.

Was he really going to throw an elderly, half-mad Holocaust survivor out of his house? Speak of madness! He could never do it, he knew that, even if she was old and emotionally damaged enough to think she was Anne Frank. Pity was a funny thing: it would be easier to throw out the real Anne Frank than it would be to throw out a Holocaust survivor so fucked up by the Holocaust that she thought she was Anne Frank. Can you imagine the headlines? Can you imagine the outrage?

Local Man Evicts Anne Frank.

Jew Drops Dime on Holocaust Survivor.

Brutalized by Nazis, Tossed Out by a Jew: One Survivor's Tragic Story of Something.

If he'd heard the story, he would join in the outcry himself; if he were watching TV one night and the news came on and they reported, with all their practiced shock and disgust, that a man had thrown an elderly, broken Holocaust survivor out of his home, would he not share in the outrage? And wouldn't he be right to do so?

The story gets weirder, the smiley anchorwoman would say: *the homeowner was a Jew.*

Boy, oh, boy, the smiling anchorman would add. *Now I've heard everything. Now I have heard everything.*

This was a hell of a way to start anew. He'd never received any love from his mother; it would have been nice to be accepted, even if only for a while, by a community. But if he turned her in, they would never forgive him. And why should they? Hi, we're from the community welcome wagon; here's a flaming bag of dog shit. They would have to move yet again.

But what could he do? Let this crazy old woman live in his attic? It was absurd. For how long? A week? A month? A year? Until whatever Holocaust she thought she was hiding from came to whatever end she thought it would come to? Until she dropped dead?

And what if she really was Anne Frank? It wasn't impossible – they'd found former Nazi officers in Rio, hadn't they, ex-camp commandants in New Jersey. Why not a famous survivor in Stockton? Could he take that chance? What if he called the police, and they came over and cuffed her and dragged her out of his house and discovered that, my goodness, my God, she really is Anne Frank. She's alive. He would forever be known as the person – the *Jewish* person – that reported Anne Frank to the authorities. Even if he could survive the shame, even if he could weather the ignominy of it all, he could never survive the look on Mother's face when she found out. He had a better chance of surviving the Holocaust itself.

My own son, she would say, ratting out Anne Frank.

You had to call the police, she would say. What's

37

the matter, you didn't have Dr Mengele's number? He doesn't make house calls?

You want Elie Wiesel's address? Maybe you could turn him in, too?

No. No, no. Hell no. There would be no police, of that much Kugel was certain. He would find another way. The old lady would die soon, from the looks of it, maybe he could wait it out. But then what? *Hello, police? There's a dead woman in my attic. Her name? Well, uh, funny story . . .*

Kugel gently placed the phone back in its cradle and, sliding quietly from the bed, knelt down beside the vent on the floor.

He listened.

Maybe he'd dreamt it.

Maybe she'd gone.

The forced-air heating system the Messerschmidts had retrofitted into the farmhouse had been usual in design for the times, but unusually poor in construction. The system pulled in fresh air through a large duct that ran from the attic to the heater in the cellar; from there, a network of secondary ducts carried the heated air through the walls, to every room in the house, where it emerged through metal vents in the floor. The better systems employed fiberglass-insulated ducts to carry the air through the walls; the Messerschmidts had gone with the cheaper steel materials, and as a result, the ducts carried sound at least as well as they did heat. It wasn't long after settling into the new home that Kugel realized he could hear every sound, from every room, of every floor in the house, clear as a bell, through the vents in the floor, a ghostly intercom system he didn't want and could never silence.

He pressed his ear against the vent.

Mother moaning.

The television laughing.

And the typing.

From the attic.

Ceaseless.

Desperate.

If only I'd found shit, thought Kugel. If only I'd found an arsonist.

It dawned on Kugel as he knelt on the cold floor of his bedroom that the very thing he'd feared the past month and a half – a house fire – might, as it turned out, have been the best thing that could have possibly happened. Combing through the smoldering wreckage, the police would find the body of some old lady, but at least she would be gone, out of his hair, and the insurance on the house would pay off handsomely.

Bree shifted, turned on her side, and mumbled something in her sleep.

She isn't going to like this, Kugel thought as he watched her. She isn't going to like this at all. He'd already allowed one crazy old lady into the house – his mother – and they were still waiting for her to die.

A physician, said Professor Jove, is but a criminal dealer of the narcotic of hope.

Kugel got to his feet and slid quietly back into bed.

Kugel first began seeing Professor Jove the previous year, soon after Jonah's illness. Kugel was having a difficult time sleeping; the anxiety and anger that had been building within him for some time were threatening to spill over, and he was determined to do whatever was necessary to be the husband Bree deserved and the father Jonah needed. He'd seen analysts in the past, but psychiatry was too narrow a scope for him now. Professor Jove, however, was a polymath; not just a Jungian or a Freudian, not just a Kantian or a Cartesian; he had studied the ancients and the moderns, the Realists and Impressionists, he had studied everyone from Aristotle to Zarathustra, from Democritus to Heraclitus and, as he liked to say, all the Ituses in between. He was, in a sense, the distillation of all of Western and Eastern thought of the past two thousand years combined, and it was Professor Jove's opinion, standing as only someone today could, on the twenty-first-century peak of all history, heir to all mankind's experience, wisdom, and knowledge, that the greatest source of misery in the world, the greatest cause of anguish and hatred and sadness and death, was neither disease nor race nor religion.

It was hope.

Hope? Kugel asked.

Pessimists, Professor Jove replied, don't start wars. It was hope, according to Professor Jove, that was keeping Kugel up at night. It was hope that was making him angry.

Give Up, read the sign on the wall behind Jove's book-covered desk, You'll Live Longer.

But you've been to Yale, Harvard, Cambridge, said Kugel.

That's how I know, said Professor Jove.

Kugel had waited weeks for an appointment.

We are rational creatures, Professor Jove explained; hope is irrational. We thus set ourselves up for one dispiriting fall after the next. Anger and depression are not diseases or dysfunctions or anomalies; they are perfectly rational responses to the myriad avoidable disappointments that begin in a thoroughly irrational hope.

Kugel wasn't sure he understood. Professor Jove smiled warmly.

Tell me, he said. Hitler was the last century's greatest what?

Kugel had shrugged.

Monster?

Optimist, said Professor Jove. Hitler was the most unabashed doe-eyed optimist of the last hundred years. That's *why* he was the biggest monster. Have you ever heard of anything as outrageously hopeful as the Final Solution? Not just that there could be a solution – to anything, mind you, while we have yet to cure the common cold – but a final one, no less! Full of hope, the Führer was. A dreamer! A romantic, even, yes? If I just kill this one, gas that one, everything will

41

be okay. I tell you this with absolute certainty: every morning, Adolf Hitler woke up, made himself a cup of coffee, and asked himself how to make the world a better place. We all know his answer, but the answer isn't nearly as important as the question. The only thing more naively hopeful than the Final Solution is the ludicrous dictum to which it gave birth: Never Again. How many times since Never Again has it happened again? Three? Four? That we know of, mind you. Mao? Optimist. Stalin? Optimist. Pol Pot? Optimist. Here's a good rule for life, Kugel, no matter where you happen to live or when you happen to be born: when someone rises up and promises that things are going to be better, run. Hide. Pessimists don't build gas chambers.

I just want my family to be safe, said Kugel. I just want the world to leave us alone. Is that asking too much?

What, asked Professor Jove, did Jesus Christ say when they nailed him to the cross?

I don't know, said Kugel. What did Jesus Christ say when they nailed him to the cross?

He said Ouch, said Professor Jove.

I don't get it, said Kugel.

There's nothing to get, said Professor Jove. It hurt. First they whipped him half to death, then they held him down and nailed iron spikes through his wrists. If he was lucky, they did the same to his feet. The weight of his body bearing down on his chest made it difficult to breathe,

42

and he died, slowly and agonizingly, from respiratory distress.

I still don't get it, said Kugel.

There is hurt in this world, said Professor Jove. There is pain. Hoping there won't be only makes it worse.

Kugel pulled the bedcovers up to his chin and moved closer to Bree. She turned over and draped her arm across his chest, burying her face in his shoulder.

While there's never a good time to find Anne Frank in your attic, this was a particularly bad time. Even with the low purchase price of the farmhouse, they needed to rent both downstairs bedrooms in order to cover their mortgage; Kugel's giving Mother the second bedroom was a decision that still angered Bree. She had been irate when Kugel suggested it, and leveled bitter accusations at him, accusations he denied even as he suspected they were true: that he put his past before his future, that his former family came before his current family. And she had been right. It had been only a couple of months since they signed the mortgage, but they were already falling behind in the payments; in an effort to find some way to make ends meet, Bree recently suggested renting out the attic in order to make up for the loss of rent from Mother's bedroom. But where would Bree write? And with that old woman up there now, what was Kugel going to do? How many more rooms was he going to let for free?

To make matters worse, their sole tenant – Haman or Pharaoh or Nebuchadnezzar or something – had, ever since moving in, been after Kugel for a corner of the attic where he could store some of his extra belongings. Kugel was afraid to refuse him and risk his leaving; he had originally requested a bit of patience on the tenant's part, claiming that the attic had not yet been organized or cleaned from the move; as soon as it was, Kugel had promised, he would find the tenant some space. But it had been some time now, and with that old woman up there now, he couldn't have the tenant traipsing in and out; what would he think of her, of her living there for free, of her filth, her stench, of her taking his storage space? And if, either in anger or disgust, the tenant suddenly moved out, Kugel worried Bree might just do the same.

Anne Frank, thought Kugel, running a hand through his hair. That's all I fucking need.

The sun was rising.

Christ, it was already morning. Sunlight crept in through the back window of the bedroom and poured slowly across the floor. All at once, the typing sounds stopped.

Bree pressed herself to Kugel and moaned softly.

There was no need to tell her about the woman in the attic, there really wasn't. Why upset her? He would deal with it on his own. How difficult could it be to get an elderly Holocaust survivor out of your house? He'd play Wagner. He'd get a German shepherd. When the UPS man had gone,

44

he'd tell her it had been a man from the Gestapo, asking a lot of questions. A *lot* of questions.

Did you *shower* yet, honey? he would call downstairs to Bree. Because if you *showered* already I'm going to *shower* now.

She'd be out in a day.

Piece of cake.

Even if she didn't leave, so what? Who would know she was there? She was hiding, after all, or thought she was; shutting up was the whole job description.

The birds flitting about on the tree branches outside his window began to warble and call, and their delicate song began to calm his nerves. It couldn't be an all-bad world, could it, not with birds who warble and call? Maybe that was the secret – to find the few things that made life just a fraction better, and to focus on those. Bird warbles. Peach fuzz. Puppies barking as if they were full-grown dogs. Nothing great, certainly nothing to justify the rest of it, but enough to keep you going. He could hear the squirrels now, clawing their way up and down the trees, chasing the birds, scaring them off.

Squirrels, thought Kugel, were assholes. That such asshole creatures could be so physically adorable suggested a major flaw in nature's schematic.

He could pull this off. He was sure of it. It would have been one thing to protect Anne Frank from the Nazis; he was pretty sure he couldn't have managed that. But protecting his family from Anne Frank? How difficult could that be?

He looked up at the ceiling.

He wondered what she was doing. She wasn't typing. Was she sleeping?

He wondered if she was hungry.

She must be hungry.

Maybe I should bring her something to eat.

Downstairs, Mother began to scream. It was a loud, piercing scream, a cry of terror and anguish that carried throughout the house.

Kugel sighed.

Mother screamed every morning. She had done so ever since reading that this was common behavior among survivors of the Holocaust.

Bree groaned, rolled onto her back, and opened her eyes.

Ah, she said. The sounds of a country morning.

Kugel kissed her gently on the top of her head.

Sleep okay? she mumbled.

So-so, said Kugel. You?

Bree nodded.

Mother screamed again. Jonah began to cry.

I'll get her, said Kugel.

I'll get him, said Bree.

Kugel stepped out of bed, pulled on his robe, and headed down to Mother's bedroom. Though she had moved in well over a month ago, Mother hadn't unpacked yet and wasn't going to; she preferred, she said, to live out of her suitcases, some

46

of which stood against the wall, and some of which lay open on the bedroom floor.

Just in case, she said.

Just in case what? Kugel had asked.

Just in case, she had replied.

The only item she had unpacked was her gilt-framed three-foot-tall by two-foot-wide photograph of the famous Harvard attorney Alan Dershowitz, which she hung, as she always had, on the wall above her bed.

Mother was sitting up in bed when Kugel entered her bedroom. She sat sobbing, her face buried in her trembling hands.

I'm sorry, she whispered.

It's okay, said Kugel.

He sat down on the bed beside her and put his arm around her shoulders.

Ever since the war, she said.

I know, he said.

Those sons of bitches, said Mother.

I know, said Kugel.

She took a deep breath and looked into his eyes.

I'm hungry, she said.

CHAPTER 6

While Bree hurriedly dressed Jonah and Mother slowly dressed herself, Kugel went to the kitchen and filled a cloth bag with vegetables from the pantry and refrigerator. He unlocked the garden door that led to the backyard – he'd been careful, every night since the arson had begun, to lock it, and careful, too, not to let Bree see that he had – and headed out to Mother's vegetable garden, where nothing ever grew.

A large rectangle of dry, dusty earth in the center of the backyard, further divided into a number of smaller raised rectangular beds and bounded on all sides by tall metal deer fencing, Mother's vegetable garden was the only area of the yard where nothing grew, that was utterly devoid of any life whatsoever; everywhere else in the garden, grasses, weeds, and wildflowers pushed up from the earth at such an astonishing rate that it was almost troublesome, requiring constant pruning and weekly mowing, Kugel's most hated chore. He tried in vain to convince Mother to fertilize the soil in her garden, to add compost, to water it more consistently, but she wouldn't listen; instead, she stubbornly continued to do what she always had, spending hours each morning raking the lifeless soil from east to west, and then from west to east, from north to south, and then from south to north, at which point she would stop for a moment, wipe her brow, fan herself with her hat, and begin the entire process all over again.

Kugel stepped inside the garden, trying his best not to let the hinges on the old garden gate creak, reached into his bag of vegetables, and began walking back and forth across the dry, loamy soil, dropping the store-bought produce haphazardly into the raised beds. He dropped radishes, tomatoes, long beans, even shucked ears of corn; later, Mother would come outside and smile to find just how much her hard gardening work had paid off. Kugel wasn't sure whether he did this each morning for Mother's benefit or for his own, but he couldn't bear to see her out there, day after day, with nothing to show for it; couldn't bear, on the days before he had begun stocking her garden with vegetables, her miserable moping and sighing about the house. The only seedlings she had actually planted were beans, herbs, and tomatoes (Kugel's heart broke to see the doomed seedlings she carried out to the garden, never to return again), but she never once questioned the many other varieties of vegetables she found there – the squash, the cucumbers, the heads of lettuce; on the contrary, she would strut into the kitchen, arms full of supermarket produce and nose in the air, gloating about her green thumb and wondering aloud if perhaps now Kugel would keep his foolish advice to himself. Some days (though he felt guilty afterward) Kugel would leave fruit out there, too – oranges, apples, honeydew, even diced cantaloupe in plastic containers – but Mother, secure in her horticultural abilities, never questioned their otherwise miraculous appearance. Her bedroom had a window that faced the backyard, as did the kitchen; if she knew what Kugel was doing out there each morning, she never said a word, though he suspected she didn't want to know, either way.

It wasn't, however, an unpleasant chore, and in fact, Kugel had come, over the weeks, to appreciate the solitude and peace. It forced him out of the house early in the morning, when the world was still quiet; where he could feel the cool dew on his bare legs, fill his lungs with the sharp morning air, where all was placidity and peace. The sun, still low in the sky at that hour, gently broke through the pines and maples, warming his face as the birds danced about in the cool canopy of branches above.

This morning, however, he felt as if he were being watched. He felt as if he were doing something wrong.

He looked back at the house; was Mother watching him?

No, he didn't see her at her window.

Bree?

Bree didn't like his wasting money on Mother's vegetables, he knew that, or that he was encouraging her (as she saw it) to stay, but thus far she'd chosen not to confront him about it. Was she watching him today? Had she finally had enough?

No, he didn't see her.

And then, higher up, just below the rising sun, he saw the darkened dormer windows in the attic.

Was she watching him, he wondered, that crazy old hag? Judging him?

Fuck her.

What was her problem, that he was deceiving his mother? That he was wasting vegetables? Yes, I know, there are people starving in the world, so what? A few turnips aren't going to save them. Or is it more than that, lady – is it my being outside on this beautiful morning while you're stuck inside? Well, you're *not* stuck inside, you're *staying* inside, there's a difference. I've been out here fifteen minutes already, and was out here all day yesterday, and I still haven't seen gas chamber one.

So fuck you.

Her judging him, what a joke! She's a trespasser, a liar, a thief, and she smells like a toilet – like a toilet that other toilets use when they need to use a toilet – and she's judging me.

Don't make me laugh.

The sun was getting higher now, and Kugel shielded his eyes against it as he tried to see if he could spot her there through the attic windows. He couldn't, but he held up his middle finger just

51

in case she was there, just in case she was watching him, and turned back to his chore.

It ruined it, being watched like this.

What did she know, anyway?

Pain in the ass.

She wasn't going to dictate what he did or when he did it; she wasn't calling the shots here.

This is *my* goddamned house, he thought.

He should just throw her out. Damn everyone else and their judgments to hell, he should just go inside and throw her decrepit ass out.

He made one more pass along the garden, dropping the remaining fruits and vegetables from his bag, all but the last apple, which he tucked in his jacket pocket before heading back to the house.

She's probably hungry, he thought.

CHAPTER 7

Where were you? asked Bree as Kugel entered the kitchen.

What? he asked, hiding the vegetable bag behind his back.

Where were you?

Where was I?

I was calling you.

You were . . .

Shh! she said. Listen!

She was in the middle of scrambling eggs for Jonah and the tenant, both of whom were already sitting at the kitchen table. She pressed a finger up to her lips and held the spatula aloft.

There, she said at last. You hear that?

He heard it. A metallic tapping sound, coming from the floor vent.

He shook his head.

No, he said. I don't hear anything.

Wait, said Bree, wait.

Tap, tap-tap.

There, she said.

She was tapping on the vents, thought Kugel. The crazy old bitch was up there tapping on the vents – tap, tap-tap, tap, tap-tap – trying to signal him, to get his attention.

That? asked Kugel.

Do you hear it? Bree asked.

I think so, he said. It's very . . . That?

Bree nodded.

That, she said.

The tenant stood.

Mr Kugel, he said firmly.

Kugel didn't like the tenant. The man was tall and dark-skinned, with an arrogant air, and a day had yet to pass without some complaint: the house smelled, the room was too cold, the closet was too small. Bree was doing her best to keep him happy, and Kugel was doing his best to avoid him. Something had happened in recent years, Kugel thought, something had changed. He remembered as a child, after Father disappeared and they were forced to move from their comfortable white house in the lush suburbs to an uncomfortable brown apartment in the barren city, how deferential Mother had been to their new landlord, how careful she had always been not to upset him in any way. Yes, Mr Rosner; I'm sorry, Mr Rosner; it's no problem, Mr Rosner. It angered Kugel to see his mother brought low before such a man, so he sometimes snuck down the stairs after dark, crept onto the sidewalk, and tipped over the garbage pails Mr Rosner had so neatly lined up alongside the curb; then he would hurry upstairs and watch from the living-room window as Mr Rosner, red-faced

54

and swearing, bent to clean up Mother's trash. These days, though, the relationship had reversed: it was the landlord who lived on his knees, answering to every complaint, heeding every call. So this morning, as angry as he was at the old woman for tapping on his vents, he appreciated the distraction from the tenant.

It's probably the heater, said Kugel.

The heater? asked Bree.

Kugel knew almost nothing about mechanical issues, but Bree knew even less.

Blower fan, said Kugel.

Is that bad?

Mr Kugel, the tenant interjected. Mr Kugel, it really is important that we speak.

Folks, said Kugel, honestly, I had a hell of a night last night, and I don't know that –

There! said Bree. Again I heard it.

Pity for everyone but me, thought Kugel. I should put some damned numbers on my arm.

The blades, Kugel said, that's what it sounds like to me. Fan blades. They're probably bumping up against the exhaust flange.

Mr Kugel, the tenant interrupted again, his voice rising, is your mother going to be screaming like that every morning?

The room grew silent.

Kugel sighed and shook his head.

Ever since the war, said Kugel softly.

Mother had never been in a war. She'd never been anywhere near a war, unless you count the

55

holiday sales at Bamberger's the morning after Thanksgiving.

I am rapidly . . . began the tenant, but at that very moment, Mother entered through the garden door, her arms full of bright fruits and shiny vegetables. She was beaming.

There's still more out there, she said breathlessly to Kugel, a triumphant smile on her face. Even the cantaloupes came in!

She placed the bounty on the counter, still beaming, until she turned and saw the tenant, whereupon her face darkened.

Mother disliked the tenant even more than Kugel did, and with far less actual cause. She suspected him of nefarious thoughts, devious plots, sexual perversion; she thought him, alternately, a Muslim, a Negro, a Sicilian; whenever she saw him, she held shut her blouse collar with one hand, and pulled down on her skirt hem with the other. And she had been, much to Bree's dismay, openly antagonistic toward the tenant from the start.

Those, she said, glaring at the tenant as she held closed her blouse collar, are for *family*.

Tap.

Tap-tap.

There, said Bree to Kugel. You must have heard that.

The taps were getting louder now.

Exhaust flange, said Kugel. Getting worse, too.

TAP, TAP-TAP.

Mr Kugel, the tenant said firmly, coming around the table and standing at the kitchen doorway, arms folded across his chest. I signed a lease with you for a period of twelve months, but given the situation here, I don't think I would have too difficult a time finding a judge who would allow me to break that contract – and to recoup my deposit, along with any and all past monies paid.

So now he's an attorney, Mother said to Bree.

Mother, said Bree. And then, to the tenant, she said, I'm terribly sorry.

Much as it had so long ago with Mother and Mr Rosner, it angered Kugel to see Bree placating this ingrate – history repeats itself, it seems, with very little concern about whether we learn anything from it or not – but Bree and Kugel knew that they could ill afford to have the tenant leave. Mother, meanwhile, took a step toward the tenant, pointing her finger at his chest.

You wouldn't be talking like *that*, Mother said to him, if Mr Alan Morton Dershowitz was here, I assure you of that.

Mother, said Kugel.

TAP.

TAP-TAP.

Pardon me, said Kugel, pressing past the tenant and hurrying out the kitchen door. We'll pick this up later, he said as he went.

Mr Kugel, the tenant called after him. Mr Kugel, you promised me space in the attic – space for which I am *paying*, Mr Kugel.

I'm so sorry, Kugel could hear Bree saying, and then, as the tapping continued and he hurried up the stairs, he could hear Mother taunting the tenant again: No, sir, she said, no, sir. You wouldn't be pushing us around if the Felix Frankfurter Professor of Law at Harvard University were here. I bet you wouldn't be so smart then, would you?

If only I'd found mouse shit, thought Kugel as he stomped up the stairs. If only I'd found an arsonist.

Maybe I could just kill her? Who would know? Who would care? If she actually was Anne Frank, everyone thought she was dead anyway.

He stopped at the hallway closet and took out his toolbox. If there was anything he'd learned from all the damned books he'd read in his life – and he was becoming more and more certain that he hadn't learned very much at all – it was that you never let the monster get away. Whatever you do, you do *not* take pity on the monster. And even if it isn't a monster – let's say it isn't, let's say the monster is, ludicrous as it may seem, Anne Frank. Then what? Let it live? What did those fool Samsas gain by waiting all that time to kill the giant pest they'd discovered in their house? Okay, sure, it was their son, or it had been, and this was Anne Frank, or might be, but how about a thought or two for the living, folks? Exactly how long were the poor Samsas obligated to keep that arthropodan pain in the ass in their

58

home? A year? Two? Ten? Sixty? Were they supposed to find him a giant bug wife, and let them have giant bug children before they could finally, without judgment, move on with their already miserable lives? Or were they never supposed to? Were they supposed to hang pictures of vermin and lice on the walls and warn their grandchildren about how they, too, might someday turn into giant bugs?

Kugel yanked down the attic door.

There was a good case to be made, in fact, when you stopped to consider it, that a family who truly loved their son, who deeply cared for his well-being, would, if they found him one morning turned into a hideous bug, have killed him right away; just gone out, found a giant boot somewhere, lifted it up over him and squashed him out of his misery. Gregor's sister could have saved the whole family – not the least of whom was Gregor himself – a world of anguish and trouble if she'd just gone into his room, day one, with a giant can of Raid and gotten it over with.

Foosh. Aaargh. The End.

You move on.

Kugel unfolded the stairs and took a deep, calming breath.

Already he could smell her.

He would reason with her, that's what he would do. There is nothing higher than reason, said Kant.

Or Spinoza.

Or Pascal.

Pascal's last words were: May God never abandon me.

A moment later, God did.

She was damaged, surely, who wouldn't be? But that didn't mean she was a lunatic, it didn't mean he couldn't discuss the issue with her coolly, with at least some degree of lucidity. Half-crazy meant half-sane, didn't it? She couldn't expect him to let her stay in his attic indefinitely, after all; a day or two, sure, just to get her things together, but no more than that. Three, tops. There was Jonah to think about; surely she, once a child herself, would understand that.

Kugel wondered, as he climbed the stairs, how Jonah would react to having to hide one day in their attic.

In the event of what, you maniac?

In the event of whatever.

Would Jonah cry? Of course he would, who wouldn't? What would Kugel tell him? How do you explain a thing like that, like hatred, like genocide? *It's not you, it's them? It's going to be okay*, when you know perfectly well that it isn't? Do you bring toys? All of Jonah's toys made loud, unpredictable noise – bells, sirens, engines, music. The toys, Kugel decided, would have to stay behind. He could probably bring the iPod and some headphones; assuming the wireless wasn't down, Jonah would be able to download movies and games. Would the wireless be down in a genocide? Would it matter? Who would help them? Who would report on them? He didn't know the neighbors very well – maybe he should get to know them better. Maybe he shouldn't. Maybe keeping to your damned self was the best idea.

Kugel wouldn't survive, he knew it. He'd last a week in that attic and kill himself. Freddie Prinze killed himself. In his suicide note, he wrote this:

I'll be at peace.

Professor Jove was opposed to suicide. It wasn't that he considered it an act of cowardice; it was that he saw it as irresponsibly hopeful to imagine a better world existed after this one, in some unnamed, unknown, unproved plane of existence. As foolish as it was to believe that this is the best of all possible worlds, said Professor Jove, it was a thousand times more foolish to believe in a best possible Afterworld.

George Eastman's suicide note read: Why wait?

Well, yeah.

Sure.

There was always that.

Hello? Kugel whispered as he climbed into the attic.

Maybe, thought Kugel, I should get a gun. A small one. Everyone else has a gun. It would be stupid not to.

Kugel stood, and though he was prepared this time for the heat and the stench, they nearly felled him.

Hello? he whispered.

Maybe he'd imagined it.

61

Maybe it had been mice.

The boxes he had toppled the night before remained on the floor, their contents spilled out, and he stepped over them as he slowly approached what remained of the western wall of boxes and crates. He peered over the top.

Her bed.

Empty.

Not a dream, then.

Not mice.

Where the hell was she?

Had she left?

Kugel smiled and shook his head. Yes. Of course she had. She'd been 'discovered,' the crazy old bag. She probably crept out just after he had gone back to bed, fled all night from some imaginary pursuers, from ghost hounds and silent gunfire, through the woods, avoiding the streets, ducking from headlights; this morning she'll wait behind a row of shrubs for some other poor bastard to turn his back, to head off to work or take his kids to school, before creeping into his attic, huddling again in those dark, dank corners where she felt so comfortable, waiting for the cessation of atrocities that never ceased. He felt sorry for her, but she was someone else's problem now, and for that, for his family's sake, he was relieved.

It was daytime now, and in the sunlight that streamed through the dormer windows and slashed through the gable vents, Kugel could see more clearly than he had been able to the night before, and what

62

he saw, there behind the walls of crates and crypts, was a remarkably devised, thoroughly hidden living space.

Whoever the hell she was, she'd clearly hidden in attics before.

Someone – say, Himmler – entering from the attic stairs wouldn't have noticed a thing; the U-shaped walls of cardboard boxes and plastic storage tubs she'd arranged around the perimeter of the attic were stacked a number of feet away from the gable and eaves, creating a hidden narrow gangway that also provided lookout views in three directions. Behind the westernmost wall were her bed and workspace, where he supposed she had spent most of her time; through the dormer window behind her she would have a watchtower guard's view of the road, driveway, and front yard. She would have known at all times who was arriving and leaving, who was home, and who was away.

Good riddance, he thought.

Standing in front of the westernmost wall, he followed it and the trail of wires to the left, around the corner to the southern gable side of the house, where, it seemed, back behind the wall, she had set up something of a kitchen; in her rush to leave, she had left behind her appliances, such as they were: a small dented hotplate, a rusty kettle, a blowtorch, some old rusted pots and pans. A four-pane window in the gable wall – small and cloudy with age, but clear enough in places to see through

– would have given her a view of the secondary parking space at the end of the driveway and the small gravel pathway that led to the back of the house.

The trail of wires ended there, but Kugel continued to follow the wall to the left, around the corner again to the eastern side of the house, where the dormer windows provided a full view of the backyard: of Mother's vegetable garden, the swing set, the sandbox, all the way to the edge of the dark, heavy woods, where the lawn ended. He wondered what else she might have used this portion of the hiding space for, and that was when, peering farther over the top of the wall, he noticed her cloudy yellow eye, watching him from the dark depths of the attic eaves.

Jesus, he hissed, jumping backward. Christ.

In the sunlight, faint as it was, she was even more hideous than he'd gathered the night before. Her hair, wiry and unkempt, hung over her face; her gnarled hands were capped with yellowed, talonlike fingernails; the floorboards behind the boxes, he noticed, were crisscrossed with long scratches and deep gouges, places where she had dragged herself, back and forth, by those very same fingernails.

Her voice, when it came, was a low growl.

I'm out of matzoh, she said.

Were you banging on the vents? asked Kugel.

I'm out of matzoh.

Don't bang on the vents.

I'm out of matzoh. I can't work without matzoh.

Don't bang on the fucking vents.

Kugel walked back to the western wall of boxes and examined her bed and workspace. His back to the old woman, he reached into his pocket, and placed the apple on top of the remaining boxes.

How long have you been up here? he asked.

A while.

What's a while?

A while.

A week? Ten days?

Thirty years, she said.

Thirty *years*?

Kugel returned to the eastern wall in time to see her scurrying, insectlike, along the floor and around the corner.

Or forty, she grumbled from the darkness. Give or take.

Kugel could hear, through the heating return vent in the center of the attic floor, the sounds of breakfast being cleared downstairs in the kitchen: of the kitchen sink running as Bree rinsed the dishes; of silverware clinking; of Jonah's feet as he stomped, squealing, about the kitchen. Down there, thought Kugel, all was sunshine and beauty and life and possibility; and yet here he stood in this attic, in darkness and suffocating gloom, surrounded by misery and death. It was as if the cosmos had flipped, or perhaps we'd simply had it wrong all along, the rapture of heaven below, the agony of hell above. The streets of the afterlife, he thought, had better be clearly marked.

You'll be glad to know, Kugel said aloud, that I've decided not to involve the police.

She was moving behind the western wall now, her breathing labored as she shuffled about in the darkness. She stopped, and he saw her hand reach up, take the apple, and replace it, a moment later, with a folded piece of paper.

What's that? he asked.

A shopping list, she said.

Then again, he thought, maybe she really was insane.

Do you know why? he continued, ignoring the list.

Why what?

Why I'm not going to call the police.

Because you're German, she said, and you feel guilty for committing atrocities.

I am not German, said Kugel.

Just then she emerged from behind the boxes at the open end of the western wall, a black mass, lumpish and dust-covered and trailing spiderwebs from her back and hair. Kugel stepped back; when he was a small boy, he would cry from fright at the sight of the mentally handicapped, certain he was going to catch whatever it was they had.

Slowly, with what seemed like great effort, the old woman brought one foot up beneath her, then the other, until she could push herself up to as upright a position as Kugel imagined she could

66

attain. Perhaps she truly had spent the past forty years in this attic, he thought, as she had seemingly come to resemble it; her body had adapted, or evolved, or devolved, into a shape most suitable for attic life: her knees seemed permanently bent at just the right angle to keep her head from hitting the rafters, and her spine and hips inclined forward at very nearly the same degree of slope as that of the roof.

She took a moment, winded from the hard work of achieving verticality, and then cocked her head sideways, fixing that hideous yellow eye of hers on Kugel's, the whiteness of which he was suddenly ashamed. She looked him up and down.

Because you're Jewish, she said, and you feel guilty for *not* suffering atrocities.

There was something familiar about her, Kugel thought, and when he realized what it was, he wondered if perhaps he was mad, too – it was something about the shape of her eyes, wide and curious; the high hairline, the cheeks, the strong chin; something, if you accounted for advanced age, decades of torment, multiple vitamin deficiencies, and a fair degree of decay, something undeniably, disturbingly . . . Anne Frankish.

Kugel backed away again as she passed him on her way to the overturned boxes in the middle of the attic floor.

What about the Messerschmidts? he asked. They knew you were up here?

She knelt beside one of the boxes, repeating in

reverse order the same slow, laborious process by which she had just risen, and nodded her head.

It hardly seemed worth it, Kugel thought, all that effort just to take a few steps. But he remembered reading that prisoners, locked in tiny cells, often walked in circles for hours, either trying not to become infirm or trying – this was the greater challenge – to remain normal, human.

The Messerschmidts, she said, were good people. Germans, mind you, but self-hating. The best kind. I prefer the self-hating. Self-hating Germans, self-hating Jews, self-hating French, self-hating Americans. We'd have far fewer problems in this world if more people had the courage to be self-hating.

Sol? Kugel heard Bree call.

He spun to face the well of the attic door; from the sound of it, she was right at the foot of the stairs.

It's eight thirty, she called up. You're going to be late for work.

In the weeks to follow, Kugel would consider that if he'd only let her come upstairs and see the old lady, then and there, it might have ended everything much more simply. If only Bree had walked up, seen her, and thrown her out, it all would have been over before it began.

If only Grete had crushed Gregor.

If only Kugel had found shit.

But Bree didn't come up, not immediately, and Kugel turned back to look at the old lady, caught there in the vulnerable open space of the middle of the attic – drawn out of hiding and safety, by him, to straighten the very boxes he had felled – and he called out to Bree: Hang on, hang on, I'm coming down.

Kugel made his way down the stairs, explaining to Bree as he did that, given the degraded condition of the interior valves on the heating-flange exhaust tubes, he was simply going to have to take the day off from work.

Another day off? she asked.

She was concerned that the company would not take kindly to this – Kugel had already taken a week off when they moved in – but Kugel insisted there was simply no choice; it was one of those problems that were easy to ignore but soon became very expensive.

Better to just get rid of it now, he said.

Get rid of it?

Fix it.

Bree asked him to call the office as soon as he could, and told him not to work all day – maybe they can have an evening together tonight? she asked. Sure, sure, said Kugel. Maybe once Jonah's asleep we can sneak up there for some privacy, she said, indicating the attic. Sure, sure, said Kugel – and with a quick kiss, she left to drive Jonah to day care.

Kugel climbed back up to the attic and stood by the side of the dormer window that overlooked the front porch and driveway. The old lady had already gone back to repacking the boxes. Kugel heard the front door close, and a moment later Bree appeared in the driveway, carrying Jonah to the car.

How small they looked from up here. How fragile. How vulnerable. How mortal.

How *unlikely*.

To be. To continue to be.

There was something nice about it, this hiding. This invisibility. This being and not being. This nothingness.

Jean-Paul Sartre's last words: I failed.

Who didn't?

He glanced over at the old woman, kneeling on the floor and heaving his books and belongings back into the boxes.

There was definitely something Anne Frankish about her.

I'm not calling the police, he said, turning back to the window, because you're going to leave on your own.

I certainly hope so, she replied.

Fantastic. I'll help you pack.

Great, she said. As soon as I'm done with it.

Bree had secured Jonah in his car seat and was climbing behind the wheel. It seemed the height of irresponsibility, putting a child into a car, strapping him like a fighter pilot into a three-ton box of steel and glass. Their car had air bags in the front and side; it had air bags, no doubt, everywhere the other car wouldn't strike it. You could line the perimeter of the damned thing with air bags – doors, windows, beams, wheels – and a tree would fall on the roof, crushing them, snuffing them out like a match light in a squall. Kugel had put safety locks on all the kitchen cabinet handles, foam bumpers on all the sharp corners, outlet covers on all the sockets. Maybe he should relax a bit. Maybe he was sending Jonah the wrong message; he didn't want him to grow into the fearful man his father was.

As soon as you're done with what? he asked her.

With my book.

Naturally, said Kugel. Of course. Because you're Anne Frank.

Because, she said, I am a writer.

Bree backed the car out, and Kugel watched her drive away, dust kicking up behind them.

We should get a bigger car. A truck, maybe. Everyone else has one. Yukons, Hummers, Tahoes. It was no longer a matter of keeping up with the Joneses; it was a matter of not getting crushed by them.

Been working on it long? Kugel asked.

Sixty years, she said. Give or take.

Well, lady, said Kugel, you really get into a role, I'll give you that.

He walked across the attic and looked out the window to the backyard. Mother was inside her vegetable garden. He watched as she pulled on a section of the fence for a few moments, then stopped, moved to the next section, and began pulling on that one.

She was stuck again.

She could never seem to find the gate, and when she did, she pushed instead of pulled, and determined thus that the gate must be elsewhere. She would slowly work herself into a panic. Kugel was certain she performed the whole tragicomic burlesque on purpose; that she liked the feeling of being trapped; that she liked needing help; that she liked suffering; that she believed she deserved it. Agony was ecstasy, ecstasy was agony.

Hell of a show we're putting on down here, thought Kugel. Don't forget to tip your creator.

So, *Anne*, he said as he watched Mother down below. Why does everyone think you died in Auschwitz?

Bergen-Belsen.

Whatever.

It's a lot easier to stay alive in this world, said the old woman, if everyone thinks you're dead.

Mm-hmm, said Kugel.

Mother was at the gate now. If she pushed, she'd be out. She pulled, and pulled again, wiped her brow, and moved on, as ever, from salvation to bondage.

There were, of course, continued the old woman, a number of financial considerations as well.

Mother fanned herself with her hat.

Sol! she called out. Solly, I'm stuck!

Financial considerations, said Kugel.

I was alone, Mr Kugel. I was eighteen, hiding in the attic of an old farmhouse somewhere between

Belsen and Hannover. Man by the name of Franz Something, I can't recall any longer, the self-loathing son of a former midlevel SS officer. Franz was hiding me, this sickly, terrified Jewish girl, from nothing, in his attic, even though the war had ended, hoping, I suppose, that the unimaginable sins of the father could be absolved by the second-rate good deeds of the son. Blew his head off ten years later, the poor bastard did. *The sins of the father shall be visited upon the sons.* What an abominable idea. Who said that?

God, said Kugel, looking down at Mother struggling in her garden. She called for him again – Sol! – and turned to look up at the house, shielding her eyes from the sun. Kugel instinctively ducked to the side of the window, though he knew she could never see him from that distance.

One day, she continued, Franz came up to the attic, carrying a newspaper in his hand. He held it out to me with tears in his eyes. Is this you? he asked. Thousands of people, it seemed, were reading my diary. I'd forgotten about it by then, to be honest; it was a couple of years later, and I was already at work on my first novel. Terrible thing, hideously conceived, something about a talking, shame-filled monkey or some such ludicrous conceit; I hope to Christ nobody finds that one like they did my diary. Anyway, I convinced Franz to take me to the publisher in Amsterdam. It was the first time I'd been out of the attic since the war ended, and the first time I'd been in Amsterdam since the war began. With my heart in my throat, I knocked on the publisher's door. May I help you, he asked. I'm Anne Frank, I said.

Mother began pulling on the gate again.

And what did he say? asked Kugel.

After a moment she replied: He said, Fuck you.

Kugel turned to her; she had finished packing up the boxes and was now pushing them with her back toward the wall.

I was taken aback, she continued, as you can imagine, and so I repeated myself, assuming he'd misheard me. I'm Anne Frank, I said. Who isn't? he replied. As it turned out, there had been, ever since the diary was published, a steady stream of girls in to see this publisher, day in, day out, all claiming to be me, all wanting a piece of the royalties. I recalled as he told me this seeing some other girls my age in the waiting area outside his office – some tall, some short, some fat, some thin – all of them, though, wearing as downcast and maudlin a countenance as they could manage, much as they imagined the woeful little girl from the attic would. The editor, naturally, thought I was a fraud as well, but when I told him about the parts of the diary my father had edited out – parts only I, back then, could have known about – he saw that I was indeed who I claimed to be. And do you know what he said then?

Fuck you? offered Kugel.

She fixed her eye on him once more.

He closed his office door, she said, sat me down in his chair and said, Stay dead.

Having finished righting all the boxes, the old lady pulled herself back along the floor to the western wall and scurried behind it. When she was gone from view, Kugel went to the boxes and began lifting them, one by one, back into place.

He said, Mr Kugel, the anger in her voice beginning to rise, that nobody wants a live Anne Frank. They want a martyr, they want to know we've hit bottom. That it gets better, because it can't get worse. They want to know that we can rise like a phoenix from our own fiery human ashes. But tell me, Mr Kugel, what is the point of a phoenix rising if all it ever does is gaze down with perverse longing at its own torched reliquiae? Stay down, you miserable bastard bird, stay down! The glory was in rising, fool, not in having burned! We all burn, everyone burns. Burning doesn't make you special!

She was shouting now, and Kugel stepped back from the wall.

He went to his desk, Mr Kugel, held up a copy of that goddamned diary, with that goddamned smiling child on the goddamned cover, and said, They don't want you. They want *her*.

Mother called out for him again.

Sol, please, I'm frightened!

Kugel took the shopping list in his hand, pressed it into his pocket, and headed for the stairs.

I told him I was working on a novel, Anne Frank

called out loudly after him. Do you know what Mr Editor did then, Mr Kugel? He laughed! Stay dead, he repeated, stay dead! I'm a writer, Mr Kugel! I am not a child! I'm not some goddamned memoirist! I am a writer! Thirty-two million copies, Mr Kugel, that's nothing to sneeze at! I will leave this attic when I finish this book, and not one moment sooner! Not one moment sooner! I am a writer, Mr Kugel, do you hear me! A writer!

Kugel headed down the stairs.

Matzoh! Anne Frank shouted after him. Get me my matzoh!

Kugel folded the stairs and let the attic door close with a crash.

He enjoyed the silence that followed.

Mother called again.

Sol, please! I'm frightened!

Anne Frank, Kugel muttered to himself as he headed outside to rescue Mother from her garden.

That's all I fucking need.

CHAPTER 8

The sun was in the sky like a something. The breeze blew like a whatever.

I was so frightened, said Mother.

The gate's right here, said Kugel. You just have to push.

He demonstrated the proper technique for her as they left the garden.

See? Like this, Mother, it's not complicated. I got no sleep last night, Mother, and there's a very complicated issue I'm dealing with, okay, very thorny, a lot of very sensitive . . . you know? I don't need to be rushing out here every . . .

Pull going in, push coming out, Mother said with a shake of her head. Everywhere else it's push going in and pull going out. They did it on purpose, those Germans, to torture me, to drive me mad.

I built that garden for you, Mother, not the Germans.

Ever since the war, she said softly.

He put his arm around her shoulders and they made their way back to the house.

I know, said Kugel.

Kugel was a small boy, no older than six years old, when he woke up one morning to find his father gone. In the days and months that followed, Mother's explanation for Father's absence varied. Sometimes she told Kugel that he simply disappeared; sometimes she told him he had died; sometimes she told him he had been murdered. Wrong place at the wrong time, she said. All Kugel knew for certain, then as now, was that he was gone. Life was good, and then, one day, it was bad. It was evening, it was morning, it sucked. Kugel sometimes wondered if it would have been better if Father had left sooner, if Kugel had never known him, never known that happier time. According to Professor Jove, it was the knowing that there had been a happy time, a place of joy and peace and security, that made the sudden absence of it all so agonizing for young Kugel. Not the agony of what was, but the agony of what was no longer; this was the source of all life's pain – not the fear of a hell to come, but rather the knowledge of an Eden that is no more. Hell isn't the punishment, said Professor Jove. Eden was.

Whatever happened to Father, it caused Mother to hate him, utterly and completely, and she wanted Kugel to hate him, too, and so Kugel did. Mother was hurt, and sad, and suffering a pain that young Kugel could not ease. Suddenly she was a single mother with two small children – Kugel was six, and Hannah, his younger sister, was not yet two – and because there had been no

78

body, no death, there were no life insurance moneys, either. Overnight, it seemed to young Kugel, Mother became older, wearier, and try as he might to cheer her up – no matter how many chores he did, no matter how well he did in school – nothing seemed to help. Hating Father was the least young Kugel could do. It was also the most he could do. Hatred was all he could offer her. And so he did.

It was soon after that Mother first began referring to the war. The first time Kugel recalled hearing about it was the day after they moved into that small city apartment; Mother had left some of the cardboard boxes in the stairway, and Mr Rosner pounded on the front door, citing all manner of violations and shouting all manner of threats. Mother opened the door, shook her head, apologized and said, in a soft voice, as Mr Rosner's tirade finally drew to a close, Ever since the war.

This seemed to extinguish the fire in Mr Rosner's heart, and he put his hands on his hips and shook his head.

It's okay, Mr Rosner said.

Those sons of bitches, said Mother.

It's okay, he said.

Mother was Kugel's whole world now, and he loved her dearly. He admired her strength, her resilience, how quickly she silenced that pig Rosner. So it didn't surprise young Kugel to learn that Mother was a war hero; she was a hero to him already.

Kugel never asked Mother which war she was referring to, or why Mr Rosner would care as much as he did. Her references were vague: Those sons of bitches, she said, or Such cruelty, or Whole families destroyed, or Never again. Some nights, she would come into young Kugel's bedroom, sit on the edge of his bed, and tell him violent tales of riots and torture and pogroms.

What are pogroms? asked young Kugel.

One evening, when Kugel was eight years old, Mother came to his bedroom, brushed the hair from his brow, and told him that it was time he learned about a terrible place known as Buchenwald. She had a large book with her called *The Holocaust*, and she showed him the photographs inside: of mass graves, starved prisoners, piles of naked corpses.

That's your uncle, she would say.

That's your grandfather's sister.

That's your cousin's father.

What's that? Kugel asked, pointing to the lamp shade she had placed beside him on the bed.

That, she said with a sigh. That's your grandfather.

Then she buried her face in her hands and wept.

I'm so alone, she sobbed. I'm so frightened. How could he leave me, how could he do this?

She cried openly now, shaking her head.

That son of a bitch, she said.

Kugel held the lamp shade in his hands and turned it over.

80

This is Zeide? he asked.

Mother nodded, composed herself.

You see what they do to us? she said. There's no peace, no peace. Wherever we go, wherever we hide. Terror and more terror and more terror.

It says Made in Taiwan, Kugel said.

Mother looked at him, disappointment and anger in her tearstained eyes.

Well, they're not going to write Made in Buchenwald, are they? she snapped.

No, said Kugel.

If the intended effect of the gifting of the lamp shade was to make Kugel fearful of people, it had, in actuality, something of an opposite result; he came to fear inanimate objects. If the lamp shade could be his grandfather, was the sofa his cousin? Was the ottoman his aunt? The armoire, he was certain, was giving him filthy looks. For weeks he crept outside and peed against the apartment house wall, concerned that perhaps the toilet was his uncle, the bathroom mirror an unknown but all-seeing relation disgusted by his most secret rituals. To this day, Kugel was a relentless anthropomorphizer, concerned for the agony of the logs he condemned to the fireplace, the terror of the underwear he imprisoned in the washing machine, the heartache and sorrow of the families of those innocent creatures – the grasshoppers, the ants, the frogs – that perished so gruesomely under the blade of his lawn mower.

Never again, whispered the spiders.

81

Never again, replied the crickets.

It wasn't until two years later, when he entered the sixth grade, that young Kugel discovered the truth. Mrs Rosengarten, his history teacher, arranged for a class trip to a nearby Holocaust museum; the children were about to enter middle school, declared Mrs Rosengarten, and they were old enough now to learn about man's capacity for inhumanity to his fellow man. The students' nervous giggling as they entered the museum was soon replaced with a timorous, reverential hush. The girls' eyes filled with tears and they sniffed as they wiped the streaks of black eyeliner from their cheeks; the boys pretended, characteristically, to be unaffected, but their uncharacteristic silence as they moved from one exhibit to the next revealed the truth. As they entered a room labeled The Transports, one image in particular seemed to arrest the young students and stop them in their tracks. It was a photograph of the exterior of a cattle car, enlarged to such a size that it covered the entire wall. Four young women waved to the photographer through the bars of the tiny window on the side of the car. Perhaps it was their young age, in their twenties, that so shook the students; perhaps it was because they were attractive, with long blond hair, and they seemed more human than the shaven-headed prisoners that filled so many of the other photos; perhaps it was because they were smiling and waving, that they didn't know what was coming, that they were so unaware of how bad things had already become, that they didn't know they would likely be dead before the train ever reached its destination. Whatever the reason, the children all stopped and stood, horror struck, before this enormous image. For a moment nobody moved, nobody said a word; and then young Kugel stepped forward, pointed to the woman at the far right side of the window, and said, his small voice cracking with emotion, That . . . that's my mother.

He buried his face in his hands and cried.

The students gasped.

Those sons of bitches, wept young Kugel.

Ellen, the pretty, dark-haired girl who sat beside him in math, looked at him with sadness in her sparkling blue eyes. Kevin, the popular star of their football team, patted him reassuringly on the shoulder.

Your mother? said Mrs Rosengarten. That's not your mother.

It is, said Kugel. She told me so.

Your mother's my age, Solomon, said Mrs Rosengarten. She wasn't even born when that photo was taken. And she was born in Brooklyn.

How would you know? demanded Kugel. You don't know anything!

I know your mother, said Mrs Rosengarten. We went to Camp Sackamanoff together. Up in the Catskills. The food was awful, young man, but it was a far cry from Auschwitz.

She shook her head and motioned for the children to follow her.

Let's go, class, she said.

Ellen rolled her eyes at Kugel as she pushed past him. Kevin gave him a forceful shove.

You're dead, said Kevin.

Over the years, perhaps as a result of this incident, perhaps as a search for some unattainable truth, Kugel became a voracious reader, hungry for facts and knowledge, and he excelled in all his classes (if he couldn't heal Mother's past, he thought, perhaps he could provide for her a better future); books seemed to hold all the answers – to life, to happiness – if one could just read enough of them. Mrs Rosengarten had been correct, he learned; Mother had been born in Brooklyn, in 1945, the year the hostilities between the Allies and Axis powers officially ended. She must have been protecting him, Kugel assumed, from some even greater horror that she had experienced. He wondered if perhaps she had been referring to a different war – had she served in Vietnam? had she seen time in Korea? – so he traveled by subway one afternoon, uptown, to his grandmother, who showed him a photo album full of old pictures of Mother's cheerful youth in Brooklyn, of her playful adolescence in the Catskills, and, later, of Mother's life as a contented young wife in northeastern suburbia.

Never suffered a day in her life, Grandmother said with a shake of her head.

Kugel, crestfallen, slammed the heavy album closed with a thud.

Grandmother jumped. She buried her face in her hands.

Ever since the war, she said.

It didn't take Kugel much digging to discover that Grandmother hadn't been in the war, either. The Kugels were fifth-generation Americans; none of them had been in the war. They had lost family in the Holocaust, of course, but most had been cousins, and most of those quite distant. A few months later, Grandmother passed away, and a few months after that, on the night of Kugel's eighth-grade graduation, Mother came into his bedroom, sat on the edge of his bed, brushed the hair from his brow, and handed him a shiny black box. The inside of the box was lined with purple velvet and the base was covered in purple satin, upon which sat a smooth white bar of soap.

What's this? he asked.

Your great-grandmother, she said.

Then she buried her face in her hands.

Those sons of bitches, she said.

Thirteen years old that day, Kugel was beginning to feel the need for individuation, for the spreading of his wings; he had less and less patience for Mother's lies – fabrications? exaggerations? myths? – and dared, once again, to challenge her. He reached in, picked up the soap, and turned it over in his hand.

Her name was Ivory? he asked.

Mother frowned and grabbed the soap from him. Her eyes filled with tears.

Well, they're not going to write Auschwitz on it, are they? she said.

It was the last time he ever questioned her about her past or about the war. He resolved from then on to show her nothing but compassion and support. She seemed to need the war, and he was pleased to be able to give it to her. At last there was something other than hate that young Kugel could give the mother he so adored: he could give her suffering.

Careful, said Kugel as he helped Mother through the garden door.

He led her down the hallway, to her bedroom, and lifted her into bed.

Get some rest, he said.

Those sons of bitches, said Mother.

I know, said Kugel. I know.

CHAPTER 9

Kugel went up to his bedroom, sat down in the small wooden chair beside the small wooden desk, took a deep breath, and phoned his office. He asked for his supervisor, and was quickly put on hold.

Post-it notes, said the recorded hold message. Pet hair. Tea bags.

Sales, said Kugel's very first manager, *is not about convincing others – it's about convincing yourself.* As a salesman, that requisite moral pliancy turned out to be Kugel's greatest challenge; he just couldn't convince himself that a Honda was better than a Chevy, that Prozac was better than a placebo (or just a long quiet walk in the woods). And so when he and Bree first began thinking about bringing a child into this world, Kugel took a sales position with the local office of EnviroSolutions, the region's leading residential composting company, hoping that by selling something positive, something he could actually believe in, he could make a difference both in his own fortunes and in the future of the world.

Eggshells, continued the hold message. Cheese. Latex condoms.

His plan had worked. Kugel could make the simple act of composting sound like the most courageous act of the most selfless superhero, and he signed on dozens of accounts. And remember, he would say at the end of his sales calls, your waste is a wonderful thing to mind. That soon became the company's slogan, and it had been his idea, too, to replace the phone system's generic hold music with a constant loop of the many compostable materials their concerned customers could turn into nutrient-dense soil.

Recently, though, the green industry, as it had become known, had exploded; there were new technologies and new companies every day, and the competition for accounts had become fierce. EnviroSolutions expanded their offerings to include recycling pickups, and Kugel proved just as adept a salesman at that as he had been with compost. The company charged their customers by the gallon; the more people recycled, the more money EnviroSolutions earned.

How much do you love the earth? Kugel would ask his clients, in a pitch that the other salesmen soon began to emulate. Seventy-five gallons or ninety-five gallons?

But I only need seventy-five gallons, they would say.

If you really loved the earth, Kugel would reply, you'd use up more.

It soon became a badge of environmental honor to bring as many bags of recycling to the stoop as possible, a trend Kugel almost single-handedly had begun.

Toenail clippings, continued the voice on the phone. Burnt toast. Goat manure.

If only he were as good with truth, he thought, as he was with bullshit.

At last his supervisor answered his phone.

Yes, said Kugel to his supervisor, yes, I know . . . Of course, yes . . . no, I don't . . . well, it just sort of came over me late last night, sir . . . A cold, I think, just a little bug . . . Yes . . . I understand that, yes, I do . . . sore throat, coughing . . . Yes, I didn't want to risk infecting the rest of the office . . . Yes, of course.

The tapping began again.

On the vent.

Tap. Tap-tap.

Softly at first, but growing louder as the conversation continued. Kugel stood and walked to the vent.

I should think so, yes, yes, he said, stomping angrily on the metal register grate. Yes, yes, plenty of liquids, *cough, cough*, I know, yes . . . Really, I am very sorry about it, sir, I just, well, better safe than sorry . . . Yes, sir, I think so, just a day is all . . .

Tap tap.

Maybe two days, you know, if it's a bad one, two or three days, tops, yes . . . Of course . . . I . . . yes . . . yes. Thank you, sir. Yes, sir, I will. Thank you.

89

Tap tap.

Kugel ended the call, slammed down the phone, and got down on his hands and knees beside the vent.

Shut up, you hear me? he whispered angrily into the vent. What did I just tell you? What did I just fucking tell you two fucking minutes ago? Don't tap on the vents! Finish your book! Eat your fucking apple! Just shut up! Shut the fuck up!

He stood, paced around the room, looked out the window, returned to the vent, and knelt down again.

Just *shut up*, he growled.

He stood, went to the window, ran a hand through his hair, and asked himself what Bree would do.

She would be calm, he knew. She would be rational. First of all, she would say, let's find out who this person is.

Yes, Kugel thought. Yes, of course.

He sat back down at the desk, went online, found the number he was looking for, and picked up the phone.

We'll see, he said, sneering up at the ceiling, who's alive and who's dead.

Kugel crossed the room, slid open the door to the closet, climbed inside, and closed the door behind him, reveling for a moment in the vent-free solitude within. He squatted down on the floor beneath his hanging shirts, coats, and pants, turned on the phone and dialed the number.

Sitting there in the dark, Kugel envied the clothing their solitude, their safety, but soon he worried that perhaps the clothes hated the closet, feared the dark – perhaps they wanted nothing more than to live, like the bed and dresser, beneath the soothing rays of the sun, beside open windows, no door no more. He worried about this often; sometimes he wore a shirt he didn't even like because he worried it felt bad, passed over day after day for something newer, sharper, cleaner. He spent the day feeling uncomfortable and ugly, and by the evening, he resented the very same shirt he had only that morning taken such pity upon, and he hung it back in the closet, swearing never to wear it again.

Good afternoon, said the cheerful woman on the other end of the line. Simon Wiesenthal Center, how may I help you?

Was it the afternoon already? Should the Simon Wiesenthal Center receptionist be so chipper?

Yes, said Kugel softly, hello. I was wondering if you could . . . .

I'm sorry, sir, you're going to have to speak up, I can barely hear you.

Hello, yes, said Kugel more loudly. I'm trying to find out if someone died in the Holocaust, I wondered if you could help me.

Of course, said the woman, her tone becoming instantly more somber. We have a vast searchable database, she continued, of all the millions of victims of Nazi brutality. Of course many died

91

outside the camps, or en route to them, so you understand that not every person that was murdered will be listed.

I understand, said Kugel.

Many died in the street.

Sure, he said.

Like dogs.

Of course.

In front of their wives.

I know.

And children.

Terrible.

Last name? she asked.

Frank.

First name?

Kugel swallowed.

Anne, he said.

Click.

Goddamn it, thought Kugel.

He climbed out of the closet and paced around the room. Now what? Should he phone the Museum of Tolerance? Should he contact the Anne Frank House? He couldn't imagine those inquiries would prove any more fruitful. What if that Wiesenthal woman phoned the ADL? he wondered. What if she told them a Holocaust denier had phoned, what if she had traced the call? Kugel imagined the ADL banging on the front door, dragging him from the house, kicking, screaming; he could see the forlorn look on Mother's face, the disappointment. She's in the attic, I swear! he would call out as they threw him into the back of the ADL van and locked the door. She's in the attic!

Tell everyone, why don't you? Mother would say.

The tapping began again.

Goddamn it, thought Kugel.

Kugel phoned Professor Jove.

Jove wasn't in.

Kugel left a message.

CHAPTER 10

Matzoh – 12 boxes
Herring – 1 jar
Borscht
Gefilte fish
Printing paper – 3 pak (no holes)
Mini-fridge

Mini-fridge? thought Kugel as he pushed a cart through the automatic doors of Mother Earth's Bounty Natural Food Market. Blow *me*.

Where the hell was he supposed to find gefilte fish in Stockton? And who the fuck needs a dozen boxes of matzoh? He hated even saying that word, *matzoh*. The Kugels had never been particularly observant, but when Kugel was young, the one holiday Mother celebrated every year was Passover.

It was a celebration, she said, of freedom.

Kugel hadn't seen it quite that way. It seemed more like a celebration of suffering, of slavery, a sacrament of hardship and abuse. Kugel, Mother, and Hannah sat around the seder table for hours on end as Mother read them stories of how their ancestors died, how babies were murdered, how rabbis were burned alive.

It made young Kugel angry. Hadn't he and Mother and Hannah suffered, too? Okay, so they hadn't been wrapped in Torahs and burned by the Romans, but it hadn't exactly been a picnic, either. Perhaps retelling the sufferings of others made Mother feel better about her own, but to Kugel, it just set up a pointless competition, a Misery Olympics he didn't want to compete in, the losers of which lost all claim to their legitimate pain, the winner of which won nothing but pity. Mother, it seemed to young Kugel, was forever going for the gold.

This, said Mother, as she handed him a piece of dry, tasteless matzoh, is the bread of our affliction.

Where, young Kugel wondered, is the seven-layer cake of our salvation? Where is the muffin of our mirth? Where is our no-longer-reduced-to-jelly doughnut?

Just eat it, Mother said.

The last words of Rabbi Akiva – the one the Romans wrapped in a Torah and lit on fire – were these:

Hear, O Israel, the Lord your God, the Lord is One.

Fuck that, thought Kugel as he made his way down the grocery aisle. Montaigne wrote of those who faced their executions with humor – not with mankind's narrow tragic perspective, but with God's all-seeing, humorous one. Said one man on

95

the gallows when asked if he had any last words: Let 'er rip! Said another as the priest pressed him to commend his soul to God: I'll just tell him when I see him.

Voltaire, on his deathbed, was asked to repudiate the devil. Is this, Voltaire asked, a time to be making enemies?

Gentlemen, said one George Appel as they strapped him to the electric chair, you are about to see a baked appel.

Funny.

Burnt Kugel.

But wrapped in a Torah? Lit on fire?

How about a little anger, Akiva? How about skipping the prayer to God above and saying a little something to His barbarous believers below?

How about, Fuck you?

How about, Fuck all of you motherfuckers?

Kugel pushed his cart to the side of the vegetable aisle, took out his Last Words notebook, and wrote that one down:

Fuck all of you motherfuckers.

He underlined it.

Not bad.

Kugel had discovered of late that he was gluten intolerant; the slightest amount of wheat in his food, and his stomach would spasm, his bowels would cramp, and the fury soon after with which his intestines attempted to rid themselves of the cursed grain was so great that he often wondered – on the train, in the car, in the mall – if he would

96

make it to the bathroom on time. It was difficult to avoid wheat, and gluten-free food was terribly expensive, but Kugel now thought it wonderfully appropriate that matzoh – the most hated food of his youth – was the one he, as an adult, would find he was allergic to, the one that his body was actually incapable of processing, the one that the lining of his gut identified as poison.

His stomach was anti-Semitic.

His bowels had assimilated.

His rectum was self-hating.

Anne Frank would be pleased.

Mother would be disappointed.

It seemed of late that everything had become poisonous. Wheat gave him diarrhea. Sugar made him sweat profusely. Caffeine gave him even worse diarrhea than wheat did, as well as intense anxiety, so that he anguished, doubled over on the toilet bowl, that the diarrhea meant something was going terribly wrong inside him, that he was decomposing from the inside out and was, in all likelihood, only moments away from death.

And that the toilet, understandably, was furious with him.

Jesus, said the toilet.

It's the wheat, Kugel said to the toilet.

Try the salad, the toilet replied.

Jonah was allergic to bees. And pollen. And cats.

How would they ever hide in an attic with Jonah allergic to bees? Winters would be fine, but spring would be impossible, with his constant sneezing

97

giving them away. Don't *ha-choo* shoot. Summer would be even worse. What if the bees got inside the attic, what then? He would have to remember to bring some EpiPens.

iPod and EpiPens; he would make a note of that. And Zyrtec, for the hay fever and sneezing.

iPod (headphones/charger)
EpiPens
Zyrtec

A list. The beginnings of one, anyway. It made Kugel feel better. He was preparing. He was fighting back. He would not be caught unawares. *Like sheep to the slaughter.* That's how Mother described the prisoners in the death camps. He wondered how Anne Frank might react to that description.

And if maybe sheep had the right idea.

Fuck all you motherfuckers.

It's okay, he would say, holding Jonah in his arms as they huddled in the eaves of their Stockton attic, soldiers in heavy boots in the hallway beneath them, shouting, cursing, shooting; he would try to calm Jonah down, try to just stop his body shaking in fear, in terror, or was that Kugel shaking, was that his own fear, was that his own terror?

Excuse me, said another shopper, trying to get by.

Fucking Anne Frank, man.

He took out her list.

Borscht? Did they sell borscht here?

Bree was allergic to color. A dye of some specific hue, some precise shade, though she didn't know which one, and doctors were unable to help. Recently she bought a pack of M&M's and ate one color a day for a week to see if she could identify the color herself – brown on Sunday, yellow on Monday, green on Tuesday, red on Wednesday, orange on Thursday, and blue on Friday. On Saturday, she rested. But every color gave her the same rash, so she assumed she was allergic to all colors. The doctors suggested she might just be allergic to dairy. Now she avoided colors as well as dairy. And wheat. And sugar.

The food at Mother Earth's was pure and natural and extraordinarily expensive. You paid more these days for the things you didn't get – no sodium, no fructose, no corn syrup, no MSG, fat-free, carb-free, dye-free, wheatless, flourless, sugarless – and with each ingredient that wasn't included, the price increased. A box of nothing – free of poisons, toxins, pesticides, a box that needed no warnings, no list of possible side effects and adverse reactions, a box that didn't harm unborn children or require checking with your physician before opening, a box of fucking air – would require a second mortgage.

Staying alive was costing them a fortune.

What kind of a monster brings a child into this world?

Jesus said Ouch.

Hitler was an optimist.

Do you have any matzoh? Kugel asked one of the Mother Earth employees.

Matzoh?

You know, said Kugel. Like for Passover.

Still, something about the store gave Kugel hope. All these remedies – plants, scents, vitamins, lotions – at least they were trying. They, too, were fighting back. With elderberry, sure, and shark cartilage. But fighting back was fighting, wasn't it?

The young man scratched his chin.

Kugel couldn't believe he was actually buying the old lady anything, but his hope was that she would finish her damn book quietly and just leave; that one morning he would awaken and go up to the attic, and Anne Frank would be gone, and he could go on with his life, Anne-free.

One hundred percent Frankless.

Now with Less Genocide.

Matzoh, repeated the young man.

Matzoh, said Kugel.

I don't think we have any of that, he said. Then, trying his best to be helpful, he snapped his fingers and added: We do have Ezekiel bread.

What's Ezekiel bread?

I'm not sure. Sounds religious, though. Biblical, you know?

Sold, said Kugel.

Crazy, anyway, buying this shit for some lunatic in my attic. Maybe getting the wrong thing would piss her off enough to leave. So she looked Anne

Frankish, so what? All old ladies look Anne Frankish. It's a misery thing.

Anything else? the employee asked.

Maybe he should get her some booze. It seemed to work for other writers. Some books, too – How to Write a Novel in a Month. A Week. An Hour.

Do you have a multi-vit? Kugel asked. Something for seniors?

He paid – that was thirty-six bucks he was never going to see again; 32 million copies and she can't pay for her own fucking Ezekiel bread – and headed out to the parking lot, stopping at the door to grab the local classified paper. If he couldn't throw her out on the street, maybe he could rent her an attic somewhere else. A little pied-à-terror, where she could cower in the corners until the world came to an end and it was at last safe to descend.

As he walked toward his car, Kugel spotted Wilbur Messerschmidt Jr, the forty-something son of Wilbur Messerschmidt Sr, from whom the Kugels had purchased their home.

Will, as Wilbur Junior was known to everyone in this small town, was a tall, fit man with a shock of red hair and a quick and easy smile, a beloved figure: a member of the town board, a part-time volunteer with the Stockton EMS, and a full-time volunteer with the Stockton Fire Department. His white pickup truck was a familiar sight; in the winter he could be seen pulling cars out of snowbanks or plowing neighbors' driveways; in the summer, he could often

101

be found helping the elderly carry their shopping bags to their cars, or changing flattened tires for grateful stranded motorists.

Will was leaning against the roof of a local police cruiser, chatting and laughing with the officers inside. Kugel approached, and Will greeted him with a hearty clap on the shoulder.

Hey, Mr K, said Will. Boys here almost got him last night.

Got who? asked Kugel.

That son of a bitch who's been burning down homes, said Will. Mr Kugel here bought Pop's place a couple months back.

The officer in the passenger seat nodded.

Tried to light another one up over on Tanglewood, the officer said.

Farmhouse? asked Kugel.

The officer nodded.

Kugel shook his head.

Didn't get very far, said Will, thank the good Lord. Our boys here showed up and gave him a good chase through the woods. Maybe the chief will find a few more bucks for you two now, eh?

Extra bucks? laughed the officer. Son of a bitch was madder than hell we didn't catch him.

Lucky he didn't can us, added the officer in the driver's seat. Good thing he had a beer in him.

They all laughed. Will slapped the roof of the cruiser and he and Kugel waved as the officers drove off.

Good guys, said Will, good guys. I know Kevin

since grade school. Didn't think he'd ever become a cop, though, truth be told – shit, the kid just about set his own house on fire trying to sneak a cigarette one night. How's the family enjoying the new place?

Well, said Kugel, now that you mention it.

Kugel glanced around, and, seeing that they were alone, said in a low voice: I found something.

Mm-hmm, said Will.

Something your father might have left behind.

Will nodded.

You don't say, said Will.

Something he left in the attic, said Kugel. In the *attic*.

He studied Will's face, looking for any sign of worry or surprise, but found there only confusion.

Like a bag or something? Will asked.

Kugel nodded.

Yes, said Kugel, like a bag. Like an *old* bag. I thought maybe your father would want the *old bag* back.

Will scratched his chin.

Hmm, he said, shaking his head. An old bag. Can't say I know of it. Truth be told, Dad took care of most of the packing. Where did you say you found it again?

Kugel glanced around again.

In the attic, he said. I found the old bag *hiding*. In the *attic*.

103

Will folded his arms and shook his head.

An old bag in the attic, he said, a bit more loudly than Kugel would have preferred. And then, like the young man in the grocery, he snapped his fingers and said: I wonder if it's Anne Frank's?

Kugel stared at Will for a moment, sure he had misheard him.

Will nodded now, certain that he had figured it out.

Yep, he said. I bet that's it. I bet it's Anne Frank's.

There was no mistaking that. Will had very definitely said the words *Anne Frank*. The shock of hearing her name spoken aloud both rattled and relieved Kugel; he wasn't crazy, that was something. That was the good news. The bad news was worse: someone – a respected member of the community, no less – believed she actually was Anne Frank.

Goddamn it, thought Kugel.

He *knew* she looked Anne Frankish.

Maybe he could order the matzoh online. Amazon probably sold matzoh; they probably sold borscht.

Did you ask her? asked Will.

Kugel, momentarily at a loss for words, shook his head.

Well, said Will, you might want to start there. I'm thinking if you found an old bag in the attic, it's probably hers. If it isn't, you might want to give my dad a shout.

Will handed Kugel one of his snowplow business cards and pointed to the phone number at the bottom.

That's the new home number, he said. How's she doing, by the way?

Who?

Anne.

Kugel looked at him a moment, uncertain how to best respond.

She's a little high maintenance, said Kugel.

Well, after what she's been through, said Will with a solemn shake of his head.

Unimaginable horrors, he added.

Sons of bitches, said Kugel.

An elderly woman pressed by, her arms full of grocery bags.

Mrs Lesko, Will called with a smile, what'd I tell you I'd do if I saw you carrying bags again?

She laughed as he took the bags from her arms and helped her to her car.

I'm calling Dr Zisman, said Will. I warned you.

Oh, don't you dare, Mrs Lesko said with a laugh.

I am.

Wilbur Junior, you call my doctor and I'm calling your father.

I can think of a few things you can call him that ain't been said before, said Will, and they both laughed again.

Kugel got into his car and slammed the door shut behind him.

He wasn't crazy.

That, at least, was something.

CHAPTER 11

U ncertain at first about the wisdom of moving homes, Kugel had consulted with Professor Jove. He described the charming house, the wooded property, the idyllic town of Stockton; he gave voice to his hopes for a new start, a fresh beginning. The professor sighed heavily and shook his head.

Why did the chicken cross the road? Professor Jove had asked him.

I don't know, said Kugel. Why did the chicken cross the road?

Because he was a schmuck, said Professor Jove.

I don't get it, said Kugel.

The chicken crossed the road, said Professor Jove, for the same reason we all cross roads – because he thought that there might be something better on the other side. Tell me, Mr Chicken: there are no wars on the other side of the road? There is no suffering, no divorce, no failure? No hunger, no disease, no tears, no pain? They don't commit genocide on that side of the road, Mr Chicken? On the other side of the road parents don't bury their children, sons and daughters always get the love they need, men and women don't grow old and bitter and die of regret?

Kugel looked down at his shoes.

Fathers disappear, said Professor Jove, his voice soft with compassion. On both sides of the road.

Can't hurt checking it out, though, said Kugel. The other side, I mean.

On the contrary, said Professor Jove. Nobody said the chicken made it to the other side. Roads are no place for naive chickens dreaming of nirvana. There are cars on roads. There are trucks. And there are a lot of flattened chickens. Few of them make it. And if one does, and he finds a Kentucky Fried Chicken there and says, To heck with this, I'm going home, odds are even higher that he won't make it back. Chickens would live longer lives if they just stayed on the side of the road they were on. And they'd live happier lives if they just stopped hoping there was something better on the other side. Kugel, I'll ask you again – why did the chicken cross the road?

Because he was a schmuck, said Kugel.

Precisely.

So you don't think I should buy the house.

Professor Jove shook his head.

I do not, he had said.

The Stockton office of Promised Land Fine Properties and Estates was located in the center of town, inside a stately old Victorian home whose interior had been converted into offices. Climbing the wide stairs of the wooden front porch, Kugel

107

wondered how the house felt about the conversion; resentful, he imagined; it probably missed having a family around; it probably missed the sounds of laughter and life and the smells of dinner, replaced so cruelly with the dead sounds of fax machines and printers and ringing phones. And, on top of that, to be used to sell other homes to the very families it so wished were living inside itself? The indignity.

Kugel tried the door.

Locked.

Goddamn it.

He knocked.

Nothing.

She can run, thought Kugel, but she can't hide.

He sat down on the bench beside the front door, put the grocery bag on the seat beside him, crossed his legs, and folded his arms across his chest.

I can wait.

So she was Anne Frank. Maybe. More to the immediate point, the man who grew up in his house was well aware of her existence – lived there with her, in fact, his entire life; if Will Junior knew about her, then Eve knew about her, too, and she had been required by law to tell Kugel everything – full disclosure, he recalled the term – which she obviously had not. She had lied to him, and Kugel now had proof. Good, he thought. The rancid grotesque in his attic was now Eve's problem; if she didn't want a lawsuit on her hands, she would get Anne Frank the hell out of his attic, posthaste.

The noon sun was directly overhead; even in the shade of Promised Land's porch it was brutally hot.

I can wait all damned day.

It's about the house, he would say to her. *We need to talk.* Her face would drop, her heart would pound in her chest, her horrible lie revealed at last. *It's about the house,* he would repeat. She would begin to sob, fearful for her job, her career, her family. She would throw herself at his feet, beg him not to report her, not to sue, she would swear to make it all right, to fix it, to make him whole. Or maybe not – maybe she would be aggressive, belligerent, denying it to the end. *You leave me no choice,* he would say, turning on his heel. *You'll be hearing from my attorney.*

Kugel stood, sat, and stood again, pacing back and forth on the porch, anxious to resolve this issue at last. He didn't want the old woman spending one more minute in his house, and if Eve would only return soon, they could get her out before Mother woke from her nap, before Bree returned home with Jonah from day care; nobody would know the hideous freak had ever been there. And even if she were Anne Frank, so what? Getting evicted wasn't the worst thing to happen to her in her life; in fact, thought Kugel, it was almost *better* that she was Anne Frank. She'd been through worse than a simple relocation, for God's sake.

Kugel stopped pacing to look over the property listings posted in the front window.

Nestled in the something.

Enjoy your own private whatever.

Unobstructed views of some goddamned thing.

If only he had picked a different house. A non-farmhouse. A house without an attic. A must-see modern contemporary with soaring ceilings, lots of light, and no survivors.

On second thought, said the first little pig, homeless now and forced to live with his brother, *I probably should have gone with brick.*

Kugel could see himself reflected in the Promised Land window, ghostlike and bedraggled over a perfect four-bedroom contemporary with an in-ground swimming pool on five gorgeous acres of rolling hills and outstanding views that wouldn't last at this price.

Ten-plus acres with something-top vistas.

Welcome to somewhere.

Leave wherever behind.

He looked like the living dead. He needed sleep.

He sat back down on the bench beside the door. The Stockton Café and Bakery was located directly across the street and, seeing it, Kugel was suddenly reminded of how hungry he was. He hadn't eaten a thing all day. His stomach rumbled, but he wasn't about to leave his post beside the door. Eve was probably inside, waiting for him to leave, so she could run out and flee.

Pathetic.

Or she was outside, waiting to run in.

People were the worst.

What was Ezekiel bread anyway?

Kugel was famished. Ordinary bread would cause his stomach to react violently, but he was starving now, and hoped there were no glutens in Ezekiel bread. Everything else in the grocery was gluten-free, he thought, why would Ezekiel bread be any different? He tore off the end of the loaf, and hungrily chewed it. He moaned with contentment and leaned back against the house. He tore off a second piece.

Fucking Ezekiel, he thought. How difficult could it be to be a prophet, anyway? Predict the absolute worst horrors you can imagine – persecutions, atrocities, fires, floods, famine – and odds are pretty good they'll come to be.

I see misery and suffering. I see pain and anguish. I see gnashing of teeth and desperate prayer but no help will arrive.

Really?

You think?

Isaiah, Jeremiah, Ezekiel – each one foresaw more misery than the one before, and what did that abject pessimism; that supernal, sorrowful, suffocating cynicism get them? It got them their own books in the Bible, that's what. Not little ones, either – fifty, sixty chapters a piece. You know who didn't get his own book in the Bible? The guy who said, *It's going to be okay, folks; honestly, I think it's coming around.* Nostradamus was no idiot – if he'd predicted peace, calm, and sunny skies we wouldn't know his name today.

The combination of the midday heat and his

now-full stomach caused Kugel to grow sleepy, and he yawned, leaned his head back against the house, closed his eyes, and fell asleep.

When he awoke some time later, his face was covered in a fine mist of sweat. He had no idea how long he had slept, but his insides were burning like the sun above; pain shot through his abdomen and stabbed at his belly. He groaned, winced, and doubled over in excruciating pain.

Fucking glutens, he grunted through clenched teeth. Fucking Anne fucking Frank.

He sat back up, and noticed a young couple on the porch beside him, standing together in front of the property listings.

They looked at him strangely.

They were quite tall.

Glutens, groaned Kugel again, forcing a smile.

The man put his arm protectively around the woman's shoulders.

Kugel, still bent over, did his best Adenoid Hynkel: Ah, the glutens, he said, shaking his fist. The glutens, the glutens.

The couple frowned and turned back to the listings. Kugel didn't like tall people, and these tall people were tanned, which made it even worse, the kind of tan that only comes from very intentional tanning; it wasn't that they had been out cultivating their garden, or even engaging in some mindless outdoor sport; no, these two had set out together, with single-minded determination, to become tan. Let's become tan, they had agreed, and after much struggle and sacrifice and aloe, they had at last achieved their goal.

Assholes.

It felt as if there was a furious rodent burrowing through his core, ripping his insides apart, desperately trying to get out, clawing at his flesh: an explosion of pain, first here, then there, subsided for just a moment before slowly building again somewhere else.

The woman's arm was around the man's waist, his arm was around her shoulders, and every time one pointed out a house to the other, they read it together and hugged and kissed.

If Kugel hadn't immediately disliked them so much he might have told them about the arsonist, might have warned them about Eve's duplicity. But he didn't like them, so he let them keep hoping. Besides, he desperately needed to get to a bathroom, and was concentrating as best he could on not allowing his bowels to move on their own; he couldn't fault his body for reacting so violently to what it regarded as poison, but it was a survival instinct that overrode any messages his brain tried to send his colon, and he knew from experience that in these situations, he only had limited control of that particular bodily function. Still, how could he leave now? He'd waited this long.

Excuse me, he groaned to the couple. Do you have the time?

The man turned and looked down at Kugel, who now felt terribly small.

No, said the man, pulling the woman even closer with his arm, but Kugel could clearly see the silver diving watch on his wrist.

Tall people appeared to have it easy; that was what Kugel found so galling. Like things just went their way. Let's go buy a house! Let's get expensive diving watches! Why not, we're tall! What could go wrong? The woman wasn't quite as tall as the man, but she was marrying into his tallness, hoping for a piece of that ever-perfect tall pie, and for that, Kugel hated her even more than he did the man.

The creature inside Kugel's gut lashed out again; a sustained blast of fiery pain; it was determined to get out, to find freedom.

I'd never make it in Auschwitz, thought Kugel. Not a week. Not a day. Bread was all they ate there, wasn't it? Soup if they were lucky. He'd die, he knew it, and not even in a gas chamber or a crematorium – no, not he, not Solomon Kugel; Solomon Kugel would die in the latrine. He'd die on the toilet. His descendants would speak of him sadly – Those sons of bitches, they would say – and they would make Great-grandfather Kugel out to be some sort of martyr, some sort of hero, but they would never speak openly about how he really died: doubled over on the crapper, dead of dehydration. Dead of glutens. Dead of the shits.

The woman pointed up at an advertisement for a large white Victorian house, in front of which stood a tall oak tree with fiery orange autumnal leaves. The man pointed to the child's tire swing that hung from one of the tree's heavy branches. The woman hugged the man and he kissed her on the top of her head.

Kugel could never survive a genocide, not with his stomach. And Bree, with her dye allergy; Pardon me, Herr Kommandant, but do you have a *clear* soup? I'm very sensitive to coloring.

Someone would have to hide them, that much was certain.

If what?

If something happened.

If what happened?

Something.

What?

Whatever.

But who? Of the roughly 2,400 residents in Stockton, Kugel knew about twenty of them by name; of those twenty, there were probably a total of seven who would agree to hide him and his family in their attic (this was assuming that those seven hadn't already promised their attics to other Jews, blacks, homosexuals, Asians, Muslims, immigrants, etc., which you had to assume at least two or three of them already had; first come, first saved). The Kugels, though, were at a distinct disadvantage for the remaining five attics: together with Bree and Jonah, there were three of them, and if Mother kept hanging on the way she was, they were four (I am *not*, resolved Kugel, taking

Anne Frank with us); realistically, they'd probably need a whole attic to themselves. He and Bree would share a bed, but Jonah was getting too old to share one, and Mother would need one, too (nobody was going to agree to share a bed with Mother, and Kugel would sooner force Jonah into a cattle car and seal the doors himself than make him share a bed with his grandmother). It wasn't a question of greed, just pragmatism, and, of course, no doubt: if the attic they wound up hiding in was large enough, Kugel would be more than happy to share it with another young couple, or maybe some children whose parents had been arrested by the authorities (they'd need constant reassuring, though, which he'd be willing to give them in the early days, but as the genocide dragged on, they were going to get on his nerves, he knew that now; man up, kids, this isn't easy for anyone). One thing was certain: with the Kugels' various dietary restrictions, whoever shared the attic with them ought to know straightaway that they were not going to be sharing their food, he didn't care how grim the situation eventually became; he'd bring an extra jar of peanut butter or something, some extra cans of corn, they can have some of that (he knew full well, too, that if they really did end up sharing the attic with two small children whose parents had been arrested by the authorities, he'd probably change his mind and share the food with them even though he was insisting now that he wouldn't; and, yeah, at the last minute, he'd probably take Anne Frank, too, so that made five people now, even before the orphans [let's face it, their parents are probably dead]). It would be nice if the attic were somewhere close by their home, not just so that he could get something if he forgot it (he'd definitely forget the iPod, he always did, and now, probably, the corn), but so that when the genocide was over, they wouldn't have too far to travel. Which is why, of the five people who might let Kugel and his family hide in their attic that hadn't already promised their attics to someone else, his first choice would be his next-door neighbors, the Ambersons, who, unfortunately, just adopted a puppy to replace a cat that had recently disappeared; even if the damn thing didn't spend all day standing in the hallway and barking up at the attic, it would only serve to remind Jonah of his confinement to see her running in the yard and chasing squirrels. The other choices were no better: the Millers down the road were Jews, so to hell with that (hiding from geno-cide inside a Jew's attic, thought Kugel, is like hiding from a lion inside a gazelle), and while the Dooners at the far end of the street were the only other neighbors Kugel knew, Kugel once borrowed their lawn mower and only remembered after returning it that he'd neglected to refill the gas; it was too awkward for him to go back and say so, so he never said anything at all. He even went out and bought a new mower of his own, not just so that he would never have to ask Dooner to borrow

117

his, but in the hopes that Dooner would see his new mower and understand, at some level, that Kugel had bought it as a way of acknowledging his earlier mistake.

Nice planet, Kugel thought; he and his family were going to die in a concentration camp because of a stupid lawn mower he forgot to refill. That's earth for you: the difference between life and death on this crap-sack planet is a half a gallon of gas.

Last words? he wondered.

Could be.

He was in too much pain to write it down, but promised himself he would later.

Anyway, even if Dooner let the mower thing slide and took them in, the Dooners themselves were going through a nasty divorce; she might report on them just to get her husband in hot water with the authorities.

The Kugels, Kugel hated to admit, might just have to, in the event of genocide, rely on the kindness of strangers.

Mother used to say: I can name six million people who relied on the kindness of strangers.

When Kugel left for college, she took him aside, held his face in her hands, and said: No matter where you go, you'll always be a Kugel.

She meant Jew, he could hear it in her tone. It was meant not as encouragement but as warning; she meant that someday he would be murdered by people he had considered his friends.

Pardon me, said Kugel, getting to his feet. He

could feel another abdominal attack building deep within his bowels. Sometimes walking helped.

Yes? asked the man.

Would you mind watching my bag for me? I desperately need to get to a bathroom.

We're leaving soon, said the man.

It will only take a minute.

We're leaving.

Kugel winced in pain.

Do you have an attic? he asked.

Pardon me?

I was just wondering, said Kugel. Never mind.

You were just wondering if I had an attic?

I was wondering, if you had an attic, ow, if I could hide in it.

What?

With my family.

Are you crazy? the man asked. Is that it?

Kugel winced in pain.

Not *now*, he said, don't be ridiculous. Ow. Ugh. I mean, you know, if something happened.

If what happened?

Something, said Kugel.

You think that's funny? asked the woman.

Ow, said Kugel. Funny?

I lost relatives in the Holocaust, she said.

So? asked Kugel.

So I find that offensive.

I lost family in the Holocaust, too, said Kugel. Oh, God.

Oh, really, she said.

119

Really, said Kugel, wincing again. Oh, God.

She crossed her arms over her chest.

How many? she asked.

How many what? asked Kugel.

How many relatives, she said.

Kugel shrank in pain.

Enough, he said, turning back to rest on the bench. Forget it.

Enough? she asked. How many?

Enough, he said.

How many?

How many did you lose? Kugel asked.

She scoffed.

More than you, she said.

The pain that had been growing exploded within him again. Kugel squeezed his eyes and commanded his organs and orifices to fight on, to resist, but it was for naught.

Oh, God, he cried.

What is the matter with you? asked the man.

Kugel hurried down the porch steps, bent over, hands on his stomach.

Watch my bag, he grunted, watch my bag . . .

There was no time, he knew it, not even enough to get across the street, and Kugel – begin-againer, starterer-anew – had no option but to scurry to the side of the house, press through the plants and shrubbery arranged along the foundations, and, squatting down, relieve himself there.

I wouldn't survive ten minutes, he thought as he did. I wouldn't even make it to head-shaving.

Nick, Sharon, he heard a woman call out, there you are. Have you been waiting long?

It was Eve.

I foresee humiliation and shame.

I foresee tortured innards and wasted days and . . .

No problem, said a male voice now. Nice to see you.

The tall man. Nick.

Eve was at the front of the house. He leaves for one damned minute . . .

This is the one, said the woman. With the tire swing. Is that as nice inside as it is outside?

Kugel straightened his clothes as hastily as he could, and stumbled out from behind the rhododendrons.

More so, he heard Eve say. Just came on the market, too. Shall we go see it?

Kugel stopped at the edge of the grass, fixed his hair, tucked in his shirt, took a deep breath, and walked purposefully, head held high, around the corner of the house.

Mr Kugel, said Eve.

You know this guy? Nick asked Eve.

Kugel clasped his hands behind his back and looked Eve in the eye.

It's about the house, he said.

Of course, said Eve.

Eve invited Nick and Sharon to wait for her beside her car, she would only be a minute.

You look tired, Mr Kugel, said Eve when they had gone. Moving can be so stressful.

121

It's about the house, said Kugel.

There's something wrong with it, said Eve, taking out a cigarette and tapping the end against her wrist.

Not *with* it, said Kugel. *In* it.

Mice?

Not mice.

Bats?

I'm referring, he said, lowering his voice, to a certain Holocaust victim.

He leaned toward Eve to emphasize his point.

In my *attic*, he said.

A Holocaust survivor? Eve asked. In your attic?

Nick and Sharon turned to her.

Keep your voice down, said Kugel.

Eve lit her cigarette and blew the smoke out the side of her mouth, a look of genuine concern upon her face.

Is it Elie Wiesel? she asked.

Don't be ridiculous, said Kugel.

Is it Dr Ruth?

Dr Ruth isn't a Holocaust survivor.

She isn't?

I think she got out before it started.

Are you sure?

Nick and Sharon approached, and asked if they could use the office bathroom. Eve handed them the key to the front door and invited them to help themselves, while they were at it, to some of the cookies on the front desk.

Eve waited for them to go inside before turning

122

back to Kugel. Kugel folded his arms across his chest.

Is it Simon Wiesenthal? asked Eve.

Anne Frank is in my attic, snapped Kugel, and you damn well know it.

Well, said Eve, I can see how that would be a problem. But I assure you this is the first I've ever heard of it.

And why, precisely, should I believe you?

I'm a real estate agent, Mr Kugel. As a rule, you shouldn't believe me. But in this case, I'm telling the truth.

She won't leave, said Kugel.

I would imagine not, said Eve. You've got a gradual roof slope and high attic knee walls.

You don't sound very surprised, said Kugel.

Buyer's remorse, said Eve, is an interesting phenomenon, Mr Kugel. It's this vague, creeping notion that one has been had, that he's spent too much money, that what he got isn't worth what he gave. So the buyer decides there is something wrong with the house, something specific, some-thing structural, and he comes to tell me about it – the boiler's shot, the foundation's a little crooked, the electrical system needs an overhaul. Little things, but real things. Maybe they can replace something, trade up, maybe they can get some money back and the remorse will go away. It usually does. Buyer's *guilt*, though, is different. The homeowner comes here, tells me there's a problem, something's not right. But they can't name anything specific with the house, nothing tangible. There's nothing I can do. They say they're unhappy, but they're wrong. They are happy. That's the problem. They're very happy and it's making them sick. You know why? Because they think they don't deserve it. They've been selfish, they've been unfaithful, they've cheated on their taxes. They've been inattentive to their spouses, cruel to their parents, absent with their children. They've taken the easy way out. They followed the money instead of following their hearts. They masturbate to violent pornography. Whatever it is they enjoy, they are certain it disqualifies them from being happy: they don't deserve the stone walkway, the master bath, the walk-in closets, the nights of lovemaking in front of the soapstone-lined fireplace, the long walks in their fifty-acre woods, the starry nights above their in-ground pool, the autumn leaves kicking up behind their white all-wheel-drive convertible Audi with cream leather interior. People in Africa are starving, and here they are with a fifteen-thousand-dollar industrial Wolf oven they never even use. People in Treblinka slept three to a wooden bunk, and they've got a California king in a bedroom so large that there's still enough room for a leather couch and a small additional seating area beside the French patio doors. There's an oil well puking black death into the Gulf, there's childhood leukemia, everything's going to hell, why should they have a screened-in porch with a slate floor and a ceiling fan that cost eight hundred dollars? They don't deserve it. And do you know what I tell them?

No, said Kugel. What do you tell them?

I tell them they're right. I tell them they don't deserve it. I tell them nobody does. Abraham was an adulterer. Moses was a murderer. Jesus jacked off, bet on it. That's why he wept. It's not an ugly world because you're in it, I tell them; I tell them they're ugly because they're in this world. You know who deserves radiant heating, marble floors, glass-enclosed showers, and Jacuzzi tubs? Nobody. Not a single goddamned person in the whole world. I sure as hell don't. I sell enormous homes to people who don't need them. I put my career before my children. I cheated on my husband, and then lied under oath that he beat me. Now I have two kids, no spouse, six bedrooms, and fifteen acres. I have a horse. I have a stable. I'm sleeping with a married employee I don't love and will fire once the lovemaking gets boring. And I'm happy. Not thrilled, not ecstatic, but happier than I deserve to be. I tell them this: there are better people than you who have less, and worse people who have more; if a proper reckoning were to be done, I tell them, if everyone in this world got what they truly deserved, most of us would be lying facedown, beaten and bloody in a fly-infested pool of steaming cow shit.

And what do they say? asked Kugel.

They say Anne Frank's in my attic, said Eve.

They say there's a bad smell coming from the vents, they say the house is tilting, or the windows are jammed or nobody told them about the winters. They want out. Not out of the house: out of happiness. Some people just can't hack it. And then do you know what I tell them?

No. What do you tell them?

She dropped her cigarette to the ground and stubbed it out with the toe of her high-heeled shoe.

I tell them to fuck off, said Eve. I tell them that's what the third-party inspection was for, and I tell them that I have their signature on a legal document indemnifying Promised Land Fine Properties and Estates from any problems with the house the owner knowingly withheld from us or which the buyer in the course of the sales transaction neglected to inform the seller and/or the seller's representatives. I tell them if they have a problem with happiness, they should call a shrink. I tell them if they have a problem with the house, they should call the former owner. And then I slam the door.

There's a bad smell coming from the vents, said Kugel.

And Eve slammed the door.

126

CHAPTER 12

When at last Kugel arrived home, he found his sister Hannah's car parked in his driveway.

Marvelous, thought Kugel.

Hannah was not taking Mother's impending death very well; when Kugel relocated to Stockton and Mother later joined him, Hannah decided to rent a small house a few towns over – so she could be close, she said. Just in case.

Just in case what? Kugel asked.

Just in case, said Hannah.

Hannah was married to an evolutionary biologist named Pinkus Stephenor. Pinkus took a teaching job at the nearby local university; Hannah visited Mother often, and often, when visiting Mother, Hannah wept. Mother would hold her in her arms and say, Come now, let's not do this.

Hannah would nod and compose herself.

You're right, she would say, you're right. Everything happens for a reason.

Then Mother would add: Let's not spend our last hours together weeping like children – which would cause Hannah to begin weeping once again.

Hello? Kugel called as he came through the front door.

He could hear voices.

Upstairs.

Mother and Hannah.

What the hell were they doing upstairs?

He put the Mother Earth's bag on the small table beside the door, dropped down beside the vent in the foyer floor, and pressed his ear against the grate. The blower was on; this not only made it more difficult to hear voices, but the stench that had been slowly returning now rushed forth from the vents, enveloping Kugel in a noxious, suffocating smog.

Kugel held his breath and tried to listen over the hum of the machinery.

Hannah (*sobbing*): Oh, Momma.
He couldn't make out the rest. He sat up,
    took another breath, and bent back down
    to the vent.
Mother: Stop that, Hannah.
Hannah: You're right.
Mother: Now, where on earth did I pack
    those photos? I know there was another
    box up here somewhere.

They're in the attic, thought Kugel with a shudder. If Mother discovered Anne Frank, he was finished. She would never let Kugel throw Anne Frank out. No son of mine, she would say, is throwing Anne

128

Frank out of his house. She wouldn't particularly enjoy the competition for his pity, either, which would only make a bad situation worse.

I foresee days of darkness.

I foresee long trips of guilt.

Pull that box down, Hannah, he heard Mother say. Maybe it's behind there.

Kugel grabbed the Mother Earth's bag and raced up the stairs.

There was a small chance that it could go the other way; Mother always had to be the biggest sufferer in the room; she might not want to have an actual Holocaust survivor in the house. It's the 500-meter Sufferer Dash at the Summer Misery Olympics, and Carl Lewis just lined up beside you. Mother might actually *insist* that he throw Anne Frank out, demand he do just that.

Hope springs eternal, Kugel once said to Professor Jove.

It doesn't have to, Professor Jove had replied.

Though he ran upstairs as quickly as he could, by the time Kugel reached the attic, Hannah had already taken down nearly half the boxes from the recently reconstructed western wall. She was leaning over the top of the remaining crates and chests and peering into the darkness behind them; Mother was sitting on the floor nearby, sifting through an opened box.

Nope, Hannah was saying, no more boxes back there; just some old blankets on the floor. And some old computer. It's on, though, that's weird.

What's on? Mother asked.

The computer.

The computer's on? Mother asked.

Kugel, in an effort to distract them, made a loud entrance, calling out to them, telling Mother she really shouldn't be lifting those boxes herself and demanding Hannah come away from that wall and say hello this instant.

It was still daylight; from the short bit of her diary that he'd read, Kugel knew that Anne Frank slept in the daytime and worked at night. They must have woken her, but where did she go?

Kugel was ashamed to admit that he'd never actually read the whole diary. By the time Mother had given it to him at age thirteen, she'd already made him read Elie Wiesel's *Night*, and *Dawn*, and *Day*, and Primo Levi's *If This Is a Man*; and sit through all three hours of Stanley Kramer's *Judgment at Nuremberg*, all seven and a half hours of NBC's *Holocaust*, and all nine hours of Claude Lanzmann's *Shoah*. Then she handed him *Anne Frank: The Diary of a Young Girl*.

I'm sick of this Holocaust shit, young Kugel had said.

So horrified was Mother at that, she didn't even yell at him; she didn't lecture him; she simply turned on her heel and walked away. Later, he went to her and apologized.

I'm sorry, he said.

She gave him a choice: *Anne Frank: The Diary of a Young Girl* or *The Sorrow and the Pity*.

He took the diary from Mother's hand and turned it over. The heartbreaking something, he read, of a tragic whatever.

He went with the documentary, all five hours of it. At least he could fast-forward when Mother wasn't looking, and he kind of knew how it ended.

Kugel gave Hannah a long, enthusiastic hug, holding her tightly while peering over her shoulder for Anne Frank.

He didn't see her. The floor, he noticed, was strewn with photos, newspaper clippings, and scissors.

Mother, said Kugel, releasing his sister. What did I tell you about that?

For some time now, Mother had been putting together a family scrapbook for Jonah. Kugel had begged her not to, but with her memory fading and her time running out, she was determined to leave behind a family history for her sole grandchild. She had requested assistance from her children, cousins, aunts, and uncles in the form of any old family photographs they could provide her with, and they speedily obliged. To her dismay, however, the photographs told a very different story from the one she remembered, or wanted to tell, or wanted Jonah to be told: faded black-and-white photos of families playing in the sand at the beach, beaming brides and proud grooms, sepia-toned families enjoying a round of badminton fun at some well-manicured Catskill resort, young lovers holding hands on the boardwalk at Coney Island as appreciative passersby smiled wistfully in their direction.

Useless.

So she began to include, here and there, a news photograph of prisoners at Buchenwald, some press clipping about pogroms in the Soviet Union, a collage of Kristallnacht, corpse piles at Dachau, mass graves at Auschwitz, until these terrifying images of history's tragic victims equaled, and soon outnumbered, the photographs of any actual Kugels.

Zelig himself, thought Kugel, would be proud. Then he would turn into a lamp shade.

Mother began the project last year, when Jonah had taken sick. From the beginning, Kugel had begged Mother not to editorialize; Mother insisted it was just adding context, making history come alive. Kugel appreciated that she wanted to leave his child something, but there was, he insisted, a better story, a truer story: her story. Mother's story. A story of moving on, he said, of a woman left alone and raising, against the odds, a pair of seminormal, occasionally functioning children with only mild sexual dysfunctions.

He should know about his past, Mother said.

You are his past, said Kugel.

Mother shook her head.

I had it easy, she said. If all you teach a boy about hurricanes is what it's like in the eye of the storm, he'll never know what to do when the wind tears the roof from overhead and the rain destroys all that he owns.

Kugel stared at her for a moment.

What the hell are you talking about? he asked.

132

I'm talking about life, said Mother.

You're talking about death, said Kugel.

What's the difference? asked Mother.

Reason rarely worked with Mother, so Kugel had appealed, as he often did, to her emotions. As destructive as her way of showing it may have been, Kugel believed she loved Jonah deeply, and genuinely cared, first and foremost, for his well-being.

You're going to scare him, Kugel said, looking deep into her eyes.

Somebody has to, Mother replied.

Hannah went to Mother and began helping her collect the loose photos from the attic floor. It was then that Kugel spotted, through a gap between the boxes on the wall behind Hannah, the cloudy yellow eye of Anne Frank.

We should get dinner going, said Kugel.

Mother sighed loudly and shook her head at the clipping in her hand; it was of the now-iconic photo of male prisoners in the Buchenwald concentration camp, crammed on top of one another on the stacked wooden planks that passed there for something like beds.

Your cousin Alex, she said.

For as long as Kugel could remember, Mother had kept a large print of this photo on the wall of their old living room in the city; every so often, she would point to one of the prisoners – the young one, using his metal food bowl for a pillow, or the one on the bottom bunk, the one with those terrible sunken raccoon eyes – shake her head, and say, poor Cousin Alex. Or, Oh, dear Uncle Morris. Or, How I miss your grandpa Solomon – you were named for him, Sol.

Kugel glanced at Anne Frank.

We really ought to get dinner started, he said.

Kugel remembered the photo, was haunted by it, less for his supposed family members and more for one of the prisoners, the naked one standing at the far right of the frame. He was emaciated, pale shrunken skin pulled tight over weary twisted bones, holding a cloth of some kind over himself in some final instinct of modesty and self-respect. And, somehow, he was smiling. Kugel was sure of it, ever since Mother first showed it to him; it wasn't a broad smile, more of a grin, a Mona Lisa thing, but a smile nonetheless.

Why is that man smiling? he had once asked Mother.

He's not smiling, she said with disgust.

But he *was* smiling, there was no question about it. Even now, as Kugel went to help Mother up, he looked at the photo and saw him, still naked, still emaciated, still smiling. Why, Kugel wondered anew, was he smiling? What was so funny? And, more important, most important: how? How can one smile in that world of misery and death? And why, for that matter, did he still play along with this game of Mother's? Why didn't he ever just call her on it, make her at last admit the unhorrible truth: that life, tragically, hadn't been so bad? That, relatively speaking, they had been, unfortunately, fortunate?

Let's go, Mother, he said. We should get dinner going.

Sons of bitches, said Mother.

It's okay, said Kugel.

Kugel helped Mother up, and she protested – There isn't much time, she said – until Kugel promised to bring the photo boxes downstairs later so that she could continue her work in her bedroom. Kugel was most concerned that Jonah not discover what Mother had been putting together, and her bedroom was the safest place for that (Jonah had not set foot in there since she moved in).

Hannah, meanwhile, was kneeling beside the box of photos, holding a small black-and-white photograph in her hand, cupping it like a broken bird. She shook her head and sighed. It was a photo of Father.

That son of a bitch, she said, hatred hardening her voice. A wife, a home, two beautiful children. What kind of a coward kills himself?

Kills himself? asked Kugel. Turning to Mother, he said, You told me he disappeared. You told me he was murdered.

What's the difference? Mother asked.

What's the *difference*? Kugel asked.

What's the difference? Hannah snapped, coming to Mother's defense. Everything happens for a reason, so what's the difference?

Then why are you so pissed off at him? Kugel asked.

At who?

135

At Father.

Just because there's a reason for what he did, said Hannah, tossing the photo to the floor, doesn't mean I can't be pissed off. And just because I'm pissed off doesn't mean there isn't a reason. There is a reason for everything.

There's absolutely no reason to believe that, said Kugel.

It was a common belief – reasonism, Kugel called it. They were a volatile bunch, the reasonists; all Christians, for example, are reasonists, but not all reasonists are Christian. Hannah was more of a general reasonist, not getting too specific about what the reason might be but certain above all that there was one – and it wouldn't irritate Kugel as much as it did if she were more honest, if she acknowledged, however briefly, that if there was indeed a reason for everything, it was as likely to be a bad reason as it was a good reason. But for reasonists, the reason was always positive: to teach us X, or so that we learn Y, to bring us closer to Z. The reason was never because life's a bummer, or because whoever or whatever the Reason for Everything is, it finds our misery kind of funny.

Hannah's face had grown red with anger, and a family feud was only narrowly averted when, just then, the tenant appeared at the top of the attic stairs.

No space, Mr Kugel? said the tenant, looking around the attic. It certainly seems to me you have plenty of space.

We've just been tidying up, said Kugel.

136

Very good, said the tenant. So then at last I can bring my belongings up?

Yes, said Kugel, of course. Let me just figure out a reasonable time . . .

Reasonable time? the tenant asked. What's wrong with right now?

It's late, said Kugel. My son will be going to bed soon, and I'm concerned the noise overhead will keep him up.

I truly hope we won't have to settle this in court, Mr Kugel, said the tenant.

Big talker, said Mother.

Pardon me? said the tenant.

Do you really think, Mother said to Hannah, he'd be opening his fresh mouth like that if Alan Dershowitz was here?

Mother, said Kugel, guiding her to the stairs. Let's just go downstairs.

You left your grocery bag, said Hannah.

I'll get it later, said Kugel.

Mother wagged a finger at the tenant.

He'd wipe the floor with you, she said, that's what he'd do. One little phone call, one little letter from Alan Dershowitz, and you'd run away with your tail between your legs.

Let's go, Mother, said Kugel.

Yes, sir, Mother continued, even though the tenant had already gone. If Alan Dershowitz was here, young man, you'd be shaking in your boots.

137

CHAPTER 13

Mother went to bed early; this was fortunate, because all through dinner, the tapping on the vents never ceased. At times it sounded to Kugel as if Anne Frank were using her arthritic, gnarled knuckles to rap on the metal register; at times it sounded as if she were using her talonlike fingernails; at times something metal – a spoon or a knife.

Tap, tap-tap.

No, he thought.

Tap. Tap-tap.

No.

Go fuck yourself.

He refused to respond to her, to encourage her.

Six million he kills, thought Kugel, and this one gets away.

I shouldn't have thought that, he thought.

At least I didn't *say* it.

But you thought it.

That's not as bad.

It's bad, though.

I just wish she'd shut up. I just wish she'd go away.

It was exhausting. Whenever the tapping began, Kugel did something to try and mask it – clanking his dinnerware, shuffling his chair on the floor, coughing.

Are you okay? Bree asked.

Wrong pipe, Kugel said, clapping his chest.

Bree probably hadn't heard the tapping anyway, thought Kugel, rapt as her attention was in the discussion she was having with Hannah about Brooklyn.

Bree loved talking about Brooklyn. When Mother moved in with them, Hannah and Pinkus had taken over her old apartment in Williamsburg, and Bree couldn't hear enough about it.

Bree had always wanted to be a writer, and though she had been writing for a while now, and applying herself with fierce determination to learning her chosen craft, she had yet to find success in the publishing world. In her darkest moments of frustration, when she swore she would never write again and swore a moment later that she could never do anything else, Kugel tried to convince her that her writing was improving, deepening, and that was all that mattered. Everyone, though, needs some external acknowledgment, and Bree was no different. She began to have regrets, doubts. She wondered if she should have gone to a different university, if she should have taken more workshops, if she should have read more books. And she wondered, lately, if she should be living in Brooklyn.

You know who I saw the other day? Hannah said to Bree, and, not waiting for an answer, continued: Philip Roth.

Brooklyn seemed to be the center of the literary world of late, and Bree couldn't help wondering if living in a more artistic, urbane location would prove helpful to her career, would inspire her. What would Joyce have been without Dublin, Miller without Paris, Kafka without Prague?

Really? said Bree. Does he live in Brooklyn?

Of course, said Hannah. Philip Roth?

Tap, tap-tap.

I thought he was dead, said Bree.

Tap, tap-tap.

Kugel stood, went to the sideboard, and turned on the stereo.

Maybe it was that other guy, then, said Hannah. What's his name?

Can you lower that? Bree asked Kugel.

Sorry, said Kugel.

What is that, anyway? she asked.

Wagner, said Kugel.

It's depressing, said Bree.

Kugel shut off the music.

Tap, tap-tap.

He ran the sink.

He flushed the toilet.

Bree said, What's with you? Sit down and eat already.

Kugel said, I'm not hungry.

Later that evening, as Bree lay beside him in

140

bed with her head on his chest, pressing her warm body against his, Kugel stared up at the ceiling and wondered what Anne might have needed. The tapping had stopped some time ago. Was she dead? She had her bread, she had her vitamins. Water? Had he given her water?

Bree ran her hand over Kugel's arm and looked up at him.

I'm worried about you, she said.

He hadn't been sleeping well for some time, she pointed out, and now he wasn't eating.

Are you really that worried, she asked, about some stupid arsonist?

Kugel shrugged.

He hated keeping things from her, hated the bottomless chasm even the smallest lie created between them.

Oh, who cares, said Bree with a smile, sliding her leg over his and snuggling tightly to him. Let him burn it down; the insurance is worth more than the house anyway.

She looked up at him.

We'll go to Brooklyn, she said with a grin.

Kugel kissed her and smiled. He assured her that nothing was wrong, that it was just the stress of the move. Bree ran her fingers gently through his hair, told him that the storm was over, that they could just settle in now and enjoy life. She lightly traced her fingertips over his lips.

The tapping on the vents began again.

Tap, tap-tap.

Bree kissed his cheek, his chin, his mouth.

Kugel turned his head from her; she kissed his neck, and he stared at the heating vent in the floor.

I can't, he said.

Tap, tap-tap.

Bree ran her hand over his chest and whispered in his ear, Of course you can. It's been so long.

I know.

What's wrong?

I just can't.

Why?

There's just . . .

He shook his head again.

There's just too many damn people in this house, he said.

Bree pressed herself up and looked at him.

It's your mother, isn't it? she said.

Kugel sighed; he knew that this had been coming for a while. They'd never really discussed Mother's moving in, or the effect it was having on them. Bree's anger, he knew, had been building for a while.

Bree stood and angrily pulled on her robe – tap, tap-tap – tying it tightly around herself as she went on a furious tirade against Kugel's mother, and against Kugel himself, leveling the same accusations at him as she had when he had first told her that Mother was to move in: that he cared only for his mother, that he was a momma's boy, that he was Abrahamically sacrificing the Isaac of their future on the altar of his miserable past. That she was getting tired of this. That there was just so much she could take.

Kugel, meanwhile, had dropped to his knees on the floor, and was busily covering the vent with as many pillows and quilts as he could gather, piling them into a small mound above it.

What in God's name are you doing? Bree asked.

She can hear us, whispered Kugel as he worked.

Perfect, said Bree. That's just perfect. I'm yelling at you for only caring about your mother, and you're covering the heating vents so she won't hear me. That's perfect, Sol.

He stopped, sat back on his heels, and looked up at her.

It's not Mother, he whispered.

Who is it, then? Bree asked. Jonah? He knows more than you think.

Kugel stood and ran a hand through his hair. It was time.

It's . . . someone else, he said as he got to his feet.

Someone else? asked Bree, crossing her arms. What are you talking about? You're fucking someone else, is that what you're trying to tell me?

Kugel pulled the chair away from his desk and sat down, his head heavy in his hands. He rubbed his face and looked up.

It's Anne Frank, he said.

Bree stared at him for a moment, hands on her hips.

You're fucking Anne Frank? Bree asked. Isn't she a little young for you, Sol?

143

Last night, he began. I heard something.

He told her everything. That she was up there, that she was old, grotesquely so, and that she claimed to be Anne Frank. That Wilbur Junior seemed to think that was who she actually was. Bree stared at him, now dumbfounded, now incredulous, but Kugel felt better already. Why hadn't he told her right away? It was as Professor Jove always said – hoping he could protect her, he had only succeeded in hurting her, lying to her, when all she ever gave him was support and encouragement.

Tap, tap-tap.

Goddamn it, said Kugel. That's her.

He kicked the pillows aside and threw himself onto the floor.

Shut up, he shouted into the vent. Shut the fuck up!

Bree stepped backward, a hand over her mouth.

You're mad, she whispered in horror. It's the move, the money, the stress . . . You need help, Sol, we'll get you help . . .

Kugel sat back on his heels and placed his hands on his heart.

The important thing, he said, is that we're communicating. That we're being honest with each other. Nothing can come between us when we're together. It's been a hell of a twenty-four hours, Bree, I'm just, I'm wiped out.

Tap, tap-tap.

Shut up, he hissed at the vent.

144

He looked to Bree, who was staring now at the vent.

She's a little high maintenance, he said.

Bree pointed to the vent.

Right now? Bree asked, her voice soft and trembling. There's someone up there? In our attic? Right now?

Kugel nodded.

Right now there's someone in the attic?

Kugel nodded.

Just calm down, he said.

Calm down?

Calm down.

Calm down? she said, her voice rising.

Her eyes filled with rage.

How, she demanded, was she supposed to calm down? How did he know that she wasn't dangerous, that she wasn't a criminal, a thief?

She can barely move, Bree.

How did he know she wasn't carrying some disease? He had a son to think about, even if he didn't care about his wife. Had he thought about his son for even a moment?

Of course I care about you.

What kind of man was he being? What kind of father? Was that why he hadn't gone to work? Was he risking his family's well-being in the middle of an economic depression to take care of this old lunatic? Where were his priorities? Had he called the police?

He stood and went to the desk chair.

I called the Simon Wiesenthal Center, Kugel said with some pride. He wasn't, after all, an idiot.

You called the Simon Wiesenthal Center.

Yes.

Before calling the police.

Yes, he said. Keep your voice down. To find out if she was dead.

You called the Simon Wiesenthal Center to find out if Anne Frank is dead.

Yes.

How did that go?

They were less than helpful.

The book sold twenty million copies, Sol.

Thirty-two, said Kugel. It's a tough act to follow.

Bree would take no more. This was just like the situation with Mother, she said – someone else always comes first, someone else always needs Kugel more than his wife and son. She demanded that he throw the woman out, immediately. And she insisted that he phone the police.

Or, so help me God, she said, I'll take Jonah and leave. I'll go to Brooklyn. I will not subject him to this.

Kugel sat in the chair, unable to fight back, unable to answer, his head in his hands as he weathered all the abuse and anger she rained upon him. He knew she was right. And he knew he couldn't do as she asked.

Tap, tap-tap.

She has numbers, he said without looking up.

She *what*?

146

She has numbers.

What numbers?

On her arm. Camp numbers.

So?

So she's a survivor.

So?

Only now did Kugel look at her, surprised by her lack of compassion.

So? he asked. *So?*

I don't understand, said Bree. If Elie Wiesel knocks on the front door tomorrow, we're supposed to give him the guest room?

Not if he shows up, no, said Kugel, not if he knocks on the door. But if we find him in the guest room?

Find him?

Yes, find him, said Kugel. Under the bed, or in the closet or something. Like I found her. You'd want me to throw Elie Wiesel out of our house?

What are you saying? asked Bree. If I'm cleaning the guest room next week and I find Elie Wiesel hiding under the bed, you're not going to throw him out?

Kugel shook his head.

No, he said, surprising even himself.

Why not?

He's Elie Wiesel, hon.

You're insane.

Keep your voice down.

You're insane.

I'm insane? said Kugel. You want to throw Elie Wiesel out of the house and I'm insane.

147

So if Simon Wiesenthal turns up in the dryer you're not going to ask him to leave?

He's dead, honey.

Hypothetically.

Hypothetically? asked Kugel.

He didn't like what he was thinking, didn't like what he heard himself saying.

Hypothetically, she said.

Hypothetically no, said Kugel. Hypothetically I'm not throwing Simon Wiesenthal out of the fucking dryer.

What about Solzhenitsyn? asked Bree. We're going out for dinner, I take a shower, open the bedroom closet to get some clothing out, and Aleksandr Solzhenitsyn's sitting on the floor. Does he get to stay?

That's ridiculous, said Kugel, relieved to have found his own limit. He'd totally throw Solzhenitsyn out.

Oh *that's* ridiculous?

Solzhenitsyn wasn't in the Holocaust, hon.

He was in the Gulag, said Bree.

The Gulag wasn't the Holocaust.

So we're specifically housing Holocaust survivors?

Keep your voice down, said Kugel.

He stood, shook his head, and turned to the window. The woods were dark, forbidding. Why couldn't he have found an arsonist, why couldn't he have found mouse shit? He knew what he sounded like, and he hated it, but he didn't like

148

what she sounded like, either. She had relatives who died in the camps, too; how could she be so cold?

Tap, tap-tap.

You know, said Kugel, this hasn't been a picnic for me, either. I was trying to protect you, to leave you out of it. I haven't slept in days, Bree, I've been berated by real estate agents, by a Holocaust foundation, who knows if they contacted the ADL – it hasn't been easy, you know?

Tap, tap-tap.

Kugel kicked the pillows off the vent and bent over.

Shut the fuck up, he shouted. I heard you, okay? I heard you!

Kugel grabbed his bathrobe from the bed and angrily pulled it on.

What about Sharansky? asked Bree. He wasn't in the Holocaust.

Bree, said Kugel as he headed for the door, I'm not throwing Sharansky out.

Where are you going? she asked.

Kugel stamped angrily down the hallway and pulled the attic stairs down. He climbed up two steps at a time; maybe, he thought, I should just throw the bitch out.

The attic was dark.

What? he called out.

Nothing.

What do you want? he called out again as he approached the wall of boxes. I'm in no mood for jokes. I'm in no mood for this hide-and-seek bullshit.

He looked over the wall. Anne Frank was on her side, sleeping. The laptop was closed, and he could hear her ragged breathing.

Tap, tap-tap.

Kugel turned to the vent in the attic floor. He approached it slowly.

Tap, tap-tap.

Kugel knelt down beside the vent.

Mother? he said.

I'm frightened, came Mother's reply.

Kugel closed his eyes and dropped his head.

Mother, said Kugel, go to sleep.

I can hear you fighting, said Mother. I don't like hearing you fighting.

We're not fighting, Mother.

I should go, she said.

Mother, you don't have to go. We weren't fighting.

I'm sorry.

Mother, go to sleep.

I'm a burden.

Go to *sleep*, Mother.

Kugel stood up, checked again on Anne, and went back downstairs, folding the attic stairs as quietly as he could. He climbed into bed; Bree lay with her back to him, on the far side of the bed.

She's not staying, said Bree.

I'm not dragging Anne Frank down the stairs, honey. I'm not throwing Anne fucking Frank over my shoulder, kicking and screaming, and dropping her on the front lawn of my house, I'm sorry, I'm just not doing it.

Anne Frank is dead, said Bree.

I wish, said Kugel.

Bree switched off her bedside lamp and pulled the covers tight around her. Kugel was thankful for the darkness that surrounded him.

She's not staying, said Bree.

Kugel turned his back to Bree and stared at the wall.

Why couldn't he have just found shit?

She just wants to finish her book, he said.

I'm in no mood, Bree replied, for jokes.

CHAPTER 14

T hat night, Kugel dreamed he was looking
out his bedroom window whereupon he
spied a long procession of derelict elderly
men and women, stretching as far as he could see,
dragging themselves along his driveway; skeletal
and withered, they moved slowly, bleating and
bawling all the way; they went barefoot, their
crumbling, emaciated bodies draped in dirty
hospital gowns and gray, soiled pajamas; they were
bent and broken and bandaged; some had their
heads wrapped in gauze, some had walkers, some
went with wooden crutches, some with steel IV
towers, the small black plastic wheels stuttering
along the crushed-stone drive. Some stumbled and
fell to the ground, unable to rise; the others took
no notice, didn't try to help them to their feet,
just kept walking on, moving ahead, even stepping
on them, trampling them, as their inexorable plod-
ding march continued. They frightened Kugel,
though he didn't know why, old and enfeebled as
they were. He hurried down the stairs and out the
front door, where he stood at the end of the front
walkway, shouting at them to get off his property,

152

warning them that he would call the authorities if they did not turn around immediately, but they paid him no attention. They moaned and groaned as they hobbled forward, sounding more like a herd of bruised cattle than human beings, drawing closer and closer to the house. Jonah had followed Kugel out onto the front porch, and Kugel shouted back to him to go inside, to lock the doors, and to tell Bree to phone the police. They grew closer. Kugel bent down, picked up a sharp stone, and threw it toward them with as much force as he could; with a sharp crack, the stone hit one elderly man square in the skull, but he didn't seem to feel it, or if he did, it didn't slow him down; his head snapped back, but he just kept on ambling forward. Kugel threw another stone, and then another, striking them on their shoulders, chests, heads, but none having any more effect than the first one had. Closer and closer they came, until they were upon him, and Kugel shouted for Bree and covered his face and shut his eyes, waiting for the beating to begin – he couldn't bring himself, even now, to lash out at them with his fists – but the beating never came. With his eyes still closed, he could feel them brushing past him, groaning and moaning and oy-veying by, as if he weren't even there. They had a stench about them like decay, like old neglected books. He opened his eyes as they shuffled by; their thin bare legs were covered in soot and mud; a few had wrapped their feet in old rags and newspapers, but they weren't English papers, they were foreign, a language Kugel couldn't recognize. When the last one had passed, Kugel turned and followed them around the corner of the house, where they had continued toward the high, sharp cliff at the edge of the property. Hey, he called to them, hey, watch out. Again, though, they took no notice of him. Hey! he called again. But they continued walking, bleating, braying, shuffling toward their doom, and soon, one by one, they were stepping off the edge of the cliff and falling, without a cry, to their deaths.

Kugel woke with a start.

He sat up, listening.

Had he heard something?

He lay back down, tried to sleep, but sat up sharply when he thought he'd heard the sound again.

Maybe when I'm dead, he thought. Maybe when I'm dead I'll get some goddamned sleep.

He wondered if there was a last line in that.

Sleep, at last. Or: *At last, sleep.*

To sleep, perchance to something.

Perchance to sleep?

To sleep perchance to sleep even more?

Something.

He picked up his notepad and wrote that down.

Byron, on his deathbed, said: Now I shall go to sleep. Good night.

How about: Don't wake me for breakfast.

Or: Cancel my subscription to the *Times*.

Or that old joke: Do not disturb any further.

That wasn't bad for a tombstone:

SOLOMON KUGEL
Born.
Died.
Do Not Disturb Any Further.

That sound again. A creaking.

Could be nothing.

Could be a door opening.

Could be two trees, their trunks rubbing together in the wind, nothing more.

Nature, he couldn't help noticing lately, was trying to scare the shit out of him. Fucking with him. He couldn't help noticing that the extremes of temperature caused the wood of the house to expand and contract, making it sound as if a roof beam were snapping, as if the house might collapse and crush them all; he couldn't help noticing, too, that lightning seemed to happen only at night, when it was most frightening; he couldn't help noticing that if nature caught you sitting peacefully on the veranda one morning, enjoying the warm summer breeze and sipping a cup of tea, WHAM, she'll cause a door somewhere to slam shut, a newspaper to fly away, a table to tip over. Sure, sure, François-Marie, all we have to do is tend our gardens. But what if your garden is trying to kill you, what then?

Again the creaking.

Kugel quietly crept out of bed so as not to wake Bree, knelt on the floor, and pressed his ear to the heating vent. He tried not to breathe; the stench was unbearable, even without the blower vomiting it up into the air. He heard Jonah, snoring lightly, and a moan of pain – that was probably Mother. He didn't hear Anne typing. At this time of night, he could usually hear her typing. Maybe the creaking was her? Maybe she was walking around the house? Was that lunatic down here, walking around the house?

Anne? he whispered into the vent.

Nothing.

Mother?

Nothing.

Ma?

Kugel tiptoed out of the bedroom and into the darkened hall. He was relieved to see the attic stairs closed, and decided to check in on Jonah. Kugel knew that parents were supposed to enjoy watching their children sleep, but Kugel did everything he could to avoid it. Jonah seemed even more vulnerable in his sleep than he did during the day, his delicate chest rising and falling and seeming at times as if it could so easily stop, for no reason, with no warning or symptoms, going one moment and then, in the next, not. It was evening, it was morning, it sucked.

Kugel thought he might get a gun.

Just a small one.

For protection.

Not too small, though.

He crept downstairs, took the flashlight from beside the garden door, and walked outside.

Hello, he whispered. Hello?

Or a dog. Something big. Not too big, though.

He switched on the flashlight; the beam seemed pathetically weak in the heavy dark of night. The air was cool. He wondered if it was any cooler in the attic now, too. Maybe he should get her a fan.

Maybe it was too cool. She was old, after all. Maybe he should get her some blankets.

Kugel swung the light across the line of trees at the edge of the woods and called out: I know you're fucking out there, motherfucker.

He waited.

Nothing.

What a world, thought Kugel; whoever you were, wherever you were, whatever time of the day or night, you could open your back door and call out I know you're out there motherfucker, and nine times out of ten you'd be right. The motherfucker might not be in your own backyard, he might not be in the neighbor's yard, he might be in the next town over, in the next state, in the next country. But the motherfucker was out there, and he meant you harm.

Why was Smiling Man smiling? Had he lost his mind? Had the photographer been joking with him? Had he made a joke himself – about his nudity, his frailty?

What's your best side? the photographer might have asked.

Looking down at his skeletal form, Smiling Man might have said: These are all my sides.

157

Maybe he wasn't smiling, after all.

Why was it so important to Kugel that he was smiling?

Because he *was* smiling, whether we wanted him to be or not.

I fucking know you're fucking out there, Kugel called again.

A .22.

Nothing crazy.

Something small.

Not too small.

For protection.

A Doberman.

Just in case.

Mother's defense against the motherfuckers out there was paranoia. Better spooked than sorry.

It's a theory, thought Kugel.

Professor Jove was opposed to guns, not because of the physical danger they posed but because of the ominous hope they represented. The whole notion of personal protection caused Jove some concern, from national armies on down, and he saw a troubling similarity between gun owners and health fanatics, the former hoping they could protect themselves from the threat of man, the latter from the threats of life, of age, of nature, of death.

You never see a happy jogger, said Professor Jove, or a happy gun owner. Do you know why?

Is this a joke? asked Kugel.

No, said Professor Jove. It's because they both

158

know they're chasing the impossible. So they run more miles, they lift more weight, they eat more protein and less carbs, or they eat more carbs and less protein. So they buy a bigger gun, a second gun, a third gun. Schmucks. Has a gun owner ever, in the history of the weapon, been satisfied with a small gun? If a small gun can save me, he figures, what can a big gun save? What can the biggest gun save? What can a bomb save? Tell me, Kugel: What did Helen Keller do when she fell into the pond?

Kugel sighed.

I don't know, said Kugel. What did Helen Keller do when she fell into the pond?

She drowned, said Professor Jove. She struggled to reach the surface, but the exertion only made her body more desperate for oxygen and her lungs began to contract and expand on their own. Soon the spasms in her chest ceased, and she lost consciousness and died.

I don't get it, said Kugel.

Maybe she jogged that morning, said Professor Jove. Maybe she had a .22 in her dresser drawer. Schmuck.

Kugel swung the flashlight back and forth across the face of the woods. Nothing moved.

Asshole, he called out.

And: Don't fuck with me.

Kugel went back inside and locked the door.

A Rottweiler, maybe. With one of those spiked collars.

After being in the fresh air outside, the stench inside the house seemed even more pronounced. The vent cleaners had suggested that perhaps it was caused by a small animal, dead in the very walls it had climbed behind for safety, but that wouldn't explain why the smell returned after they had cleaned it, or why it seemed of late to be getting worse.

Awake anyway, he thought. Might as well try to find out where it was coming from.

Kugel got down on his hands and knees, nose up, sniffing and crawling as he went, out of the kitchen, into the living room. Here the stench weakened somewhat, but after crawling into the hallway and foyer, he picked up the scent again. At the tenant's room, the smell seemed to grow stronger.

He knew that bastard had been up to something.

He considered knocking, demanding to know what the tenant was up to in there, but it was three o'clock in the morning, and he decided to wait until morning. Before he left, just to be certain, he sniffed along the rest of the hallway, and indeed the smell was at its worst in front of Mother's bedroom door.

He quietly got to his feet, knocked gently on the door, but heard no reply. He wrapped his hand around the doorknob; turning it slowly, he silently pushed the door open.

Mother? Kugel whispered.

Nothing.

He stepped into the room. The bed was empty.

Mother?

He heard a sound in the darkness from the far side of the bed. He switched on the light and stepped around the bed.

Ma? he called.

And then he saw her, squatting down beside the bed, over the heating vent, just the silver halo of her hair at first, as she was peering down between her knees. Kugel said, Mother? again, and she looked up, and he recognized the expression on her face, it was the same expression he'd had on his own face, every day and night for a week after Passover, after eating that damned matzoh, that cursed bread of affliction, and she saw him there, and she shook her head and said, her face red with exertion, Ever since the war.

I know, said Kugel.

Alan Dershowitz looked on.

Those sons of bitches, said Mother.

It's okay, said Kugel.

It's okay.

CHAPTER 15

Kugel awoke early the next morning, turning his face from the harsh rays of intruding sunlight that stretched across the room like some goddamned thing that stretches across some other goddamned thing.

Why did children always draw the sun smiling? he wondered. It's a giant ball of *fire*, kids. It's rage and fury. Whatever it's doing, it isn't fucking smiling.

Kugel sat up, dressed, went out back, left vegetables for Mother in her garden, gave Anne Frank the finger, and decided to go for a bicycle ride.

Bree had given him the bike as a gift when they first moved in – that seemed like so long ago now – all titanium and carbon fiber and bright yellow paint, hoping he would use it to relieve his stress, to change his mood. It hadn't quite worked out that way. He found bike riding stressful – the worries about flat tires, the concerns about getting up the next hill, the cars and trucks speeding by only inches away. Still, he couldn't give up on the idea – riding a bike *should* be calming, even if it wasn't so for him – and he didn't want Bree to think that he didn't appreciate the gift or, worse, that he was incapable of enjoying it, of enjoying anything (anhedonia, a psychiatrist once told him by way of diagnosis, the inability to feel pleasure; it isn't the inability, Kugel argued, it's the knowledge that pleasure is just a prelude to pain; exactly, said the psychiatrist). So Kugel rode, hoping it would calm him, knowing it probably wouldn't, hoping it would mollify Bree's anger, knowing it probably couldn't. Perhaps, he hoped, she would see him riding back up the driveway, and think, Well, he's trying. Perhaps she'd spy him through the living-room window, struggling up the impossible gravel drive, and she'd think, That's why I love him. That's why I've always loved him. He's made some mistakes, sure, but they were with the best of intentions, and isn't he doing what he can now to correct them, to make things anew? This can't be easy on him, either, can it? Perhaps, she would think, an apology was in order.

Kugel set off, the wind in what would have been, some years ago, his hair.

Everything this morning was dead.

Crushed turtles.

Burst raccoons.

Flattened chipmunks.

Of all the roadkill Kugel passed, chipmunks were always the most troubling. Maybe it was because they seemed so innocent. They weren't, though, he knew that; he had watched them now and then in the garden, fighting, stealing food, attacking

163

birds. They were adorable, territorial pricks. They were survivors, and survival wasn't pretty. What, then, was so disturbing about the flat ones? Maybe it was because they always seemed so desperate to survive, forever darting, running, fleeing. Maybe it was because they always seemed so terrified, and Kugel hated to see their fears validated for future generations of chipmunks. This patch of hair, Mother Chipmunk would say to her children, was your grandfather; this bloodstain was your aunt. Or maybe it was because when they darted across the road, more than any other animal, they seemed so certain they would make it to the other side. Deer, like Kugel himself, seemed certain they wouldn't make it. Tentatively they stepped into the road, frightened, waiting for the truck that would slam into them, for the car that would split them in two. Maybe, he thought, stopping his bike and kneeling down beside the furry remains of one such now two-dimensional chipmunk, it was just the way they popped. He picked up a nearby stick and prodded it. Most other animals seemed to get flattened, pressed like a dress shirt onto the roadway, everything staying tight and contained and crushed. Chipmunks seemed to pop, from the inside out, like a tube of toothpaste squeezed from the bottom up, like hairy little ketchup packets, the rolling pressure of the enormous vehicle above them forcing all their guts and brains right out through the tops of their little heads. Pop. The chipmunk at Kugel's feet lay there like all chipmunks lay there: a furry, flattened body with a red/gray ejaculation of blood and brains having burst from his little exploded head. To Kugel, chipmunks looked as if they'd died of a good idea; a great idea; an idea so unbelievably revolutionary that it made their lovable little heads burst. Like they'd cured some disease. Like they'd proved (or disproved) the existence of God. Like they'd figured out the meaning of life.

Well I'll be damned, Stan, we're only here to *ka-pow*.

The irony, thought Kugel, as he peeled the dead chipmunk off the road with the stick, was that what they'd actually died of was a bad idea. A terrible idea. They'd died of the worst idea in the world, an idea that always seemed like a great one at the time: they died of 'Let's cross the road.' They died of 'Let's see what's over there.'

I wonder if life is better on that *splat*.

That looks like a nice place to raise a *wham*.

Well, we can always come back if it doesn't *oof*.

Maybe they bothered him because in their desperate hope they reminded him of himself. Maybe Professor Jove had been right. As this hopeful chipmunk's corpse was beginning to disintegrate, Chipmunk Anne Frank was at home, storing her nuts for winter and letting all the foolish dreamer chipmunks try their luck on the other side of the road.

What if she died? Kugel wondered.

Anne Frank.

What if she was dead already?

He flicked the dead chipmunk to the side of the road, happy to help the little believer, albeit in death, reach his dreamed-of destination, got back on his bike, and continued riding. He wasn't so much concerned for Anne Frank's passing as he was that there would be a corpse in the house, even for a small amount of time. What if she died in her bed, directly over Jonah's bedroom? What if she died of a great idea? Kugel was surprised to realize that he had gone, in such a short time, from wanting to kill her to worrying that she might be dead. Who could blame her, after all? Maybe hiding in an attic your whole life wasn't insane; maybe not hiding in an attic your whole life was. Ask the chipmunk.

What would Anne Frank's last words be? he wondered as he rode.

Gas is running low, said Amelia Earhart in her last radio communication before her plane disappeared. Of course those were just the last words she ever said to anyone else – her actual last word, as the plane went down, might just have been *Fuuuuuuck*. Most likely it was *Fuuuuuuck*, why wouldn't it be? Nobody is going to admit that *fuuuuuuck* was someone's last word, even if it is the most appropriate last word of all. It's possible she didn't die going down, of course; she might have landed safely on an island, thanked God, and then discovered the island was deserted and had no food sources. Last words: Fuck, now what?

He liked that.

Now what?

He would write that down when he got back home.

Now it has come, said Laurence Sterne.

He meant *Fuuuuuuck.*

More light! shouted Goethe. More light!

He meant *Fuuuuuuck.*

Fuuuuuuck isn't a bad way to go. To hell with all the profundity and wit and pithiness; Anne Frank struck him as someone who might just want her last word to be *fuuuuuuck.*

Let's do it, said Gary Gilmore.

Toodle-oo, said Allen Ginsberg.

Kugel, thinking of last words and Anne Frank's demise, drifted into the middle of the road. A black van sped by, horn blaring.

Asshole! called the driver.

Kugel steadied his bike and held up his middle finger. The driver leaned on his horn in reply.

Vans are the vehicles of murderers. Serial killers, rapists, thieves. Nothing good ever happens in a van. Police should be allowed to arrest van drivers without cause. The van is the cause, asshole.

Kugel spent the rest of the ride worrying that the black van would return. He worried the driver would force him into a ditch, or mow him down, or drive by and shoot him in the head. Then he'd steal the bike Bree gave him and sell it on eBay. *Like new. Ridden once. Light scratches on frame.*

The attic life, thought Kugel, is the life for me. I should go for a bike ride, it will help me *ka-blammo.*

167

I need to learn to stop and smell the *wham*.

It's a wonderful *ka-pow*.

Kugel entered the house, covered in sweat, glancing back at the road before closing the door to see if the black van had followed him.

He locked the door behind him.

Then he unlocked the door, wheeled in the bicycle, and locked the door again.

He stood and listened. He could hear Bree in the kitchen preparing breakfast, but that was all. He went to his knees and pressed his ear against the vent. No tapping, that was good. He could hear the tenant, though, speaking on his phone. Laughing. What was he laughing about? He was probably laughing at Kugel, mocking him.

Dad? asked Jonah.

Kugel looked up. Jonah was standing before him, still in his Spider-Man pajamas, which were covered in crumbs.

Oh, said Kugel, hey, buddy.

What are you doing?

I was just checking the heat.

Is it broken?

No, no. It's fine.

Dad?

Yeah, buddy?

Why is the bicycle in the house?

Why? I thought it would be safer here. What are you eating?

Jonah held up the piece of bread in his hand.

Grandma's bread, he said.

Grandma's bread? asked Kugel.

Jonah nodded.

Was she eating it? Kugel asked.

Jonah shook his head.

I got it from the couch, he said.

Kugel sighed. Mother had been hiding bread around the house ever since reading that this was common behavior among survivors of the Holocaust. She hid it under her mattress, beneath the rugs, in between the cushions of the couch.

Did Grandma say you could have it? Kugel asked, getting to his feet.

Jonah nodded, taking a bite out of it.

She did?

I saw her putting it there last night, said Jonah.

And she said you could have it?

Mm-hmm, said Jonah. She said I would thank her for it.

Joney, said Kugel, bending down to kiss Jonah on the head, don't eat Grandma's bread. If you want bread, just ask me.

Dad? asked Jonah.

Yeah, buddy?

How come Grandma puts bread in the couch?

Well, said Kugel, she's old, buddy.

Are you going to put bread in the couch when you're old?

Probably, said Kugel.

Am I?

I hope not.

Mother came into the room then, wearing her

sun hat and carrying her basket full of vegetables. Kugel asked Jonah to go into the kitchen for breakfast.

I asked you, Kugel said to Mother when Jonah had gone, not to do that here.

Not to do what?

Not to hide bread.

Mother waved at him with annoyance.

They don't have Holocausts in Stockton? she asked.

No, said Kugel. They don't.

We'll see.

Mother, I asked you not to. I was concerned my son might discover it.

And?

And he has.

And?

And I don't want to get into the meaning of genocide with him just yet, Mother.

Why not?

He's three.

So?

So I don't want to frighten him.

He'll thank me when they kick his doors in.

When who kicks his doors in?

Whoever.

Whoever?

What's the difference? said Mother. A kicked-in door is a kicked-in door. You care so much who's doing the kicking in?

Kugel decided then and there that he would die

170

a happy man, that he would consider his meager life a success, if in years to come, somewhere, someday, someone kicked in Jonah's door and Jonah was surprised. Shocked. Amazed. Let him be utterly bewildered, dear God. Let him wonder, raised-eyebrowed and slack-jawed, They kick doors in now? Since when? Hang on, hang on – they're putting people in *ovens*? You can't be serious. Since when do people put other people in *ovens*?

If you have to hide it, said Kugel, hide it in your own room.

Mother waved him off again and headed for the kitchen.

Oh, please, she said. That's the first place they'll look.

Let him be floored, O Lord, thought Kugel.

Let him be stunned.

Let him be flabber-fucking-gasted.

After checking that he'd locked the front door, Kugel entered the kitchen. Bree was at the stove, scrambling eggs; Jonah was at the table, which Bree had set and filled with plates of bread and muffins; through the window, Kugel could see Mother back in her garden, filling a second basket with store-bought groceries and rejoicing at the bounty she had brought forth into the world.

Kugel watched Bree as she worked at the stove, her hips swaying slightly as she did, and fresh desire rushed through his veins.

Kugel had only loved one other woman in his

life, an African-American woman named Aleeyah, whom Mother disapproved of for not being Jewish. She would, Mother wailed, be the end of the Kugels, which only made Kugel want Aleeyah even more (so much did he want her that he was willing to overlook the fact that her name, in Hebrew, meant *to go up*, and was the idiomatic term used to describe immigrating to Israel; Kugel hated the superiority and judgment implicit in that term, and though he loved Aleeyah and thought the world of her, he was concerned that a part of him, however small, just wanted to 'fuck Aleeyah'). Unfortunately, Aleeyah was an intensely political member of the African-American community, and all she seemed to want to speak about with Kugel was the suffering of her people, of slavery and Tuskegee and Birmingham.

Can we talk about something else? he asked one night.

Can we talk about something else?

I don't want to talk about the past all the time.

The past, said Aleeyah, is the present.

Then let's talk about Auschwitz, he said. Let's run a warm bath, fill it with bubbles, undress, climb in, and talk about Auschwitz.

I'm sick of that Holocaust shit, said Aleeyah.

When he met Bree a few months later, the fact that she was Jewish was mitigated by the fact that her connection to that part of her history was tenuous at best; she neither hated nor adored it; she simply didn't give it much thought. He admired that about her, emulated her, wanted to become like her; how much happier he could be, he thought, if he could just turn ambivalence into indifference.

Well? asked Bree as Kugel sat down at the table.

Well what? Kugel asked.

Bree glanced at Jonah.

Did you talk to h-e-r? Bree asked.

Kugel sat down at the table beside Jonah.

She's a s-u-r-v-i-v-o-r, hon.

Bree brought over the plate of eggs and dropped it with a clang onto the table in front of Kugel.

Who isn't, she said.

Bree had suffered physical abuse when she was a child – her father had been a violent man with a drinking problem, her mother a weak woman with a self-esteem problem – and the moment she turned eighteen, she left her home and moved to New York City; she hadn't spoken with them since. At the beginning of their relationship, Bree wanted to talk about it and Kugel wanted to listen. Like his own mother, though, he felt that, compared to Bree, he hadn't quite suffered enough, and wasn't qualified to advise or even relate to her. What was an absent father compared to an abusive father? Was a good father leaving as bad as a bad father staying?

Which is worse? Kugel had asked.

They're both bad, Bree had said.

Yes, said Kugel, but which is worse?

It's enough that you listen, Bree had said, but

173

Kugel couldn't help wanting to help, even if the only way he could think to help her was to help her help herself. With books. Books had always been his answer, and he bought her so many self-help books – Overcoming This, Getting Past That, Coming to Terms with Your Whatever – that she soon stopped wanting to talk about it at all, concerned that this part of her past she just needed to talk about, to share with him, was now becoming, for Kugel, her defining feature. She was no longer Bree; she was becoming Bree of Sorrows, Bree of the Leather Belt, Bree of the Thrown Shoe; Bree, Patron Saint of Adult Children of Alcoholics.

I suffered, Bree maintained. I'm not a sufferer.

Kugel wasn't sure he understood the distinction.

The tenant appeared in the doorway. Kugel was not in the mood for him. He didn't want to hear about the damned attic. There were dead chipmunks all over the road. Did this jackass even know that? Did he even give a damn about the poor dead optimistic chipmunks?

The tenant did not enter, remaining instead in the doorway, arms folded across his chest.

This house, Mr Kugel, said the tenant, smells like *shit*.

Kugel felt a searing rage grow in his heart, a rage he could feel throughout his entire body, in his fingers, in his toes. Maybe the rage was due to lack of sleep, maybe it was all of it – Anne and Mother, Bree and Eve, bicycles and chipmunks, the past and the present – but he was suddenly certain that his situation would not have become as dire as it was – indeed, there would be no difficulties at all – were it not for the damned tenant; were it not for his damned complaining, his damned insolence, his damned arrogance; were it not for his damned covetousness, duplicity, and selfishness, would this situation ever have gotten so out of hand or seemed so insoluble?

I shouldn't be surprised, the tenant continued, unaware of the hatred building within the man before him, that it smells like piss. It smelled like piss when I first got here. But the smell of shit, Mr Kugel, that is not . . .

Kugel stood suddenly, knocking his chair over backward and pointing an angry finger at the tenant.

Get out! he roared.

The tenant stepped back.

Get out, Kugel continued loudly, stepping toward him, or shut the hell up. Stop threatening me, stop complaining to me, stop it all, or so help me God, I'll throw you out on your ass.

The blood was pounding in Kugel's ears; if it came to blows, he thought, he might kill the son of a bitch.

Solomon! said Bree.

Jonah began to scream.

The tenant turned on his heel and left.

Bree lifted Jonah into her arms and now it was Kugel's turn to have an angry finger thrust in his face.

You better make sure he doesn't leave, Bree

hissed. And then, pointing to the ceiling, she added, And you better make sure she does.

She grabbed Jonah's lunch bag from the kitchen counter and stormed from the kitchen.

Bree, said Kugel, as he followed her.

She stopped when she reached the front door and glared at him.

And if your mother doesn't drop d-e-a-d soon, she said, I'm going to k-i-l-l her myself.

She slammed the door behind her.

Kugel stood with his hands on his hips, his head lowered. The silence that rushed in after them, at least, soothed him.

Tap.

Kugel closed his eyes.

Tap-tap.

Don't tap on the vents, said Kugel aloud.

TAP.

TAP-TAP.

Don't tap on the vents, he said again, louder this time. He threw himself to the floor and shouted into the vent, tears of anger and frustration clouding his eyes.

Don't tap on the vents! Don't tap on the vents! Get out of my house, would you? We all have our problems! You're not special! You're average, you're ordinary – do you know that? You're fucking boring, you're a quitter, your troubles are over, you have the damned attic, stop complaining. I'm down here, trying to live, trying to deal with the real world, while you're hiding, bitching,

176

fucking everyone's shit up but your own, so shut up, just shut the fuck *up*. Thirty-two million copies, thirty-two million copies, that's what you got for your pain. What do I get for mine? What does anyone get for theirs? Nothing, not a fucking thing, they get another goddamned day of it and another goddamned day of it after that, so just shut up, will you? Will you just shut up?

Kugel heard the back door open. A moment later, Mother appeared.

The corn is coming in so nicely, she said. And avocado – who knew? I always knew I had a green thumb. But who can tend a garden when you're always running, always fleeing, always being chased? *Feh*. There's no end, no end. They won't give us a moment's peace.

She sighed heavily.

Why are you on the floor? she asked. Who are you talking to?

TAP.

What's that noise? Mother asked.

TAP-TAP.

And that was when Kugel – on the floor, on his hands and knees, shouting into a foul-smelling vent, bowed like that before his mother, standing in front of him, gloating over an armful of vegetables she never planted – realized the solution to his Anne Frank problem.

She was standing right in front of him.

He'd considered it before – Mother always had to be the biggest sufferer in the room – but now he was sure of it. There he was, tears running down his cheeks, and she's talking about being chased from her garden.

Mother, said Kugel, getting slowly back to his feet, there's something I have to tell you.

She wouldn't suffer another sufferer in the house for one moment, particularly one who had the numbers to prove it. There was no way.

He led her to the couch in the living room and sat down beside her.

Who died? she asked.

Nobody died, said Kugel. I don't want you to be frightened, okay, but the other night, I discovered someone – an old woman, far older than you – hiding in our attic.

Mother gasped.

In *our* attic?

Kugel nodded. There was a loud crash from above.

That's her now, said Kugel.

You're putting me on, said Mother.

Kugel shook his head.

And there's something else you should know.

Kugel watched her face closely as he said the next words: She's a survivor, Mother.

Mother frowned and stiffened, crossing her arms over her chest.

Bingo.

A survivor? said Mother. Please. Of what?

A Holocaust survivor, Mother. She has numbers. And she says – and here's where I need your help, Mother – she says she's Anne Frank.

178

Oh, for goodness' sake, said Mother. Is this some kind of a joke?

Kugel slowly shook his head. He explained that he had tried to find out for certain if she was who she claimed, that he had made certain calls, certain inquiries, but it wasn't easy, and she did look like Anne Frank, and her story did seem to contain a certain degree of plausibility.

Did you call the police? asked Mother.

No.

Did you call the Simon Wiesenthal Center?

I did.

And?

TAP, TAP-TAP. TAP, TAP-TAP.

Kugel glanced down at the vent.

She's calling me, said Kugel.

How?

She's tapping on the vents.

Why is she tapping on the vents?

She's a little high maintenance, said Kugel. Come, let's go up.

Now?

Mother was frightened, but Kugel assured her as they headed upstairs that it would be okay, and that if she was really uncomfortable – well, this was her house too, and she should feel free to tell the old lady to leave, to just get the hell out, to find another attic somewhere else. He added that, due to her own time in the war, she was certainly better qualified than he to know if the woman was lying or not, not just about being Anne Frank but

179

about having been in the war at all. If, Kugel assured Mother, she decided the old lady was a fraud, and that she needed to go immediately, well, then, he would act on her wishes. This was, after all, her house, too.

Kugel pulled down the attic door, and unfolded the stairs.

I'm frightened, said Mother.

There's nothing to be frightened of, Mother, she's quite old. She couldn't hurt a fly.

Kugel called up the stairs for Anne to come down.

Anne? he called. Anne, are you there?

Nothing.

She sleeps during the day, he said to Mother.

This is absurd, said Mother.

He waited another moment.

Anne, he called, it's me. I heard you tapping. I thought I'd come see if you needed anything.

He smiled at Mother and winked as he made the 'She's crazy' sign with his finger, twirling it at the side of his head.

It's all right, Anne, he called again. I'd like you to meet my mother, I've told her all about you. She loved your book.

There was still no reply, and Mother asked Kugel if he was pulling her leg, if maybe the move had been too much for him. Just then, they heard a loud crash as a storage box fell on the attic floor above; Mother jumped and grabbed at Kugel's arm.

It's okay, said Kugel.

Overhead, something began shuffling, sort of

dragging its way to the stairs, and at last the hideous old woman peered over the edge.

Mother gasped.

Oh, dear God in heaven, she said.

So far, so good, thought Kugel. In the daylight, he knew, she was even more repulsive than she was cowering in the darkened attic eaves. Kugel could hear Mother's breath catch in her throat.

Anne Frank, said Kugel, this is my mother. Mother, this is Anne Frank.

Mother held her hands over her mouth, her eyes wide open. Anne Frank, leaning on one hand, held up the half-eaten loaf of Ezekiel bread in the other.

What the *hell*, said Anne Frank, do you call this?

Ezekiel bread, said Kugel.

Did I ask for Ezekiel bread? she suddenly shouted. Did I?

No, said Kugel, taken aback at her ferocity. But I . . .

Of course I didn't, shouted Anne Frank, because I don't even know what it is. But I know what it isn't, Mr Kugel. It isn't matzoh!

With that she reared back and threw the bread down the stairs. Kugel had to duck to avoid being struck by it, and it landed heavily on the floor behind him.

You wouldn't have lasted five minutes in Auschwitz! Anne Frank berated him. Not five minutes!

Kugel straightened up and watched the bread

181

skittering down the hallway behind him. He turned to look up at Anne Frank.

Bergen-Belsen, said Kugel.

I was in Auschwitz first, you idiot, Anne Frank said. Did you even read my diary, did you?

Mother looked at him reproachfully and sighed.

I read *Night,* offered Kugel. When Oprah had it. You know, in her book club.

At this Anne Frank shrieked and picked up the heavy glass bottle of seniors' multivitamins from beside her and threw it, too, at Kugel; this projectile, unfortunately, hit its intended target right between his eyes, and Kugel felt the sharp pain stab through his skull. At first he wasn't sure if it had been the bottle or his bones that had shattered; it turned out to be both. He fell to his knees, covered his face with both hands for a moment, and then held them before his eyes, as if in prayer or supplication, stunned at the blood he found covering his palms.

When I ask for matzoh, Anne Frank said, I want matzoh. I'm trying to write, Mr Kugel. To compose prose, to limn the . . . Do you think it's easy? Thirty-two million copies, Mr Kugel. And what do I get from you for it? Elie Wiesel. Oprah Winfrey! No matzoh! No herring! No borscht! Vitamins! Vitamins!

She picked up a rope Kugel hadn't noticed before, which she had tied to the stairs in such a way that by pulling on it, which she now did, the attic stairs lifted and folded onto themselves and then the attic door was pulled shut with a slam.

They could hear her, overhead, shuffling back behind her boxes.

Still on his knees, Kugel could feel that his eyebrow was already beginning to swell; blood from the gash made by the shattering glass bottle trickled down the side of his nose, and his head was throbbing with pain.

He looked up to Mother, who was looking up at the closed attic door, eyes wide, mouth open, her hands pressed together on her chest.

She's a little high maintenance, mumbled Kugel.

Mother shook her head.

She's wonderful, she gasped.

Goddamn it, thought Kugel.

CHAPTER 16

It was already well past noon when Wilbur Messerschmidt Sr answered the front door in his bathrobe and slippers.

Kugel, he said.

Senior, said Kugel. Senior was what all the locals called him, and Kugel, preparing for a fight, for denials, thought that it might be helpful to establish some intimacy first.

Senior leaned over to get a better look at the golf-ball-size bump on Kugel's brow and the purple, half-swollen eye below it. The gash was nearly an inch long. He had iced it for a while that morning, while Mother busily phoned every grocery in town looking for matzoh; he even considered going to the hospital for stitches, but thought that *Anne Frank threw vitamins at me* wasn't going to go over that well in the ER. Also, he thought this:

They didn't have stitches in Auschwitz.

They didn't have Tylenol.

They had roll call at four in the morning that lasted for hours.

I wouldn't have lasted five minutes.

Senior tutted and shook his head.

Looks like you picked a fight with the wrong person, he said.

The past is the present, said Kugel.

Not sure I follow, said Senior.

Kugel could smell the whiskey on his breath.

It's about the house, Kugel said.

What about the house?

Kugel sighed.

About the old bag I found in it, said Kugel.

He waited for a response, a tell, a flicker of recognition. None came.

The old bag? said Kugel. In the attic?

Senior shook his head.

Nerves of steel, thought Kugel. If you had to hide in someone's attic, Senior wasn't a bad choice.

Did your son mention anything to you, Kugel asked, about the old bag I found in the attic?

Oh, he's in and out, that one, said Senior with an angry wave of his hand. All hours, coming and going. Takes care of everyone but his own damn family.

Did you leave something behind? asked Kugel, trying not to get sidetracked. In the attic, Senior, did you forget something there?

Like an old bag?

Exactly.

Nope. Don't recall leaving any old bags behind. What was in it?

I'm referring, said Kugel, to a certain well-known Holocaust victim.

185

Senior cocked his head.

In the attic, added Kugel.

Senior scratched his chin.

Elie Wiesel? asked Senior.

Kugel crossed his arms over his chest.

You sold me a house with Anne Frank in it, said Kugel.

Senior looked to the ground and sighed heavily. Then, slowly, he began to nod his head, and, turning and heading back into his house, he motioned with his hand for Kugel to follow.

The Messerschmidts were one of the founding families of Stockton, having originally come to the States during the great wave of German immigration in the mid-1800s. They had arrived by ship in New York City, but the Messerschmidts were farmers and builders, as were many of the German immigrants. Those early years were difficult, and so the next generation moved out to the countryside, where they could find more suitable work. They took what money they had and purchased a rocky, dry patch of land, which they wrestled into producing some meager but desirable crops. In a short time, their small patch of land grew into an impressive farm. As their family and business grew, the Messerschmidts bought more land, upon which they built more farmhouses, and many of the houses they built then still stand today. The original Messerschmidt farm – a photo of it hung over Senior's living room couch, and a framed reproduction of it still hangs in the Stockton Town

Hall – and a second, larger farm built by their son Angus, were two of the homes struck by the arsonist. These burnings were particularly painful to the people of Stockton, and they had begun a small drive to raise funds in order to rebuild exact reproductions of them in the very places where the originals had once stood.

Anyway, said Senior – they were in the living room of his small ranch house, and Senior was at the table behind the couch, pouring himself another drink – the Messerschmidts came here wanting pretty much nothing more than to be left alone. That was the real promise of America back then. They weren't pursuing much of anything but a bit of space and solitude.

Carrying the whiskey bottle with him in one hand and his glass in the other, Senior sat down heavily in the wingback chair beside the fireplace.

My ancestors weren't proud Americans, he continued, I'll admit that, but they weren't proud Germans either. Nothing more dangerous than to be proud of soil, that's what I say. Dirt's dirt, all pretty much the same. Well, things were pretty good for them back then, building and growing and whatnot. Then WW One came around. Teddy Roosevelt, that fat son of a bitch, starting raising hell about what he called *hyphenated Americans*. Well, soon enough the libraries removed all their German books, German-named streets were renamed. Hell, us hyphenated Americans were running around buying war bonds just to prove our loyalty, changing our names, pretending we were something we weren't, when we weren't really either of the two things to begin with, just like all them Islams, sticking flags and whatnot on their cars after nine-eleven. Nothing changes. My great-grandparents changed Messerschmidt to Messersmith, which my grandparents, a few years later, chopped all the way down to Smith. Went from Messerschmidt to Smith in about five American years' time, so you can God bless my ass. If you can't beat 'em, join 'em's what they say, but I'll tell you what I say: I say most of the time you can't beat 'em, and the rest of the time they won't let you join 'em anyway, so where's that leave you? Whiskey?

No, thank you, said Kugel. About Anne Frank, though.

Well, Senior continued, the war ended, and my father and his wife decided to change their name back to Messerschmidt, just in time for WW Two, and then here we go again. Germans were interned in camps, but lucky for us, Americans hated them Japs more than they hated us, or maybe we just looked more like them, so we got off a bit easier. My parents were third- or fourth-generation Americans by then – my father's the one who built that house you're living in now – and a whole hell of a lot more Yankee than Nazi, but I'll tell you what – when the stories came out about what them Nazis did to the Jews and whatnot, well, they felt

188

just as if they had gone and done it themselves. Terrible thing that, I'll never forget it. I was a small boy at the time, but they showed me all them pictures of the camps and the bodies. Said I needed to see them, said I needed to see what my people had done. Terrible thing. I'd bet money I ain't got and never had that there wasn't a soul within a thousand miles of our house that hated Germans more than my parents did. Didn't want a speck of that German blood in them any longer. Anyway, I met my beloved Esther, rest in peace, when I was in my early twenties, we married some time after that. Wasn't long then that my father died, my mother joined him pretty soon after. Well, that about left the house in our name; me and the wife, we set about gathering up their belongings, cleaning up and whatnot, and, well, that's when we first discovered her in the attic.

The old lady.

Senior nodded and threw back his drink.

Anne Frank, he said.

She's not Anne Frank.

Oh, yes, yes, sir, I know that she is. That's her, all right, said Senior. Crazy bitch, too. Can't blame her, though, I suppose, after what she been through and all. Terrible thing, just terrible. You can imagine Esther wanted me to throw her out, of course, toot sweet, but then Esther wasn't German. I begged her not to make me do it. How could a German throw Anne Frank out of his attic? I asked her. Can you imagine the headlines?

Nazis Strike Again? Local Man Makes It Six Million and One? No, no, thank you; I'm kind of a private man. Well, I gave Esther the diary to read, and it got to her in a big way, and she agreed to let Anne Frank stay on a bit, until she finished the book she was working on at the time.

She's still working on it, said Kugel.

Senior shrugged.

Can't be easy, I suppose, he said. Thirty-two million copies, that ain't chicken feed. Anyway, those first few years weren't so bad. She slept during the day and worked at night. I brought her food every so often, but that was it. When Wilbur Junior came along, well, things got a bit rocky then. Junior cried a lot when he was a baby, and played a lot when he was a little boy, and he just about drove poor Anne Frank crazy with all that noise. He got to calling her his Aunt Frank, though, and once he got a bit older, they actually became quite close. Esther passed on when Junior was only fifteen or so – bad ticker – and well, I guess I took it pretty hard. Pretty hard. I'm not a perfect man, Mr Kugel, or even a very good one, I figure. Too much drinkin', not enough thinkin', what can I say? Didn't do right by that boy, I'm afraid, don't think he'll ever forgive me, neither. Can't say that I blame him. Terrible things I done to him, terrible things.

You lied to me, said Kugel, getting to his feet. You said there was nothing wrong with the house.

You want to sue me? said Senior. You're looking

at all I got. I didn't mean to saddle you with her, Mr Kugel; when that lady from the real estate office told me you were a Jew, I thought the Lord Himself had sent you, like He had his Jew son, Jesus. A German can't throw Anne Frank out of his house, but a Jew sure as hell can.

A Jew can't throw Anne Frank out of his house, said Kugel.

Quicker'n a German can, that's for sure, said Senior. Look, Mr Kugel, I'm sorry, I am. But, hell, I've done my share. I spent the best years of my life atoning for something I didn't do, something my parents didn't do, something done just about before I was ever even born. I got no complaints with that, but I'm about all atoned out, and I ain't yet gotten round to atoning for the things I did do. You'll forget she's there. It might take a while, but soon you'll forget. Sure, you'll have to spend a little bit more on food, maybe you hear a thing or two at night, but that's about it. She keeps to herself pretty much, doesn't do much up there but sleep and write.

Unbelievable, muttered Kugel.

Senior poured himself another whiskey.

We all got our crosses to bear, Mr Kugel. Didn't you ever want to hide somewhere? Didn't you ever think the world was just too damn ugly to face for one more day? Didn't you ever ask yourself what kind of a world you'd been dragged into, what kind of world you'd dragged your kid into? Can't protect them, not from anyone, not even from

191

yourself. Nah, I don't blame her, not a bit. Not for hiding and sure as shit not for writing. We all make mistakes, Mr Kugel. God knows I have. You'll get there. There comes a point where you realize that this is it; more of your life has been written than there is left to write, and you're not all that enthused about the pages you've got so far. Maybe it's too sad and you wish it were happier, maybe it's too happy and you feel bad, wishing it were sadder. So you start to rewrite. We all do it. Add a little here, take away something there. Maybe you're not old enough yet, God bless you, but I'm coming on seventy-two this January. Everyone I knew my age is dead, and everyone I know younger than me is waiting for me to go. I double-lock my doors, make sure I'm home before dark. I don't carry a wallet anymore. My wallet days are over. Did you know there is an end to the days when you can carry a wallet? You never think of it. Your whole life, you worry about how much is in your wallet, where you left it, where'd I put that receipt, where's my credit card, why can't I ever find my license in this goddamned thing, and you never think, there will come a day I am so weak and vulnerable that I can't carry this goddamned thing outside anymore. I carry some cash, a few bills – gotta keep some cash with you to give to the kid who holds you up. They'll beat you worse if you don't have anything, that's the theory anyway; I don't know if that's true, but I'm not too keen on finding out.

Now, I never went through what Anne Frank went through; I never seen a death camp or a gas chamber in the flesh, but fear's fear. Don't you ever wish you could take your lovely wife and that innocent little boy and lock yourselves up in an attic somewhere? Don't you sometimes wish you never had to come out again at all, that you found the one person kind enough – one kind person would be enough, too – who would bring you some food now and then? Well, I know I do. Take it from someone who knows, Mr Kugel, the only thing golden about the golden years is that it's almost over, the whole shebang. If I could find someone who'd let me hide away in their attic, rewriting my life story and waiting for the end, I'd do it in a minute.

Hearing a car door slam, Kugel went to the window. Outside, Will had pulled up in his truck, and was now heading up the front walk.

I've been thinking about getting a dog, said Kugel.

I've been thinking about getting a gun, said Senior.

Something big, said Kugel.

Something small, said Senior.

Will walked in, glumly at first, but smiled to see Kugel there, and said, Hey, Mr K, how are you?

Good, said Kugel.

Senior slid the whiskey and glass on the floor beside his chair, where Will couldn't see them.

Glad to hear it, said Will, glad to hear it. Looks like you took a fastball to the noggin there, Mr K.

Something like that, said Kugel.

193

How's our friend doing?

Kugel shrugged.

She's a little high maintenance.

You give her my best now, said Will.

Kugel promised that he would. Will walked to the kitchen, passing by his father without so much as a word. Senior watched him go.

Yep, said Senior, picking up his whiskey glass. Could do with a few rewrites myself.

CHAPTER 17

Can I help you? asked the young woman at the bookstore help counter.

I'm looking for *The Diary of Anne Frank*, said Kugel.

The . . . Diary . . . of . . . Anne . . . Frank, she said as she typed the title into the computer. I haven't read that, she added. I should.

Mmm.

I saw the movie, though, she said. That was great.

Kugel nodded.

Which movie was that? he asked.

Oh, you know, said the young woman. The one with what's her name? I can't remember the actress's name . . . you know, her teacher, and she teaches her sign language at the end?

That's Helen Keller.

She snapped her fingers.

Yes, she said, yes, that's right. Helen Keller. What a story, huh? So, you know . . . just, wow.

Inspiring.

Yes. Very inspiring. She dies, right?

That's Anne Frank.

Okay, good, she said cheerfully, so I wasn't

totally off. Here we go, it's in the memoir section. I'll take you there.

He hadn't intended to buy the diary; after speaking with Senior, though, Kugel began to think his best option for getting rid of Anne Frank might just be to help her finish her book; he didn't want to say it to her directly, but maybe a novel was not the same as a diary; maybe she needed some help. He picked out a handful of writing books for her – The Guide to This, the Handbook for Whatever – and then decided to get a book or two about the Holocaust.

We have one, said the young woman at the help counter, squinting as if in pain at the word on the computer monitor. *Butcherworld: A History.*

Buchenwald, said Kugel.

He wondered if Anne Frank was hungry.

And one, she said, on Austerlitz.

Auschwitz, said Kugel.

He wondered if she needed more printer paper.

That was when he asked about the diary.

Kugel paid for the books and left (the Holocaust books, he couldn't help noticing, were twenty percent off), and stopped on his way home at Vince's, the local hardware store.

My cat, Kugel said to Vince, peed in the heating vent.

Get rid of the cat, said Vince.

I'm working on it.

Once a cat starts peeing in a vent, likely as not she's going to keep peeing in it.

I'm working on it.

Vince recommended scrubbing the vents and ducts with a mixture of water and vinegar and then sealing the damned thing up.

Better yet, said Vince, get rid of that damned cat.

I'm working on it.

Kugel purchased a plastic bucket, a wire brush, and a box of latex gloves, and spent the rest of the day cleaning up from a cat that didn't exist and a mother that did, who was suffering post-traumatic effects from a genocide that happened, but not to her. Afterward, he went out back to the small gardening shed at the edge of the woods, where he found an old wooden-handled hammer and a rectangular scrap of pine board, which he nailed over the heating vent in Mother's bedroom floor. He drove the nails through the board, crushing the wood fibers with the end of his hammer, sealing it like the lid of a coffin. He didn't feel bad for the wood. He didn't feel bad for the nails. Problem solved. That was the old Kugel. Large and occasionally in charge.

He liked this hammer.

He liked this hammer a lot.

A fourth farmhouse burned that night.

It was near midnight, and Kugel had been telling Bree about his conversation earlier that day with Senior. He told her that Senior believed the woman really was Anne Frank, that she had been in his attic for over forty years.

Has everyone in this town, said Bree, lost their mind? What are we doing here?

That was when the firehouse alarm rang.

Kugel stood by the open bedroom window, listening to the long, mournful wail of the siren, rising and falling slowly in the night air. He was certain he could smell smoke, but it may have been just a neighbor's woodstove. He pitied the wood. He hoped the wood's children would remember him. He shivered and closed the window.

He said we'll forget she's there.

You actually sound like you agree with him.

It's some food and water, Bree, it's no big deal. She'll be done soon. We won't know she's there.

No, we won't, said Bree. Because she's leaving.

At least, Bree argued, Kugel's mother had given birth to him – Bree could understand why he'd feel some responsibility to house her, care for her. But what had this woman in the attic done that Kugel should feel such a responsibility to her, a responsibility even greater than the one he felt to his family?

Tell me, she said, I just want to know. Okay, so she's Anne Frank. Let's say she is. What has she done, Sol? She hid? She wrote a diary? She got caught? I could almost understand, almost, if it was Miep Gies hiding up there. She was a hero, she risked her life for another, she did something.

Keep your voice down, said Kugel.

She could be crazy, said Bree. She could be violent. Look at yourself – one eye half-swollen shut, a gash across your forehead. How much do you have to suffer before you can be done with this? She could be sick, Sol, she could be diseased. Your child is in this house, your family, your future. What are you trying to fix? What are you atoning for? What she went through? Or what you didn't? Could another Holocaust survivor throw her out, would that be okay? Could we have Elie Wiesel come by and throw her out? Maybe he has a sideline business, something to supplement his income.

In the distance, Kugel could hear the fire engine sirens beginning to scream.

If Bree couldn't understand Kugel, Kugel couldn't understand her, either. So Anne Frank stays in your attic for a while, so what? So you toss her a bit of matzoh and you put up with her annoying writer bullshit now and then, so what? When she's gone, when she's finished her book or dropped dead trying, they can all go up there, toss her shit away, lock the attic door behind them, and live happily ever after. A Nazi's son took care of her for ten years; a Jew is going to throw her out after forty-eight hours?

He turned from the window to face her.

Did you even read the book? he asked her.

What book?

The diary.

No, she said. I didn't. Did you?

No, said Kugel, I didn't. But I know the story.

Everyone knows the story, so what?

So it's tragic.

No, she said, it's not. It *was* tragic. We *thought* it was tragic. But she lived, right? She's upstairs in our attic, Kugel, that's what Will said, that's what Senior said. It's a happy fucking ending.

That doesn't make it any less tragic.

Dying is always more tragic than surviving, said Bree. Just listen to your mother on that one.

Kugel was discovering something about Bree that he had never known, and it worried him; he wondered if this whole incident had revealed an unbridgeable gap between them: how could she think that dying was always more tragic than living? Kugel was a firm believer that death was not always a bad thing – that life often reached such levels of crapitude that dying was preferable to living. Maybe that was why Smiling Man was smiling? Maybe he realized it would soon be over. Maybe he wasn't happy – maybe he was *relieved*. Maybe the rest of them, looking on in misery, were still holding on to the idea – Bree's idea – that any life is better than death, which, given their situation, was tremendously bad news. Maybe Smiling Man – emaciated, diseased, his loved ones murdered, his earth a hell – maybe he knew it was almost over, and maybe he was glad.

Fuck all of you motherfuckers.

Toodle-oo.

Surviving? said Kugel. She's been living like a rat in attic after attic for the past seventy years. That's much more tragic than if she had been murdered.

How can life be more tragic than death? asked Bree.

You can spend it in an attic, said Kugel.

Do you really think, said Bree, her voice rising, that anyone would have read that fucking book if she had survived?

Keep your voice down, snapped Kugel. He imagined Anne Frank upstairs, her ear to the vent, listening to them, listening to Bree, hearing those words. They would cut her to the bone.

Of course they would have, he said loudly for Anne Frank's benefit. It was a terrific book, heartfelt and beautifully written.

Because she *died*, said Bree. There are a dozen other books by survivors – a dozen dozen – and nobody reads them. You know why? They're by *survivors*. People read Anne Frank because Anne Frank died.

What's your point, Bree?

My point is that death is more tragic than life, than any life, because every life has hope of some kind. She's alive, Kugel – and she needs to go.

Kugel covered the vents with their bed pillows.

Jesus Christ, said Bree.

Imagine, Kugel said in an angry whisper, just imagine, that you heard that a black man found Martin Luther King Junior in his basement, alive, and kicked him out. What would you think of him?

You need help.

He got shot, sure, but they dragged him away, patched him up. But it fucked him up, messed up his head – he couldn't go out there anymore, so he decided, Bree, to let the world think he *had* been assassinated, that sometimes it's easier to live on

201

this planet if everyone thinks you're dead. And we're sitting in the living room one night, you and me, watching TV, and the story comes on that MLK isn't dead: some guy found him hiding in his basement. A black man. And he threw him out. A black man, a son of slaves, threw Martin Luther King Junior out on his ass. What would you think, Bree? You'd look at me and shake your head and say, What a piece of shit. And you'd be right.

Is that what this is about? asked Bree. What other people think? When does what your family thinks start to matter?

It's about what's right.

So you're going to tell Jonah? Who she is, what a Nazi is, what happened, why she's here?

No.

So you're going to lie to him. Is that what's right?

Kugel's head throbbed. He hated arguing with Bree, they almost never did. It was one of the cornerstones of their relationship that no matter what they were discussing, they remained rational, calm, able to compromise.

I'll tell him she's his Aunt Frank, said Kugel.

The hell you will, said Bree.

And this she added with a quiet, chilling calm:

You want to live with Anne Frank over your head, be my guest. But I'll be damned if my son will.

And Bree slept that night on the floor of Jonah's bedroom.

CHAPTER 18

Kugel returned to his office the following morning, trying to return some measure of normalcy to his life, but he was preoccupied, tired, and nervous, and he remained that way over the course of the day. He was uninvolved in meetings, and when asked his opinion on some matter or the other, could not recall what subject they had been discussing. He phoned home often, every hour or so, hanging up if Bree answered (though relieved to know that the house hadn't been burned to the ground), and if Mother answered, asking how Anne was doing.

She's sleeping, Mother would say.

Are you sure?

Should I check?

No, no, you'll wake her.

I think she's okay. Do you think she's okay?

She's probably fine.

Should I check?

Can you hear anything?

Hold on . . . No.

Maybe you should check.

The effect of the recent economic downturn upon

203

Enviro Solutions had been severe; they had lost revenue, market share; in response, they expanded their product offerings to include environmentally friendly, eco-conscious office furniture. The pressure to bring in sales was intense.

Kugel had been out a while, and he had some lost time to make up for. He phoned his client, Mr Thomason, the superintendent of the largest local school, whom Kugel had, some time ago, signed on as one of EnviroSolutions' biggest recycling clients. It was a contract that caused the whole company to celebrate, and Kugel was heralded as a hero, but the reality was that he'd just gotten lucky; under pressure from environmental groups, the state and local government had begun offering financial incentives to any organization that instituted a comprehensive recycling plan, and Mr Thomason had negotiated such a low-cost contract with Kugel that he was actually making money off the new plan, and pocketing the extra incentive fees for himself. But nobody was offering incentives on eco-friendly furniture, and Mr Thomason had already turned down two other EnviroSolutions salesmen in the past week alone.

Hello, Mr Thomason, Kugel said into the phone, Solomon Kugel here from EnviroSolutions. Did you know that your students' chairs might be affecting their minds? Off-gassing from plastic seating has been . . . Yes, of course, I understand. Yes. Of course, yes, but for only a few dollars per unit, your students could be sitting on eco-friendly bamboo chairs that save their minds and save the planet.

Kugel sighed and rubbed his eyes with the fingertips of his free hand.

That's probably overstating it, to be honest, he added. Wouldn't that be great, though, Mr Thomason, if some chairs could save the planet? If chairs could save the planet, I'd be the happiest motherfucker alive, let me tell you. We have hemp office chairs, Mr Thomason, made of sustainable something or other. Can I interest you in hemp office furniture, Mr Thomason? When the oceans rise and drown us, at least you can smoke the goddamn things. But the oceans won't rise, Mr Thomason, I don't want to worry you about that; God Himself promised, after the whole Noah thing, he promised he wouldn't drown us, and, fuck, Mr Thomason, if you can't trust God, well, we're all fucked. You know who wanted to save the earth? Hitler. Mr Thomason? Hello?

The line had gone dead a while ago, but Kugel soldiered on.

Perhaps I can interest you, he continued, in some handmade recycled cardboard office partitions? Handmade by, well . . . by hands, I suppose. That's better than partitions not made by hands, wouldn't you agree, Mr Thomason? We all have hands, you know. We all have hands and we have feet and we have heads. Did you know that repurposed printer tables are a great way to save . . .

something? To protect the whatever? The sun? Have you thought about the sun, Mr Thomason? Have you?

He was beginning to shout.

Have you ever thought about the sun, Mr Thomason? Think about the sun, man, just once, for God's sake, think about the sun!

If you'd like to make a call, said the phone, please hang up and try again.

Kugel hung up, and after a moment phoned home.

Is she okay? he asked.

I think so, said Mother. She's hungry.

She said that?

No, but I think she is.

It should be there soon.

How soon?

Soon.

Okay.

Let me know when it gets there.

Okay.

Okay.

Last night, he had gone online and ordered Anne Frank a twelve-pack of Streit's matzoh (*4 stars – Light and crispy! Great packaging!*), and he went back online now and ordered her a jar of thick-cut herring (*3 stars*) and a six-pack of Gold's Russian borscht (*no reviews*).

A salesman named Neil stuck his head into Kugel's office.

You okay? he asked. I heard some shouting.

Customers, said Kugel. Can't see the big picture.

Nasty shiner, said Neil.

In this difficult financial atmosphere, supervisors brought quick attention to the slightest of their employees' failings and mistakes, and coworkers privately made it known to those same superiors that, in regard to Employee X or Y, they were in complete agreement with their superior's judgment and shared his or her concerns. Kugel didn't blame them; he understood and accepted the nature of business, and what it meant for the way others behaved. That's business, said Kugel, suggesting that people were less treacherous and self-serving in everyday life. This concerned Professor Jove, who insisted that the regular world was no different from the business world, and attempted to get Kugel to see it that way, too.

What do you call five lawyers in quicksand? asked Professor Jove.

Kugel shrugged.

Fucked, replied Professor Jove. And if one has to step on another's head to get himself out, that's what he'll do.

Because he's a lawyer?

Because he's a human being. Survival has its own morality, Kugel. Only a fool would expect someone drowning in quicksand to behave any differently. And, brother, we're all in quicksand. Up to our eyeballs, from the moment we're born. And do you know how to get out of quicksand?

Is this a joke?

No.

I don't know, said Kugel. How do you get out of quicksand?

There are two ways. The first one never works.

What's the first one?

You wait for someone to save you. You rely on the kindness of strangers.

What's the second way?

You save yourself. You step on something. Living or dead, you step on it and get the fuck out.

Ten years earlier, Kugel had been at a sales conference in Los Angeles when a perfect series of perfect storms left flights across the nation canceled and airports closed. It was a few days before Christmas, and even once the storms had passed and travel was restored, the backups and delays meant many would be stranded away from home over the holidays. The company, though, decided to charter a small plane from Los Angeles to New York, reserved for just those employees with family back east – wives, husbands, children. It was a tremendous show of corporate sensitivity at a time of terrible uncertainty. As soon as word of the chartered plane got out, though, senior executives, similarly stranded in Los Angeles, began to complain: Why should I have to stay here? one asked. Why does that nobody get to go home before me? asked another. And so the higher-ups soon began using their rank and seniority to force their way onto the plane, until one by one all the mothers and fathers of lower rank were bumped off, and all that remained on the flight were senior executives and their personal assistants.

You step on something.

You get the fuck out.

According to John, author of the Gospel by the same name, Jesus, dying on the cross, said this: It is finished.

Was he referring to his life? Or, supposed Kugel, to mankind, to humanity, to the species that could do such a thing to one of its own? You never see a lion crucifying another lion. You never see a bear just randomly murdering salmon for anything besides food; bears don't form armies, invade rivers, tear the heads off male salmon, rape the female salmon, and enslave their salmon children.

It is finished, to Kugel, sounded a hell of a lot like Fuck all of you motherfuckers.

Kugel wondered if Miep Gies would have done what she had if she'd had children of her own. Would anyone blame her if she didn't? Maybe, on the contrary, they would have thought her irresponsible if she had?

At lunch that day Kugel asked Neil: Would you hide me?

Hide you?

Hide me. And my family. Wife and a child. He's three. Maybe a dog.

What are you talking about?

If something happened.

If what happened?

Whatever.

Whatever?

Whatever.

You're freaking me out, Kugel. People are starting to talk.

Would you hide us? That's all I'm asking.

Where?

In your attic.

I have a lot of shit up there, Kugel.

But would you? If we had to hide?

From who?

Whoever.

Whoever?

What's the difference?

What's the difference?

What's the difference? Would you hide us or not?

I have a lot of shit up there, Kugel.

Is that a no?

Are you okay, Kugel? That's a nasty bump on your head.

Of the seven people in his office Kugel asked that day if they would let him and his family hide in their attic, three said they had a lot of shit up there, one said he would love to but was allergic to dogs, one said he didn't have an attic but Kugel could stay in his garden shed (on condition that, if discovered, Kugel would back up his claim of ignorance), and one said he could probably stay in his attic, but he didn't want to commit to anything at the moment and Kugel should ask again when the time came.

He left work early, complaining of a headache. As he was driving home, he received an e-mail from his supervisor:

Your performance of late has been subpar.

A last line?

A tombstone:

SOLOMON KUGEL
His performance, of late,
had been subpar.
Born, unfortunately. Died eventually.

As Kugel pulled into his driveway that evening, the UPS man was there, delivering packages.

Kugel knew all too well that this would be a terrible time to lose his job. Nobody was hiring, Mother wasn't paying rent, and their only tenant was threatening to leave, if he wasn't already out looking for a new apartment.

The twelve-pack of matzoh cost $64.95, and would last Anne Frank about three days. The borscht cost $74.95. A nine-cubic-foot mini-fridge cost $265.43.

Kugel wondered if in these days of the Internet you would even need a Miep Gies anymore, if you could make it through a genocide these days with just a smartphone and a credit card, and he was hopeful that in the event of another Holocaust, he would have some sort of broadband Internet access. Still, somebody would have to sign for the packages and bring them up to the attic, so he was back to square one. Also, they would probably be tracking Amazon orders, or at least UPS deliveries, so he'd probably have to have the packages delivered to an alternate address and brought to him by Miep (assuming Amazon even took orders from Jews once the shit started going down, which they probably wouldn't).

Bree looked at the UPS packages piled up on the front porch and shook her head in disgust.

The house was beginning to smell again.

Kugel phoned Professor Jove.

Jove wasn't in.

Kugel left a message.

CHAPTER 19

That night, lying in bed, staring up at the ceiling, Kugel thought he heard a gentle tapping on the vent, but decided that he hadn't.

Maybe he had.

He hadn't.

The noises from the ducts were loudest and most oppressive at night. Mother below, moaning, groaning, belching; Anne Frank above, tapping, shuffling, wheezing, typing, printing, bitching; and Kugel, trapped in the middle of this miserable suffer sandwich, with all the wretched clangor of their failing mortal coils – the farts, the grunts, the gasps, the coughs; the nightly performance of the Judeo-Misery Orchestra, a distressing cacophony of *oy-veys*, *gevalts*, and *Gott in himmel*s played against the endless laugh track that emanated from the tenant's television, culminating in the big finale, when Mother woke them all with her daily morning screams of her not-traumatic-enough-stress disorder.

Burp.

Groan.

Moan.

Ha ha ha!

Oy vey.

Freeze, police!

Gottenyu.

This is *Sixty Minutes.*

Oof.

God in heaven.

Tonight on Jay Leno.

Ugh.

Fart.

Grunt.

Applause.

And, on top of that, the creaks, the cracks, the pops that sounded, each and every one, like an arsonist, whatever an arsonist sounded like, just outside his window, just outside the door, preparing to burn them all alive.

Tell them I said . . . something.

What, though, goddamn it? What?

Kugel already had the perfect tombstone for Mother. He'd had it since he was a teenager, had thought of it on their trip one summer to a German concentration camp. Mother had taken him to Jerusalem for his bar mitzvah (You should know your history, she said as the Israeli soldier eyed them suspiciously and tore through their suit-cases); when she realized the return flight required a stopover in Berlin, she decided this was the perfect opportunity for the two of them to visit a death camp.

You with your comfortable American life, she said. You wouldn't last five minutes in Auschwitz.

Young Kugel wondered how Chelmno felt. Nobody ever talked about Chelmno.

He wouldn't last five minutes in Chelmno, either.

They decided to spend the night in Berlin, visit a death camp in the morning, and continue home that afternoon. Unfortunately, Mother soon discovered that all the really famous death camps were far away, much too far for a day trip, so she had to settle for the concentration camp in Sachsenhausen.

Sachsen what? she had asked the hotel concierge.

Sachsenhausen, he said. It's about a thirty-minute train ride from Berlin Central Station.

Never heard of it, she said. And then, holding her hand up to her mouth, she said to Kugel: They don't want us to see the *real* death camps.

The concierge assured her that many thousands of people died there.

How many?

Many, miss. Very many.

Was there a gas chamber?

After a long pause: Of course, yes.

You're sure.

Oh, yes.

I don't want to get out there and find some sanitized park grounds.

No, no, not at all. It's very disturbing.

They set out by train the following morning, but

215

as neither Mother nor Kugel was yet aware of his gluten intolerance, she packed only some bottles of water to drink and a loaf of bread to eat, since anything more than that, she declared, would insult the memory of the deceased. They would have killed, she said, for a loaf of bread like that.

By the time they arrived, Kugel was doubled over in pain, and he raced to the bathroom the moment she handed him his ticket.

And there he stayed, on the toilet, for the bulk of their available time.

He made a few attempts to leave the restroom and walk to the camp, but he'd only get as far as the gates – Work Will Set You Free, they read – before having to turn and run back, hoping his stall was not yet taken. With little more than forty minutes to go before their train to the airport, Kugel managed to gain some control of his quivering innards, and he and Mother hurried together into the camp. Kugel did his best to keep up with Mother's angry, purposeful stride through the camp gates.

Well, I'm never going to see it all now, said Mother, looking at the map of the camp in her hands, thank you very much. I can forget about seeing the Jewish barracks, they're way the hell over there. And the medical center is a twenty-minute walk all by itself. Walk faster, Solomon, for crying out loud.

She decided, with the limited time they had, to just see the gas chamber, marked with the letter Z on the camp map. They followed the map closely, but to Mother's growing frustration, couldn't seem to find 'the damned thing' anywhere. With just twenty minutes left, she stopped the leader of a small tour group standing at the center of the camp.

Pardon me, she said, can you direct me to the gas chambers?

Ah, he said, no problem, we were just heading there our-selves.

He clapped his hands to get the group's attention.

This way for the gas, ladies and gentlemen, he said.

He led them to a small patch of grass at the far side of the camp, where they gathered around him in a tight, solemn circle. It was silent for a while, as the visitors let the reality of the horrors of what happened here, on this very spot, only a few short decades ago, sink into their minds and tear at their hearts.

This, said the leader of the tourist group, is where thousands of men, women, and children were systematically murdered.

One woman began to cry. Her husband put his arm around her.

Where? asked Mother.

Right here, said the group leader.

Where?

Here. Where you're standing.

Where'd they go? she asked.

They died, he said with irritation.

Not the people, said Mother, the gas chambers. They knocked them down.

Who?

The SS, he said.

Sons of bitches, she said. Still they torture us.

The guide nodded.

One of the visitors placed his hand on his head and made a blessing in Hebrew. Everyone closed their eyes and when he finished, they nodded and said: Amen.

After a moment, Mother said, Are there ovens at least? The trip shouldn't be a total waste?

The guide pointed them to the infirmary, in the basement of which were half a dozen steel crematoriums built into the foundation wall. Mother had Kugel stand in front of one of the ovens for a photo.

Open it, she said to him. So we can see.

Kugel reached over, pulled the heavy door open, and faced the camera.

What are you doing? she asked.

What?

Stop smiling.

Oh.

Look into the oven. Not all the way in, Solomon, just with your eyes.

Like this?

Sadder. Good. Now get one of me.

They hurried back to the train, Kugel again walking quickly to keep up with Mother's furious gait.

I hope you're happy, she said once they had taken

their seats. You ruined the whole concentration camp for me, you know that? You ruined the whole damn camp.

Kugel felt bad. She had been so looking forward to it.

We saw the ovens, though, he offered. Those were pretty cool.

She waved her hand at him in disgust and looked out the window.

Ah, she said, never mind. I'm sure I'll see the inside of a gas chamber before long. I'm sure they're already building them, getting them ready.

Who? he asked.

What's the difference?

She lay back, closed her eyes, and went to sleep. And that's when he looked at her and thought, instantly, of her tombstone:

MOTHER
Here she lies.
Big surprise.

Now, he thought as he lay in his bed, I just need one for myself. And for Mother to drop dead.

I shouldn't have thought that, he thought.

At least I didn't *say* it.

But you thought it.

That's not as bad.

It's bad, though.

There it was again. That sound.

Maybe it was just the wind.

It was probably just the wind.

Kugel crept quietly from bed, knelt on the floor, and pressed his ear against the cold metal vent.

Anne? he whispered.

I'm hungry.

Mother? he whispered.

I'm hungry, Mother repeated.

Mother, go to sleep.

I'm hungry. Can you bring me a little something?

Kugel looked over his shoulder to check on Bree, who stirred in her sleep, rolled onto her side, and pulled the quilt over her head.

I'm hungry, Mother called.

Go get something, then.

I'm frightened.

Mother had claimed, after he'd found her befouling the heating ducts, that she'd been doing it because she was frightened of the tenant, that she didn't feel comfortable leaving her room at night, that she often barricaded the door with a chair.

That's dangerous, Mother, he had said.

Not as dangerous as not barricading it, she had replied.

Bree rolled over again, mumbling in her sleep.

Will you bring me something? Mother asked.

Okay.

Bring me something to eat.

Okay!

He'd do anything for a night of silence, a no-groan, no-moan, no-*oy* night.

220

Kugel went downstairs to the darkened kitchen, shone the flashlight out the back door to see if the arsonist was there, gave him the finger in the event that he was, made Mother a plate of cookies and a cup of tea, brought it to her in her room, asked her twice if she needed to go the bathroom while he was there, and, enjoying the silence that followed, climbed back upstairs.

Sol, he heard Mother call through the hallway vent. Solly, I spilled.

He pulled the attic stairs down and headed up to check on Anne, hoping to find her picking out cover art and packing up her belongings.

It was dark up there, the only light visible being the blue-green glow of a computer screen coming from behind the boxes on the western wall. A positive sign.

Hello? he said softly. Hello?

A sigh of frustration came from behind the wall.

Enter, said Anne Frank, *the son.*

Kugel noticed the heavy black fabric hung over the windows. He crossed to the window nearest him and tugged on it.

Your mother, said Anne Frank, in addition to having an inordinate amount of time on her hands, has a rather sepulchral design sense.

During the day, as Anne slept and Kugel worked, Mother had covered the windows of the attic dormers with heavy black cloth, as, she had read, had been done in the original Frank attic, which left the Kugel attic even darker and more depressing

221

than it had been before. Kugel worried that Mother might be annoying Anne Frank, disturbing her, slowing her down and interrupting her work.

I'll talk to her, said Kugel.

He peered over the wall of boxes; the pile of papers beside the computer didn't seem to have grown much, if at all.

It may have even grown smaller.

He walked back to the window that faced the driveway, looking over the dark cloth Mother had stapled to the frame.

I'm curious, Anne Frank said. Which do you think it is? Does she not want others to see in, or does she not want me to see out?

Both, said Kugel. Kind of her whole parenting philosophy, really.

It's a funny thing, said Anne Frank. My mother and I never got along very well. We clashed, for any number of reasons. In the end, what brought us closer together was genocide.

That *is* funny, said Kugel.

We cried in that camp, said Anne Frank, and held each other, shivering, dying, and she told me how special I was, and I told her how much I loved her, and we both apologized, again and again, for all the time over the years we had wasted bickering.

Hilarious.

What do you imagine would have happened, continued Anne Frank, if she had survived? If we had reunited somewhere in Europe after the war;

if we'd gotten a small flat in Paris, Milan, Berlin, somewhere? We'd have killed each other, that's what, Mr Kugel. We'd have hated each other more than we ever had before.

What's that got to do with my mother? Kugel asked.

Don't let death fool you, Mr Kugel. Death holds no red pen over the decades of life that came before it. It changes nothing. A free man, said Spinoza, thinks of death least of all things. That should be true of the death of others as of his own.

Kugel pulled on the black cloth covering the window, but it held fast.

Well, Anne Frank continued as she typed, our elders fail us, more often than not. They should teach us how to live, yes, but more important, they should teach us how to die; teach us that to obsess about death is cowardice, and that to run from death is to run from life.

She said from her attic, said Kugel.

You'll not shame a turtle for its shell, Mr Kugel, said Anne Frank.

Silence. Typing.

I kind of like it up here, Kugel said. It's got a certain fatalistic charm, a certain *je ne sais fucked.*

He pulled again at the fabric, tearing it slightly from the window, and peered outside. Not enough attics in the world, he thought. Not enough attics in the whole goddamned world.

How's the book coming? he asked.

There was no reply for a moment, and then

Anne Frank said: I'm sorry to be the cause of such friction in your marriage. I suspect, though, the causes are deeper underlying faults that have nothing at all to do with me.

Kugel tore the rest of the black fabric from the wall and looked out the window into the darkness below.

He should really get a dog.

Yes, he said, you're right. I suppose we should have discussed how we'd deal with finding Anne Frank in our attic before getting married. Most couples do, but we were in a rush. We had a plan for finding Simon Wiesenthal in the pantry, but this is a whole different—

Simon Wiesenthal, Anne Frank spat, was full of shit.

Silence.

So how's the book coming? asked Kugel.

I have a world of characters in my head.

Mm-hmm.

A novel has to be given room to breathe, Mr Kugel.

Sure.

Thirty-two million copies, said Anne Frank. That's nothing to sneeze at.

So I hear.

Anything less than that, she added, will be a failure.

Kugel went to the window on the other side of the attic and tore at that covering as well, though he found he had to step back behind the eastern wall of boxes to do so. It was dark there, and it gave him a strange comfort to be back there, an unfamiliar but welcome sense of safety. He wasn't so sure he wanted to leave. He grabbed the corner of the black fabric and pulled, but the staples held tight.

Aren't you setting the bar a little high? he asked.

I've sold that many before, she said.

Yeah, but that was . . .

That was what?

That was different.

He pulled again, but his hands slipped. Mother must have used a staple gun over here, and he thought he might have to go downstairs and get a screwdriver.

Why was that different? Anne Frank asked.

You died.

People didn't buy my book because I died.

No, of course not. I didn't mean . . .

They bought it because of the quality of my prose.

Of course. I just . . . I don't think people read so much anymore, that's all.

As he stepped backward, he felt something small and stiff crack beneath his shoe, like the shell of a walnut, only larger.

What is that supposed to mean? she asked.

He lifted his foot and felt around with the tip of his shoe; he felt many of the shell-like things, and he pulled hard on the fabric to try to get some light in. At last the corner gave slightly, and a small pool of moonlight spilled onto the attic floor.

Maybe you should do it as a screenplay, he said.

A screenplay? she said. I am a *writer*, Mr Kugel. A prose artist. I create worlds with language, with image, with character. I peer into the abyss and welcome the abyss as it peers into me.

Mm-hmm, said Kugel, bending down; with a splinter of wood he found beside his foot, he began nudging the items beneath his feet into the nearby moonlight until he could see what they were: here a mound of small white bones, here the severed head of a squirrel, here the eviscerated body of a crow, the burned flesh pulled from its bones.

Pulitzers, Anne Frank continued, not Oscars. Art is not convenient, Mr Kugel, art is not safe.

Kugel stood, his hand over his mouth; the stench was unbearable. He pulled on the black window covering again, moonlight now illuminating a number of small rodent carcasses – mice, squirrels, and what he was sure was the cooked body of the Ambersons' missing cat, Sunshine. Beside the bodies were a small pile of their heads, torn or cut off, and a pile of innards in various states of decomposition.

Everyone wants a Van Gogh in the living room, Mr Kugel, Anne Frank went on, but nobody wants Van Gogh in the living room. It is the price of genius . . .

Kugel gagged. It made sense, of course; anyone living in attics for that long . . . but the bile rose in his throat, and his head began to spin.

. . . and I shall gladly pay it, Anne Frank declared.

Kugel wasn't listening, he just needed to get away, to get some air, and he staggered away from the wall, fast, away, away – was this in his house? was this him? was this her? was this survival? – his feet stumbling beneath him, and suddenly he was tripping, falling, and the attic seemed to recede into the darkness as he tumbled, backward, down the attic stairs.

Solomon! called Bree from the bedroom.

Jonah began to cry.

CHAPTER 20

There was no doubt about it – in the days since Kugel had told Mother that Anne Frank was in the attic, he noticed some distinct, troubling changes in Mother's behavior. To begin with, she had stopped collecting the vegetables Kugel left in her garden each morning. She had, she said with a disconcerting air, far more important things to do now. Kugel continued to put the fruits and vegetables out each morning, regardless, but now he had a second, more tedious chore, that of collecting the same fruits and vegetables again that very evening. And his new injuries weren't making those chores any easier.

Most of the bruises Kugel suffered in the fall down the attic stairs were contusions and scrapes, some simple, some severe; his right thigh, from buttock to knee, was covered in a large purple-and-red bruise that ached whenever he put any weight on it. So painful was it to step on that leg that he thought he had broken his ankle, but the X-rays revealed no leg fractures at all, and the doctors gave him some painkillers and a hospital cane to ease the pain of walking. His left wrist suffered the most damage: hairline breaks on two of his metatarsals and a fracture on the end of the radius; he was in a cast from elbow to fingertips, the end of which was shaped like a flat paddle in order to keep his wrist and fingers straight. Thanks to the painkillers, however, it was the first night he'd slept soundly in some time. Still, he found the underlying Christian ethic in emergency rooms troubling: if you suffer enough, you get the Vicodin; if you suffer not as much, you get the codeine; if you suffer not at all, you get Tylenol and a bill. So deep was his slumber that night that when he awoke the following morning, he didn't recall a single dream, and was grateful for that, too. How wonderful, he thought, to recall not at all.

Bree was already dressed and out of bed, straightening up the bedroom and putting things away. Kugel groaned in mock agony, hoping for a show of concern.

Nothing.

He stood, went to the dresser, took a pill out of the prescription bottle, and once Bree turned in his direction, made a show of lifting it into his mouth and wincing at the excruciating pain that resulted from even that small amount of movement.

Bree walked past him and out the door.

Goddamn it, Kugel thought.

He phoned his office and asked for his supervisor.

Tampons, said the recorded hold message. Nail clippings. Urine.

His supervisor wouldn't be happy about his missing another day, but he was lucky he hadn't broken his neck, and surely they would at least be relieved to hear that.

Yes, Kugel said to his supervisor, I know . . . Of course, yes . . . my own fault, really . . . nasty fall, it was, right down the attic stairs . . . The left wrist, sir, yes . . . Ha ha, no, no, that shouldn't be a problem. Yes . . . yes, these are difficult times, I understand, my clumsiness is not your problem, no . . . Well, it shouldn't be more than a day, no . . . Yes, tomorrow, of course . . . Thank you, sir, yes.

He went down to the kitchen and began filling a bag with vegetables for Mother's garden. He put in a couple of tomatoes and a zucchini.

Her stupid fault I broke my arm, he thought to himself.

He put in a handful of strawberries and a package of sliced turkey breast.

If I hadn't been up making her tea, I wouldn't have been up visiting Anne.

He put in a package of frozen asparagus tips and a plastic tray of California sushi rolls.

He slid his good arm through the handles of the bag, picked up his cane, and hobbled out to her garden. The whole damned routine was now a much more complicated affair. For each item, he had to step forward, lean the cane against his leg, place the bag on the ground, take out the produce, put the bag back on his arm, give Anne Frank the

230

finger, pick up the cane, take a few more steps, and repeat the whole process. After completing a few steps of this complicated routine, however, Kugel noticed something strange in Mother's garden: life. A number of young green seedlings were somehow, against all odds, pushing through the top of the soil. At first he thought they were weeds, surely they must be, but the one- and two-leafed shoots were aligned in perfect parallel rows; without Mother's constant tilling and scraping, they had at last been given a chance to grow.

Kugel placed the end of his cane on the first shoot, and crushed it into the ground. He did the same with the rest; it took him some time, but after an hour, he was sure they were all dead. He tossed the package of turkey breast to the ground, sprinkled some California rolls around the beds, and limped inside.

There was a still more troubling change in Mother's behavior since she had learned about Anne Frank's presence: she seemed rejuvenated, revived, energized, and this disconcerting liveliness was on display that morning as she buzzed around the kitchen preparing a tray of food for Anne Frank. It tormented Kugel to see it: she was indefatigable when she was supposed to have been terminal. She strode through the house more quickly, more busily, her posture more upright, with an uncharacteristic sense of purpose and determination. The very same stairs that only days ago caused her to moan in agony, to pause every few steps with a heavy sigh and a hand on the small of her back, she now ascended and descended speedily, without pause, without complaint, with the energy of a woman half her age. In the morning, which was Anne Frank's evening, Mother removed her trash and dishes from the night before; in the afternoon, as Anne Frank slept, she went with Bree to town, where she purchased food and writing supplies; in the evening, she prepared Anne's breakfast and coffee and double-checked that she had all she needed for the night of crucial writing that lay ahead.

On a positive note, Mother's inexplicable turn for the better concerned Bree as well; over coffee that morning (Have you seen the sliced turkey breast? she had asked Kugel), Bree suggested the change in Mother warranted placing a call to her physician, an eminent geriatric specialist named Dr Lamb. If Mother was well enough to take care of Anne Frank, Bree figured, maybe she was well enough to take care of herself – maybe she could at last get out of their house, leave them alone; maybe they could at last rent the second room, could at last get on with their lives. As for Kugel, his newfound tolerance for Anne was accompanied by an equal but opposite lack of tolerance for his mother, and he was relieved to have something he and Bree could agree on. So once Mother had finished her breakfast and went back to her room – That scrapbook, she sighed, isn't going to collect itself – Kugel and Bree sat together at the kitchen table and rang Dr Lamb's office.

Dr Lamb had first diagnosed Mother many months ago. He was a tall man whom Kugel remembered for his rare, untarnished honesty. As Mother lay resting in the hospital bed, Dr Lamb had asked Kugel to step into the hallway, in order to keep from upsetting her, and there, with compassionate austerity, he said to Kugel, Your mother is dying. I'm sorry. There's nothing we can do for her. We can try to make her comfortable. We can try to minimize her discomfort. We can try to reduce her suffering.

No, Kugel had answered.

We just want to make her feel better.

Making her feel better isn't going to make her feel any better.

Dr Lamb looked at Kugel with concern.

What will make her feel better? he asked.

Feeling worse, said Kugel.

Dr Lamb nodded.

I understand, he said. We can stop the pain medication. We can discontinue the antidepressants. We can restrict her desserts, and prescribe hours a day of grueling exercise.

I think she'd like that, Kugel had said.

Kugel put the call on speakerphone; Bree sat with a notepad beside him.

It's about Mother, said Kugel.

Mm-hmm, said Dr Lamb. What seems to be the problem?

Well, said Kugel, she seems to be getting . . . I don't know . . . better.

233

Better?

Better, yes. She seems very . . . energetic. For someone as close to death as you suggested. You did say 'close to.'

I said 'brink of.'

That's right.

I see, said Dr Lamb. And now you want me to tell you that she's going to be okay, that she's turned a corner, that she's out of the woods? I'm not going to tell you that, Mr Kugel.

Bree scribbled on the pad: Move out.

Well, no, I wasn't . . . I was just wondering if you thought she could live on her own again, get back to normal. I think she'd like that.

And you'd like that, too, said Dr Lamb. For it to be over.

Well, I think she'd be happier. I love her, and just want her to be, you know. Happy.

Mr Kugel, said Dr Lamb, the disease your mother has is degenerative; it is not one from which she, nor anyone else, can recover.

Kugel glanced at Bree and raised a hopeful eyebrow, though he knew that more waiting was not the suggestion Bree wanted to hear.

I understand, Dr Lamb continued, how difficult that can be for a child to accept about a parent. And there are certainly experimental treatments you can try. There are pills and injections and scans and scopes; you can try acupuncture, home-opathy, bioresonance, massage therapy; you can feed her colloidal silver, shark cartilage, monkey brains, and elephant semen. They won't hurt her. Nor, I can assure you, will they help her. They may temporarily prolong her life, yes; they will also only delay the inevitable while protracting her suffering.

Elephant semen? asked Kugel.

My advice, said Dr Lamb, is to let the disease take its course. If there were something we could do, we would be doing it; we're doing everything we can, which is why we aren't doing anything. There is a time to be born and a time to die. Et cetera.

Energy? wrote Bree on the pad. <u>PARANOIA?</u>

What about all this energy, asked Kugel, and this paranoia?

It is not uncommon, said Dr Lamb, for sufferers of your mother's condition to exhibit a certain burst of energy or spirit; unfortunately, this heralds not a recovery but the beginning of the end. A last hurrah.

Kugel glanced at Bree and shrugged.

The paranoia, said Dr Lamb, would seem to confirm that.

So all we can do is wait? asked Kugel.

Bree shook her head, and folded her arms across her chest.

We can't go on, said Dr Lamb, we go on.

And then what? asked Kugel.

Then, fortunately, we drop dead. Yes, at least, at last, there's that.

It was not the prognosis Bree was hoping for,

and with a chilly I'm going to town, she went upstairs to get her purse and keys.

Mother's paranoia had begun to present itself only recently. Kugel noticed that she'd begun locking the windows at night, and she ceased conversation, whatever the subject of discussion, if either the tenant or Bree so much as entered the room. She was becoming increasingly suspicious – of neighbors who waved and of neighbors who didn't, of phone callers that hung up, of cars that passed by too quickly (or too slowly, which was even more suspicious) as she walked down the road. But she narrowed her eyes at nobody quite so much as she did at the UPS man, who was arriving these days on a fairly regular basis. Boxes of matzoh and jars of borscht and herring arrived every other day, and books on death camps and how to be your own best editor every day in between; Mother watched him from the bedroom window, from the living room window, from the peephole in the front door.

The now-familiar honk of the UPS truck brought Kugel hobbling quickly to the front room; the arrival of the daily packages infuriated Bree, packages they could ill afford, and Kugel would have liked to be rid of him before she came back down.

Mother was already at the living-room window, peering through the blinds. She tutted and shook her head as Kugel limped up behind her.

Not good, she said.

Mother, said Kugel.

We should get her an electric book.

A what?

An electric book.

She was talking about an e-reader.

We're not getting her an electric book, Mother.

She could download anything she wants, said Mother. This delivery thing is too risky. I don't like it.

Forget it, said Kugel.

There was no money for an e-reader. There was no money for anything.

He's onto us, Mother added.

Onto what?

He knows too much. I don't trust him.

There's nothing to know, Mother.

The UPS man set the boxes down on the front porch and checked his scanner. Mother's voice dropped to a whisper and she said, He knows that we get a lot of packages all of a sudden.

And?

What if he puts two and two together?

Two and two equals Anne Frank in our attic?

Mother turned to face him.

That other woman's been snooping around a bit, too, she said.

That other woman is my wife, Mother.

I don't trust her.

The UPS man knocked on the door. Kugel went to open it, and Mother followed behind him.

Careful, she whispered as he opened the door.

Morning, said Kugel.

Morning, said the UPS man with a smile. Ouch, he added, looking over Kugel's various injuries. You get the number of that truck?

You should see the other guy, said Kugel.

The UPS man laughed and handed Kugel the scanner and a stylus he pulled from the pocket of his brown shirt.

That's far enough, said Mother.

Kugel glanced at her.

Sure getting a lot of books these days, said the UPS man.

I'm a reader, said Kugel.

Oh, me, too, said the UPS man. Thing of the past, though, I'm afraid. Wife got me one of those e-reader things for the holidays this year. It's something else.

That's what I hear, said Kugel as he signed for the packages.

Noticed you blacked out your windows up top, said the UPS man.

Mother nudged Kugel.

Drafty, said Kugel.

Yep, said the UPS man. Got to save every penny these days, I'm afraid. Well, I'll see you folks tomorrow.

I'll see you, said Kugel.

The UPS man got back in his truck, waved, and headed down the driveway.

He knows, said Mother.

He doesn't know anything.

He's probably already reported us.

To who?

Whoever.

Mother, please.

She turned and went back inside. Kugel watched the UPS truck turn down the road with a friendly toot of its horn.

Kugel smiled and waved.

He sure did ask a lot of questions, though, didn't he?

CHAPTER 21

Mother decided to join Bree on her trip to town. Hannah and Pinkus were coming for dinner, and Bree needed to stop for groceries and meat; Anne Frank needed printing paper, said Mother.

And a microwave, she added.

Kugel walked them to the front door; he was relieved to be getting them out of the house, and to have some time alone with Jonah. It had been a while.

We're not getting Anne Frank a microwave, said Kugel.

Do you know what she eats? asked Mother.

The thought of it still haunted him.

I'm aware of what she eats, he said.

So?

So we're not getting her a microwave.

Then get her a bed.

A bed?

That woman, said Mother, pointing at the ceiling, sleeps on *rags*. That will be Anne Frank's deathbed, thanks to you, will it? A pile of soiled rags?

Bree pressed by without a word and headed for the car.

240

Mother, said Kugel, we don't have money for a bed.

She looked at Kugel with great sadness in her eyes.

My mother, she said. Do you know what *her* deathbed was? A wooden board in Auschwitz. But what could I do? I was a child, you understand, just an innocent child. I wanted to bring her food, but where would I find it? We were all starving, all of us.

Kugel stamped the end of his cane on the wooden floor.

Mother, he said through clenched teeth, surprising even himself, you weren't in Auschwitz. And neither was Grandma. She died in the cardiac unit at St Vincent's Hospital in New York City, surrounded by her husband and children.

Mother looked at him for a moment, stunned, and then she began to weep. Kugel sighed.

The past, she sobbed. It's disappearing like so much gossamer before my failing eyes, like a child's writing is wiped from a . . . from the . . .

She shook her head, trying to jog her memory. Kugel waited a moment before offering, Blackboard?

Mother nodded.

Bree tapped on the car horn.

It's all disappearing, Mother sobbed.

Lucky you, thought Kugel. He could go for some of that forgetting stuff right about now. Forget her, forget Father, forget it all, just for a day, a weekend. Heaven is a place with no memory, no history, no past; sure, some warm memories would be sacrificed along with the bad, but all in all, an improvement. A step in the right directionlessness.

There's no money for a bed, Mother.

How can there be no money? Mother asked. She's Anne Frank. Thirty-two million copies, that's not exactly small potatoes.

She can't touch it, Mother.

Why not?

Because she's dead.

Bree leaned on the horn.

Mother wagged a finger in his face.

When I get home, she said, I'm phoning Alan Dershowitz.

You're not phoning Alan Dershowitz.

The hell I'm not, Mother called back as she headed for the car. Spineless, just like your father. If you had even half the courage in your whole body as Alan Dershowitz has in one finger.

Mother, Kugel shouted back, you're not calling Alan Dershowitz. And if you get Anne Frank a microwave, I'm bringing it back.

Which is exactly, Mother said, cinching her coat belt before getting into the car, what Alan Dershowitz would *not* say.

Kugel gave Jonah a quick lunch of peanut butter and jelly and chocolate milk, and after a couple of cookies, took him out back to have a catch.

I'll be the Yankees, said Jonah, you be the Mets.

Why do I have to be the Mets? asked Kugel. The Mets stink.

Jonah laughed.

Though Jonah was still young, it was obvious to everyone that he was an exceedingly bright child, and his intelligence only exacerbated the guilt Kugel felt for bringing him into the world. It was one thing to have condemned a child to life, that was criminal enough, but life was a sentence more easily served by fools.

Congratulations, the obstetrician should say, your child is an idiot.

Oh, thank you, Doctor. We were so worried.

Not at all. He's a schmuck.

Too much brain, wrote Gogol, is sometimes worse than none at all.

Perhaps, wrote Dostoyevsky, the normal man should be stupid. Perhaps it is very beautiful, in fact.

Perhaps, thought Kugel, Smiling Man was stupid. Perhaps he was smiling because he was too blessedly dumb to know how completely fucked he was. You wouldn't call anyone in Buchenwald lucky, but the dumb ones were luckier than the smart ones, the sensitive ones, the aware ones, of that much you could be sure. You didn't want to be in Auschwitz at all, but you sure as hell didn't want to be a poet in Auschwitz.

Or Chelmno. Chelmno was bad, too.

With the vegetable garden behind Jonah acting as their backstop, Kugel tossed him the ball. He watched Jonah's little legs as he ran and chased it into the weeds.

I should have dropped him, thought Kugel.

When he was a baby. If I really loved him, I would have picked him up, turned him over, and dropped him on his delicate eggshell skull. I would've shaken him. A truly good father, a caring father, a protective father, would sit that child in front of the television set all day and let that sharp, curious mind turn to spongy, uncomprehending, witless mush. It would have been the least I could do. I brought him into this world, didn't I? I should at least have the courtesy to ensure he go through it in a mindless, drooling stupor like the rest of the goddamned species. Two and a half thousand years later, it was becoming undeniably apparent that an *un*examined life is the only one worth living. Examined lives tended to end hanging by the neck in the shower. Life examiners tended to go out sucking on the barrel of a shotgun.

Life: examine at your own risk.

Last words?

Not bad.

The ball hit Kugel in the crotch, and Jonah squealed with glee.

Shh, Kugel said, glancing up quickly at the attic windows.

He didn't want Anne Frank to hear them, and his concern for her surprised him. He worried that their happiness would make her sad, and wanted to spare her what he imagined was the pain of his joy.

Come on, buddy, said Kugel, let's go to the side lawn.

Jonah grabbed the ball and ran ahead of him, disappearing around the corner of the house. Kugel wondered why Anne Frank hadn't contacted her father after the war, once she'd learned that he'd survived. Would he contact his own father if he'd discovered he was alive? He thought that he might. And that Professor Jove would be against it.

The north side of the house was the only side completely hidden from Anne Frank's view. There was nothing much on this side of the house, though, just a few bramble bushes and a small patch of grass, and Jonah wanted to return to where they had been playing before.

Jonah grabbed the ball and ran, shouting, to the backyard.

Not so loud, called Kugel after him. The neighbors . . .

No poetry after Auschwitz, said Theodor Adorno. How about laughing, though, Ted? How about giggling? How about fucking? Those are much worse than poetry, and poetry was dead anyway (there was a death, at last, you couldn't pin on the Nazis). Kugel doubted that Anne Frank would mind very much if Jonah sat outside and read a sonnet or two aloud, but he was sure that child's laughter would cut her to the bone. Perhaps it would remind her of happier days. Whether there had been happier days or whether she could recall them any longer, he was unable to say with any certainty. He didn't even know that she was

245

unhappy now – disfigured, sure, half-mad, perhaps, but sanity has never been a prerequisite for happiness; it often seemed to be its biggest hurdle – so he couldn't say for certain that overhearing other people's happiness would cause her sadness. But he didn't want to take the chance.

Dad, called Jonah. Hey, Dad, come here.

Kugel walked around the corner of the house, and Jonah motioned him over to something he'd found in the grass. Kugel went over and knelt beside it.

Don't touch it, said Kugel. Don't touch it.

There in the tall grass at the side of the house, as if napping peacefully, was the severed head of Sunshine, the neighbor's missing cat. Kugel looked up at Anne's window, directly overhead.

Where's the rest of her? Jonah asked.

I don't know, said Kugel.

What happened?

Kugel shook his head.

Something must have killed her, he said.

Did they hate her?

Kugel shook his head.

Just hungry, he said.

Using a pair of sticks they found lying in the grass nearby, Kugel and Jonah dug a small hole in the ground in which to bury Sunshine's head. Jonah squatted down beside the cat's head and lifted it up by its ear.

I don't want you to die, said Jonah, looking at Sunshine's face.

I'm not going to die, said Kugel.

Jonah dropped Sunshine's head into the shallow grave, and together they covered her up. They sat there for a while, talking; Jonah asked Kugel what happened when you died, and where you went, and what it was like. Kugel answered as best he could, covering Sunshine's head while explaining that some people believe there's a world after this one where we all meet, and other people believe in reincarnation, where we all come back to life as something else. Jonah looked upset.

Someone once said, Kugel said to Jonah, that a free man thinks of death least of all things.

What does that mean?

How should I know? said Kugel with a smile. Go ask the guy who said it.

Jonah laughed – You're silly, Dad – and placed a small stone on the grave of Sunshine's head.

I want to come back as candy, said Jonah.

Candy?

Jonah shrugged.

Everyone likes candy, he said.

When children aren't saying something incredibly stupid that we in our need for answers decide is incredibly wise, they are saying something that makes you want to lift them up, hold them tightly in your arms, climb up inside an attic, and never, ever come back down.

Joney wouldn't make it in Auschwitz either, thought Kugel. Not a chance.

CHAPTER 22

After six years together, Hannah and Pinkus were still childless, though it wasn't for a lack of dogged, relentless trying; regardless of company or occasion, they were unashamedly physical with each other – perhaps this was because they were still attempting to have children (said Kugel), perhaps it was because they were ashamed of their pathetic previous failures (said Mother) – and it was difficult to find a time when one wasn't touching the other in some overtly sexual manner, standing close together, adjusting the other's clothing or playing with the other's hair. Family members or anyone else unlucky enough to witness these public acts of fore-foreplay either attempted to pretend not to notice or, more commonly, attempted distraction by engaging Pinkus or Hannah in unrelated, prosaic conversation.

Purely natural behavior, Pinkus, ever the evolutionary biologist, would proclaim as he grabbed Hannah in the kitchen, nuzzled her neck, and ran his hands over her hips and legs. I'm simply a male of the species obeying his natural imperative.

How about those Yankees, Kugel would say.

As desperate as they were to conceive, neither of them wished for a child of their own as much as Kugel wished one for them, as their unfortunate childlessness made Jonah the sole focus of Mother's intense melodrama. When Jonah was still an infant, Mother would hold him in her arms, look into his eyes, shake her head, and whisper, The last Kugel.

What she meant was Jew.

She used to say the same thing to Kugel when he was younger.

The last Kugel.

They had cousins, of course, and uncles and nephews all over the world. But somehow, for thousands of years, every Kugel was the last Kugel, just as every Jew was the last Jew; Tevye the Terminal, every single one. Yet, Kugel couldn't help but observe, in all that time – no last Jew. There had been a last Assyrian. There had been a last Ammonite. There had been a last Babylonian, a last Mesopotamian, a last of the Mohicans. But no last Jew. There had been a final Aztec, a departing Mayan, a Phoenician of Completion, an ultimate Ottoman, a conclusive Akkadian. There had been an Incan who closed the lights and shut the door on his or her way out. But no last Jew. Rocky Balboa took a beating, sure, but the story is: he won. Or tied. Or just: didn't lose. Ask an Arawak about who lost and who won, ask a Pequot, ask a Herero. Where were the stories of the *non*-last Jews, he wondered – the ones who thrived; the ones who prospered; the ones who married, had children, and died not of pogroms and Zyklon B and Inquisitions, but of old age? Surely some Jews died of old age; that's what Florida was for.

Pinkus had written a number of books attempting to prove, historically and mathematically, how much better the world was getting. We were becoming, his last book insisted, better people – more humane, more caring, less violent. The book, titled *You've Got to Admit It's Getting Better, A Little Better All the Time*, was a tremendous best seller. Professor Jove had written a book on the futility of hope entitled *Hello, Darkness, My Old Friend*. He was still sending out query letters.

As Bree passed the potatoes to Mother, and Mother passed the chicken to Kugel, Pinkus explained to everyone how things were taking a turn for the better, and had been for hundreds of years. It was the subject of his forthcoming book, *Here Comes the Sun, and I Say It's All Right*.

It would seem absurd, Pinkus said, to suggest so, no? It would seem insane to suggest such a thing in the face of Rwanda, in the face of Darfur, of Cambodia, of the Holocaust; naive at best, criminal at worst. But those *are* the facts, you see. Those are the *numbers*; it is something we can measure, a knowable thing: are we more or less violent now than a hundred years ago, five hundred years ago, a thousand years ago? Are we getting worse, or are we getting better? The answer is, we're getting better. Nobody wants to hear that answer, which is fascinating in its own right, but we don't have more killing now than then, that is the fact – we simply have more reporting.

Bree asked Hannah: How's your writing coming?

Hannah said: I haven't had much time.

My great-grandparents, continued Pinkus, lived through the Armenian genocide, I know how inhuman these events were. I'm not suggesting they weren't. But compared to life in the past – the everyday brutality and violence, the endless conflicts and bloodshed – well, the Holocaust wasn't so bad.

Kugel glanced nervously at the heating vent in the floor beside his feet.

I should thank the Nazis, Mother said to Pinkus, for being so evolved.

Pinkus, said Hannah, you're upsetting Mother.

My point, said Pinkus, is that we're doing something right. Why should that be upsetting? I know about Auschwitz and Hiroshima and My Lai and the Killing Fields, I know. But the numbers tell the real story, no? We are getting better. We are more caring, more giving, more moral. We are less violent, less callous, less hateful. Ten thousand years ago the odds of a simple hunter-gatherer dying at the hands of another – through wars, territorial disputes, tribal conflict – could be as high as sixty percent. That is a fact. In the last century, though, the supposedly worst century of war ever, it was

251

less than one percent. That includes two world wars, mind you. And just look at the homicide numbers, the numbers of random killings due to crime or foul play: in Europe, in the Middle Ages, there were a hundred murders per every hundred thousand people. Today, in modern Europe, that's down to less than one per every hundred thousand. Less than one. Shouldn't we be asking why? Shouldn't we be trying to understand the nature of this progress, to ensure it continues?

That wonderful European soil, said Mother, is soaked with the blood of my parents.

Pinkus shook his head.

Bree said to Hannah: Williamsburg must be fun.

Hannah said: Yes, but here you have the trees.

Which is precisely what fascinates me, Mother, Pinkus continued. We're doing something *right*. We *are* getting better. We should be trying to figure out why, and how, but to even suggest that we are getting better makes people furious, no? It is as if mankind *needs* the world to be getting worse, even if it happens to be getting better. Of course we'll happily admit that it's getting better for other people, but we'll adamantly refuse to include ourselves in that group. No, no – for us, it's always getting worse. Here's what I believe: we dream of utopia, but could never bear one. The impossibility of heaven is less a function of theology, in my opinion, than it is a problem of nature – *our* nature. How many days in the eternal sphere of goodness will it take before you complain, before you find someone that hates you, that oppresses you? One day? A week, tops. Pursue happiness all you want, but may God help us if we achieve it. Nothing would make us more miserable than joy. What would we have done without Hitler?

Kugel glanced again at the vent in the floor. He let his napkin fall from his lap and pushed it with his foot onto the vent.

Mother threw her napkin onto her plate in disgust.

I've heard enough of this, said Mother.

Listen, said Pinkus, nobody's saying it wasn't horrific. I wrote a paper on the effects of the Rwandan genocide years after it was over . . .

Genocide? said Mother with a dismissive wave of her hand, please. It was a summer. A few bad months. The UN calls everything genocide. The Holocaust lasted years, years of suffering and systematic murder. *That* was genocide.

Mother, said Kugel.

Pinkus, said Hannah.

What about the Armenian genocide, then? asked Pinkus. That lasted years, too. Does that make it as bad as the Nazi genocide?

Armenian genocide? said Mother. How many people died? A million?

A million and a half, said Pinkus.

Call me when you break three million, said Mother, then we'll talk. Genocide, my eye.

She stood and pointed her finger at Pinkus.

Maybe you need to suffer yourself, she said, before you determine so casually that things are getting better. What a fine example you are of the arrogance of science, of the audacity of math. Perhaps if you had spent three years with me, hiding in a darkened attic from the bloody hands of those damned Germans, perhaps then you wouldn't see life through the rosy glasses you have strapped to your head. A child I was, nothing more, trembling in fear in a cold, bare annex, never knowing which hour death would come but knowing, yes, knowing that it would.

Tap, heard Kugel. Tap-tap.

Kugel took Mother's napkin from her plate and dropped it, too, over the heating vent.

Tap, tap-tap.

But there you sit, Mother continued, having trembled in darkness over what – grades? degrees? – in your fancy dormitory room at MIT or Stanford or Harvard, and you dare to tell me that life is getting better? *Feh!*

And with that, Mother stormed from the room.

Mother, called Hannah, and looked to Kugel for help.

You see? said Pinkus to the rest of the family. This is why I'm writing this book. It's fascinating! It's as if a man goes to his doctor and, upon hearing his tests are negative, that not only isn't he unwell, but that he is in fact in perfect health, he flies into a violent rage. *Liar! Quack! Can't you see I'm bleeding, can't you see I've bled? Can't you see the scars? The damage?* I have the temerity to suggest that the human patient is not as hopelessly consumptive as we thought, and they call for my head. We're sick! they say. We're not so bad, I say. We're dying! they cry. What would we have done without gas chambers and ovens?

Tap, tap-tap.

What would we have done, Pinkus continued, without Dresden, without Srebrenica, without the Katyn Forest and the Killing Fields? I'll tell you my worry: my worry is not that we are becoming more violent. On the contrary, my worry is that we will someday reach such an unsettling level of peace, such a level of happiness and joy, that we'll engage in the most brutal war of all, a thousand Holocausts rolled into one, because peace frightens us. Expecting hell, we're ill prepared for heaven. It is like watching two men carry a pane of glass across a busy highway: we expect it to break, we know it will, the situation itself is so precarious that we almost *want* to see a car drive through it, we pick up a rock and shatter it ourselves. Smash it already! I know it's going to fall to pieces, I know it can't remain, stop getting my hopes up, stop letting me believe!

Tap, tap-tap.

Mother, called Kugel as he stood and hurried from the room. Once out of view of the dining table, though, he turned from her bedroom and headed upstairs.

One morning, he recalled as he climbed the

stairs, a few weeks after Jonah's illness, Kugel found himself on a subway, late for an appointment with Professor Jove, when the train came to a screeching halt. The anger inside the train was palpable. Fuck, muttered the man to Kugel's left. Fucking bullshit, Kugel had replied. After a moment, an announcement was made by the conductor: the train, tragically, had struck a waiting passenger, and they were going to be stopped a while as police and emergency workers arrived and saw to the passenger's health. The mood in the subway car now changed considerably, and everyone, including Kugel, seemed ashamed for having been so callous and rash. Soon more facts became known: the victim was an elderly blind woman; she worked at the station for years; she had gotten disoriented and stepped off the platform just as the train was arriving.

F Train? Kugel imagined her thinking. *That's how I die? The F train?*

The horrific news deepened the passengers' solemnity; some wished her well, some prayed, others told stories of similar tragedies: of the friend who died in the World Trade Center attack, of the family member who lost everything in Hurricane Katrina, of the child struck down by swine flu. It annoyed Kugel, this wallowing, this cheap pseudo-mourning. Shut up, all of you, he thought, keep your damned horror stories to yourself.

There was no need to confront them, though; their compassion lasted only as long as their patience, which wasn't very long, and as the minutes ticked by, their sympathy slowly turned back to anger. They began to grumble about missed meetings and angry clients. After fifteen minutes, the mood in the train returned to the same indignant, griping space it had occupied before. What is taking so long? someone muttered. Ridiculous, sighed another. Kugel, late now for his expensive Jove appointment, thought, Just move the train, for fuck's sake, she's not getting any deader. At last the train lurched forward, and the passengers, Kugel included, sighed with relief.

Kugel pulled down the attic door and warily climbed up the stairs, worried about being met by flying borscht bottles and jars of herring. He was relieved to hear Anne Frank typing away behind her wall.

I'm sorry about that, he said to Anne Frank as he approached the wall. He's a scientist, you know, his world is facts, not feelings.

The typing stopped. Kugel looked over the wall, and Anne turned to face him. The stack of manuscript pages beside her computer had grown.

What is she, said Anne Frank, stealing my bit? What?

Your mother, said Anne Frank. What's with all the attic crap?

Kugel's immediate concern became Jonah; if Anne Frank could hear Mother, so could he.

If she wants to steal something, said Anne Frank, let her steal from Wiesel.

How much more does the little guy need to know, anyway? thought Kugel. Burying one severed cat head a week was enough, wasn't it? Did he have to get into attics and Nazis?

I don't know what's worse, Mr Kugel, continued Anne Frank, your mother's auto-hagiography or the people like you who permit it to be written.

She began typing again.

The Brothers Grimm, she muttered, were never so grim.

Kugel often wondered how he would explain it all to Jonah. Other fathers worried about the Big Talk, but sex would be easier to explain than mass murder. How was he to do that? *In terms he can understand*, advised the books he'd purchased on talking to young children about death. *Well, Jonah,* he would say, *you like SpongeBob, right? Well, some people don't like SpongeBob, like Plankton. Plankton hates SpongeBob, right? Now, imagine if there was a whole bunch of Planktons, and a whole bunch of SpongeBobs, and the Planktons all got together and said, Things in Bikini Bottom would be better for everyone if we got rid of the SpongeBobs. Do you know what an optimist is? Anyway, one day, the Planktons rounded up all the SpongeBobs, and put them in, well, a sort of a camp. What kind of camp? Well, a death camp. And what happened was, you see, the Planktons tried to exterminate the SpongeBobs. What does exterminate mean? Do you know what annihilate means? Anyway, one very brave SpongeBob managed to hide from the Planktons in Mr Krabs's attic. Was it a happy ending? Well, that's where it gets a little tricky, son . . .*

I have to check on Jonah, he said.

Anne began typing again.

Have you told him about me? asked Anne Frank.

I was going to talk to him about fucking first, said Kugel, preparing to go back down the stairs.

Protecting a child from the outside world is easy, said Anne Frank as Kugel struggled to descend; his leg ached and he could only hold on, awkwardly, with his one good hand.

Protecting him from his inner world, Anne Frank continued, is quite a bit more complicated.

And other parenting tips, said Kugel, from hideous lunatic shut-ins.

Some terrible parents before the war were great parents during it, said Anne Frank. The convenience of an enemy, Mr Kugel; no nation has more enemies abroad than the one failing at home; no father yells more loudly at the Little League coach – He was safe! – than the father of the child who is utterly unsafe at home.

How's the book coming? he asked.

But there was no reply.

Kugel made his way down the attic stairs.

The train incident, or rather his reactions and those of his fellow passengers to it, had bothered Kugel, so he mentioned it to Professor Jove when he arrived at his office later that morning.

Why did it bother you? Professor Jove had asked.

It was awful, said Kugel, *we* were awful. In our

259

anger we were unfeeling, and in our sympathy we were self-involved.

So?

So we should be better.

But we're not.

But we should be.

What, Professor Jove asked Kugel, did the bartender say to the homosexual?

Goddamn it, thought Kugel.

I don't know, he said, what did the bartender say to the homosexual?

He said we don't serve faggots.

I don't get it, said Kugel.

He stood upright, Professor Jove continued, pointed to the door and said, Get out. Other customers likely joined in. The poor man agreed to leave, didn't want any trouble, just wanted a beer, but it was too late. They beat him half to death. They broke his teeth. They stripped him bare. They shoved a plunger up his ass. They wrote Fag on his back with the point of a knife and left him to die in the gutter.

I still don't get it.

There's nothing to get. We're ugly. Have you been to the zoo lately? You should go. Take Jonah with you, it will be good for him. See the placid zebra strolling in his field. Witness the mighty lion lazing in the sun. Smile at the droopy-eyed camel enjoying a mouthful of grass. Then go to the monkey house. Go see your forefathers. They are, by far, the most dangerous creatures in the zoo.

260

They rape, they kill, they form gangs. They're terrifying, your greatest-grandparents. Look at the warnings they post on the monkey cages, warnings not posted anywhere else: Do Not Taunt the Monkeys; Do Not Stare at the Gorilla; Do Not Put Hands in Cage. No other species requires such caution as the one from which we came. They're missing only one sign, the most important sign of all: Do Not Evolve From This Species.

That's depressing, said Kugel.

Only, said Professor Jove, if you thought we'd be better. Stop expecting more from us than we can possibly provide, and you'll stop being so disappointed.

Jonah was sound asleep, and Kugel returned to the dining room.

How is she? asked Hannah.

She?

Mother.

Oh. Okay.

Soon after, Mother, too, returned to the dining room; in her hands, she held the lamp shade she had given Kugel when he was a boy.

Goddamn it, thought Kugel.

Mother walked mournfully to the head of the table, a look of dignified grievance on her face.

We stayed in that annex for as long as we could, said Mother.

Kugel placed his foot over the heating vent.

But a man we considered a friend, Mother continued, soon turned us in. I don't blame him;

he was protecting his own family. What's another dead Jew in the grand scheme of things?

She held the lamp shade in both hands, and presented it to Pinkus, as one presents a crown to a king.

Of thorns, thought Kugel.

This, my dear Pinkus, said Mother, is my aunt.

Kugel shook his head.

Pinkus took the lamp shade in his hand.

Why don't you tell *her*, Mother said, how much better things have gotten. Why don't you tell *her* what a wonderful world this is.

Pinkus turned the lamp shade over in his hand.

It says Made in Taiwan, he said.

Well, they're not going to write Made in Buchenwald on it, are they?

You told me it was my grandfather, Mother, said Kugel.

What's the difference? said Mother. You're related to that lamp shade, suddenly you care so much how?

Later, as Bree and Hannah cleaned up from dinner, Kugel went outside to the vegetable garden and picked up the produce he'd left there that morning.

When he got into bed, Bree said, They have to go.

I know, said Kugel.

All of them.

I know.

Bree turned over and closed her eyes.

Ripping off Anne Frank, said Bree. That's a new one, even for her.

Maybe Jove was right. Maybe he wasn't just expecting too much from people, maybe he was expecting too much from himself. Sparing Mother, shielding Anne, sheltering Jonah. Maybe he should just be an asshole. Maybe the answer to a happy life, thought Kugel, was just being a son of a bitch.

It wouldn't be easy.

He hoped that he could be.

CHAPTER 23

As Kugel was driving to work the following morning, he came around a corner and saw a small group of deer standing – waiting, it seemed – on the far side of the road. A buck and several does stood at the edge of the road, where the tall roadside grass gave way to the dark pine forest, with three nervous-looking fawns behind them. Kugel slowed down as he approached, expecting them to dart across the street or scatter into the woods, but none moved; even the usually skittish fawns stood frozen still. He slowly drove closer, until he was almost upon them, but the small congregation remained motionless, their attention focused on the field of brush on the far side of the road.

Kugel pulled over, came to a stop, and switched on his hazard lights. He tapped lightly on the horn. The large buck turned to him briefly, but with a dismissive twitch of an ear looked back again toward the brush. They seemed anxious, their bodies tense, unsure of whether to stay or to flee, and in anxiety and ambivalence, they stamped in place and flicked their tails.

Kugel opened his car door and stepped out.

Still they didn't move.

Hey, he said, slamming his door to scare them off.

Nothing.

Kugel walked to the area of brush where the deer seemed to be looking; there, in the weeds and brambles, just a few feet from the side of the road where it had been struck, lay the broken, bloody body of a young fawn, a deep gash along her belly.

Kugel pushed the weeds aside and knelt beside her. Her eyes were wide, fixed straight ahead as she concentrated on the suddenly difficult task of breathing; she didn't move, couldn't, her legs shattered, her back broken; Kugel could see the slight pulse of her heart, and recalled with a stab in his own heart Jonah in his too-big hospital bed – it seemed long ago now, but never far away, perhaps today, perhaps tomorrow – having lost so much weight that Kugel could almost see his tiny heart pumping through his skin. It seemed such an inadequate device, the heart – so finicky, so easily stopped, so Japanese when it should be so German. One moment it's pumping, the next it's not. *And they lived. The end.* Kugel stroked the side of the fawn's nose while whispering to her the planet's oldest untruths: it was going to be okay, he wasn't going to hurt her, he was going to get her help. She yelped, tried to lift her head. *Shh.* The deer across the way watched him closely, with – you couldn't say it was anything less – hope

265

in their eyes. He rested the tips of his first two fingers on the fawn's chest – *shh* – feeling her heart underneath, racing, desperate; slowly, delicately, Kugel pressed his two fingers into the gash on her belly. She blinked, licked her lips. She felt warm inside, and wet; Kugel moved his fingers slightly, pressing them in deeper until he could feel her terrified heart thumping against the tips of his fingers. Kugel glanced up to the deer watching him from across the way; they seemed to think that he was helping, or that there was a chance he might, and for a moment he felt remorse for giving them such hope. Was that such a crime, though, Professor? Was a moment of false hope going to make their loss any greater? What was the greater kindness? Wasn't pretending like this, lying, faking, his fingertips on her heart, a crease on his brow, the least he could do? The few moments he kept his fingers inside her – doing nothing – were a few moments more that they could believe in some answer; wasn't that the kindest thing he could do for them?

The Lord is my shepherd, I shall not want.

Ask and thou shall receive.

For God so loved the world that He gave His only Son, that whosoever believes in Him will not perish but will have everlasting life.

Bullshit, sure, but good bullshit. The best bullshit. A lie, but the whole thing was a lie, what was one more to ease the pain?

And then the fawn sighed deeply, and rested her

266

head, and Kugel pressed his fingers against her heart, and it stopped. After a moment, Kugel gently removed his fingers from her wound; they were warm, wet, covered with dark red, almost black, blood. Kugel held his fingers up to his nose, inhaled deeply, and then, slowly, slowly, he placed them into his mouth and closed his eyes.

Fuck all you motherfuckers, he thought.

Toodle-oo.

And then the blare of a car horn, and the scattering of deer, and the squeal of tires and the shattering of glass.

Nobody was hurt, though Kugel was shaken and the other driver was furious. The police arrived (Are you hurt, he asked Kugel; Yes, Kugel responded; the officer glanced down at his cast and cane; From a previous accident, he asked, or this one? A previous one, said Kugel; I'm not interested in previous accidents, said the officer; Lucky you, said Kugel), insurance information was exchanged, and after writing tickets and helping Kugel load his rear bumper into the backseat of his car, the officer said they were free to go. It was, however, almost eleven o'clock, and past lunch when Kugel finally arrived at his office. His supervisor had left a note for him on his desk:

If you're not here, read the note, we assume you don't care.

An Indian chief named Isapwo Muksika Crowfoot said this on his deathbed: A little while and I'll be gone from among you. Whither I cannot tell.

From nowhere we come, into nowhere we go. What is life? It is the flash of a firefly in the light. It is the breath of the buffalo in the wintertime. It is as the little shadow that runs across the grass and loses itself in the sunset.

That seemed a lot to cover in a last moment. Kugel imagined he would manage to choke out the first few words – A little whi . . . – and drop dead before he could finish the rest. A little why, Bree would wonder. What did he mean by that? Remember your grandfather's last words, Jonah would tell his children: Life is nothing more than a little why.

Kugel thought the supervisor's note might make for a good tombstone:

SOLOMON KUGEL
*Just Because I'm Not Here,
Doesn't Mean I Don't Care.
Born. Died.*

The morning's incident with the fawn, despite its tragic outcome, had left Kugel in a surprisingly upbeat mood. Maybe there was something to this hope thing, after all. Fuck Jove, he thought. He imagined the professor at the scene of the accident, counseling the horror-stricken buck: *She's fucked, you know,* he would say. *Standing here forlornly? I would advise against it.* And so, though initially concerned with the threatening note from the supervisor, Kugel decided that in retrospect, it

268

was, when you looked at it, a generally positive development. The fact is, he hadn't been fired – he'd been warned. They could have fired him – they'd fired others for less – but they hadn't, clearly because he was a valued employee and clearly because they understood that he was going through a difficult time at home. All goodwill has its limits, of course, he was no fool, and of course he was going to have to reapply himself, prove to them that their trust in him was warranted and well deserved. Troubling? On the contrary, this was just the kick in the pants he needed. He had a family to think about, after all. Beginning Monday, he decided, he would apply himself with focus and determination; why, by the end of the following week, they'll be leaving him letters of thanks and encouragement, he would see to that. All he needed was a bit of a push – that's only natural, everyone does from time to time – and his supervisor, sensing that (he was a very good supervisor), had at last given him one.

Very well, he thought. Pushed I am, and pushed I shall be. A new beginning. A fresh start.

That evening, when Kugel returned home, he found Bree and the tenant arguing on the front porch. The tenant had his suitcases in hand, and Bree was trying to block his way. As Kugel made his way from the car to the porch, the tenant began calling to him, demanding to see the attic and to move some of his belongings there, or he would vacate the premises immediately.

I have paid for that space, Mr Kugel, said the tenant as Kugel approached. This is theft, and I will no longer stand for it.

Kugel, feeling buoyed from the positive new direction he'd taken at work and determined at last to take the same step at home, tried to calm the tenant, asking politely if they could discuss this issue like adults; it quickly became clear, however, that the tenant was going to leave and leave now if he didn't get a chance to see the attic.

Sir, said Kugel, you know that my mother lives with us because she is old and unwell.

That is not my concern, said the tenant.

It is not, that's true, said Kugel. We have our own problems, and can't always save the world. But the world is getting better, we are becoming better people, were you aware of that? The numbers don't lie, they do not lie, because, after all, there is a reason for everything, wouldn't you agree? But what is the reason for this delay? you wonder. My mother's illness, as I just mentioned, which necessitated her moving in here, with us. No one is less happy about that than I, I assure you, but because we could not rent out the room in which my mother is now living, and because the income from that room is required for us to maintain our own expenses, I must tell you that we were forced to rent out the attic as well.

Bree turned to Kugel with surprise.

You rented out the attic, said the tenant.

I'm afraid so, said Kugel.

Bullshit.

I should have told you sooner, said Kugel. I'm sorry, but we were assured by the doctors that Mother would have passed by now, and I was hoping to move the new tenant into her room, in order to give you all the space you need and, as you point out, so rightly deserve.

The tenant folded his arms across his chest.

There's someone in the attic, he said.

Yes.

Right now.

Absolutely.

I don't believe you for a minute, he said.

Why is your car all smashed up? Bree asked Kugel.

Why, why – life is a little why, is it not? A little why here, a little why there. More whys than becauses, precious few becauses, and a mountain of therefores that don't quite add up. She is quite old, Kugel said to the tenant, and rather infirm. The woman in the attic, I mean, not the car, ha ha. I had reservations about renting the space without telling you, but she seemed in quite desperate straits. Would you like to meet her? You'll see what I mean. She hasn't moved many of her belongings in, I doubt very much that she has many, and she sleeps most of the day on a small pile of blankets, but she's there if you would like to see her.

I would, said the tenant. I would like that very much.

Very well, said Kugel.

Kugel headed upstairs, the tenant close behind him, with Bree, in turn, close behind the tenant. Kugel wasn't concerned; he knew that this being daytime, Anne Frank would be sleeping, and if she wasn't, so much the better. He could argue with the tenant afterward, they would air their respective grievances, and Kugel was certain he could convince the tenant to stay – both Mother and Anne Frank were terribly old, and as soon as one died, the tenant would have his space.

I suppose the poor woman has her own bathroom, too? the tenant asked, his voice heavy with sarcasm.

Oh, no, said Kugel. Nor a private entrance. It is not at all convenient; you'll see soon, sir, the room you have is the best of all possible rooms.

Kugel was surprised that he hadn't thought of this plan earlier. Sometimes problems seem quite thorny, but they have a rather simple solution that was staring you in the face the whole time. His only concern was that this would be the first time Bree was seeing Anne Frank, and he expected her reaction to be quite negative, as, admittedly, his own reaction had been. But who knew? Perhaps seeing her in the flesh would cause her to feel pity, for him if not for her, and she would then understand all that had transpired.

Kugel pulled down the attic door, held a finger to his lips to indicate silence, and then began climbing up the attic stairs. They moved slowly; Kugel pressed himself onto the attic floor, while the tenant and Bree remained, apprehensively, on the ladder, only their heads rising up into the attic space. Kugel turned to motion them up after him, glad that in a moment at least one of his problems would be resolved. And that's when he saw her: Anne Frank, on the other side of the stairwell, very much awake, very grotesque, squatting over the heating return, her skirt lifted around her waist, her face red with exertion.

Ever since the war, said Anne Frank.

Bree and the tenant turned to look.

I'm out of here, said the tenant.

Bree stumbled down the stairs and ran to the bedroom. The tenant was not far behind her, fleeing down the stairs and out the front door.

She's a survivor, Kugel called after him. She's a survivor!

Kugel stood in the empty hallway, hands on his hips, and took a deep breath through his nose.

Well, at least he now knew where the rest of the smell had been coming from.

He wasn't crazy.

That, at least, was something.

CHAPTER 24

Saturday morning, Kugel returned to the hardware store for some additional latex gloves and a new brush. Upon arriving, though, he realized he had forgotten his wallet, and had to return home to get it.

Perhaps he was coming down with the same forgetting disease Mother had. Perhaps soon he'd forget it all.

She did it again, didn't she? said Vince.

Who?

The cat. She peed in the vents.

Shat.

Shat?

Shat.

You have got to get rid of that cat.

Vince recommended an industrial cleaner this time – We got Miracle-Away, he said, and Forever-Gone, but I'd go with Erase; toxic as hell, but gets rid of 'most anything, he said – and a two-pack of disposable odor-valved respirators.

And get rid of that cat, he added.

It was the last weekend in June. Next weekend would be Independence Day, the Fourth of July, and as Kugel walked back to his car, he noticed that all of town – the cars, the stores, and the homes – was festooned with flags, streamers, and large signs. July Fourth had always been one of Kugel's favorite holidays; it had never failed to stir within him, even when he was a child, a feeling beyond patriotism – a feeling rather of belonging, of oneness with a nation of strangers.

So what had changed? he wondered as he made his way back to his car. Why did these banners and flags today suddenly make him nervous, anxious? Was it something in the country, or something in him? It seemed now the basest form of patriotism; not pride, but fear; not celebratory, but suspicious, fearful. Was it the nation – a nation at war? – or was it him? Was it Anne Frank? The signs no longer seemed to express unity; they seemed like threats, dares, provocations, a grabbing of a stranger's shirt collar instead of a straightening of one's own spine:

United We Stand.

These Colors Don't Run.

Love It or Leave It.

A black silhouette of the twin towers and the words Never Forget, in blood red.

Why not? wondered Kugel. Why not forget? Isn't that what they would have wanted, the terrorists, that we never forget? That's probably what they said to one another when they came up with the whole plan: Holy shit, said one, they are NEVER going to forget this. They are NEVER, said another, going to forget this.

So forget it.

Gone.

Over.

Were there lessons to be learned? What, then? Did we know anything the day after, some kernel of wisdom or truth or knowledge that we hadn't known the day before? That life is short? Who knew? That men kill and are killed in return? What?

Nothing.

Not a goddamned thing.

I see floods, said Nostradamus, and fires and wars.

No shit, really?

So forget it.

Me and my friend Mohammed here are going to the Giants game.

Mohammed? Don't you remember 9/11?

No, why?

What's the harm in forgetting? What does remembering do? Kugel had read that the war in the Balkans was referred to as the War of the Grandmothers; that after fifty years of peace, it was the grandmothers who reminded their offspring to hate each other, the grandmothers who reminded them of past atrocities, of indignities long gone. Never forget! shouted the grandmothers. So their grandchildren remembered, and their grandchildren died. He had read that Darius the Great, so as not to forget the harm done to him by the Athenians, had a page whisper three times in his ear, every time he sat down to the table, *Remember the Athenians.*

276

Asshole.

If you don't learn from the past, said someone, you are condemned to repeat it. But what if the only thing we learn from the past is that we are condemned to repeat it regardless? The scar, it seems, is often worse than the wound. If only there was a Miracle-Away for the past. A Forever-Gone for brutalities, atrocities, indignities great and small. A lemon-scented life, that was what he wanted; for Jonah, for Bree, for Mother, for Anne. A pine-scented, cleaned, polished, revitalized life. Leaves no residue. Resists fingerprints. Sixty-four ounces of New, price on Amazon – who cares. Click to add to cart. Rush delivery.

Forget the Alamo.

Fuck it.

It's over.

This sort of patriotism worried Kugel, a worry he had inherited from Mother, who always told him it could happen here.

What?

It.

What it, Mother?

It it.

She seemed almost disappointed that it hadn't.

Kugel put his bag in the backseat of his car, and as he stood and closed the door, spotted a small For Rent sign on a high window of a small white house.

He knocked on the front door but there was no answer. He peered into the windows, knocked again, and made his way around to the rear of the house, where he found the back door unlocked. He opened it slightly.

Hello? he called.

He stepped into what was the kitchen, and called again.

Hello? I'm here about the room.

The house was tidy and well kept, the dishes cleaned and standing upright in the rack beside the sink. He made his way into the living room and den, and out to the front foyer.

Hello, he called up the narrow stairway.

Hello?

He walked slowly up the stairs. There were three bedrooms upstairs, one cleared of all furniture and smelling of fresh paint. The For Rent sign hung in the window. It was a small room but well lit, with a large central window that overlooked the street.

Kugel sat on the floor. He lay down on his back and folded his hands across his chest. He stood. He closed the door and opened it. He went out into the hallway, looked up at the ceiling and spotted a pull-down attic door.

Hello, he called again.

Kugel pulled down the attic stairs and climbed up.

The attic was small, much smaller than his own, and yet so filled with the owner's belongings that it was difficult to maneuver past the desks, chairs, rugs, bicycles, boxes, and old steamer trunks, all piled haphazardly, one atop the other. There were no windows, and the only light came from the meager rays of sunlight peeking through the gable vent.

Kugel found a box tied and held together with a long section of rope; he removed the rope, climbed down the stairs, and tied the rope, as he'd seen Anne Frank do, to the bottom rung. He climbed back up and pulled on the rope, and the attic door closed behind him with a satisfying thump. He made his way through the attic until he came to an old dining table standing against the back wall. He crawled underneath, lay down, closed his eyes, and fell asleep.

It was the deepest sleep he'd had in some time.

When he awoke sometime later, he heard voices below him. The owners. A man, a woman, their words muffled; Kugel pressed his ear against the floor, but beyond the occasional word or two, all he could make out were intonations, cadence, rhythm; he recognized the long pauses, the impassive delivery, the lackadaisical alternation of comfortable familiarity. They had been married for some time.

Him: Mmm mm mm mmm mm?
Long pause.
Her: Mmm mmm mm.
A door closing.
Walking.
Her: Mmm mm mmm.
The television coming on.
Him: Mmm. Mmm mmm mmm.
They were arguing about something. Bickering.
Her: Mmm mmm mmm?
A cabinet door slams shut.

Him: Mmm! Mmm mmm mmm!
Kugel chuckled.
Her: Mmm mmm. Mmm!

He held a hand over his mouth, trying not to laugh out loud, but it all seemed so comical, he was soon throwing back his head in silent uproarious laughter.

Someone slowly walking up the stairs, down the hall, below him now.

Silence.

Kugel composed himself.

A light coming on. And then, directly beneath him, groaning, farting.

Oh, God, he heard her grunt.

Kugel chuckled again.

She was in the bathroom.

More farting, more appeals to the Lord above.

Kugel tried desperately not to laugh out loud, but the flush of the toilet killed him; he lost it. He buried his face in a quilt and hoped the sound of the flushing toilet would cover the sounds of his laughter. Tears streamed down his face and his ribs ached. Then the creak of bedsprings, a groan. Then, for a while, nothing but the tinny sound of the television downstairs.

Minutes passed, ten, maybe fifteen.

Kugel pressed his ear to the attic floor.

He heard snoring.

Kugel crawled out from beneath the table and quietly pushed some boxes into the corner until he had built a small wall, and placed behind it a number of quilts and blankets. As quietly as he could, he made his way back to the attic door, slowly pressed it open, and descended from above.

He crept down the hallway to the bedroom; the old woman was on her side, fast asleep. Kugel smiled again, remembering it all; he tiptoed across the room and lightly, ever so lightly, kissed her on her head.

He thought that perhaps he loved her.

Downstairs, an old man sat sleeping in the brown recliner in front of the television. Kugel slowly moved back through the house, into the kitchen and out the back door.

The sun was beginning to set.

Kugel made his way around to the front of the house and knocked on the door.

Hang on, called the old man.

After a moment the door opened.

I'm here about the room for rent, said Kugel.

The old man shook his head.

Already taken, he said. Sorry.

Tall guy? asked Kugel. Beard?

The old man nodded.

Something like that, the old man said, suddenly wary.

Kugel looked over the house.

Well, he said, I'll see you.

Reckon so, said the old man.

He closed the door and Kugel could hear the locks clicking shut behind him.

Kugel spent most of the following day cleaning the vents and registers. He dragged a bucket of water and cleaning supplies up to the attic, scrubbed the grilles first, then the sides of the ducts, and poured the leftover mixture down into the ducts to let it make its way through the house; still the smell lingered in the air, the smell of Anne Frank, much as it did on his fingers and hands, no matter how much he scoured them.

By the time he went to bed Sunday evening, Bree had already fallen asleep. We think of the obvious signs of love – tenderness, concern, care – and yet somehow, nothing said more about the health of a couple's relationship than whether or not they went to bed at the same time.

Kugel lay down on the bed, fully clothed, and closed his eyes.

Maybe Mother was right, he thought. Maybe she shouldn't die on a pile of rags.

Spinoza declared: I call him free he who is led solely by reason.

Spinoza also declared: True virtue is life under the direction of reason.

Kugel wondered if Spinoza declared those things before or after he dragged his mother's deathbed across the Netherlands; Kugel had read that he took it with him wherever he went. He took it from Amsterdam to Rijnsburg, from Rijnsburg to Voorburg, from Voorburg to The Hague. That didn't seem all that reasonable to Kugel; it seemed pretty unreasonable. This was not some inflatable bed. This was not some futon. This was a full-size wooden bed. There may have been a box spring, for all we know.

The story troubled Kugel. If she had died when Spinoza was a middle-aged man, perhaps you could say she meant the world to him, that the loss was of a mother who was more than simply a mother, but of a necessary, trusted, and wise guide who had passed on, and that Spinoza was having trouble saying good-bye. It would still be weird, frankly, damn weird, but you could cut him some slack. But Spinoza's mother died when he was six years old. If even the High Priest of Reason could be so unreasonable about a deathbed, perhaps he should give it more thought himself. And so the following morning, on the way to work, Kugel stopped at the local mattress store.

Everything, shouted the sign in the window, Must Go.

You don't know the half of it, said Kugel to the store.

He wasn't comfortable with the idea of buying Anne Frank a marked-down deathbed – it didn't seem like the kind of thing one should go bargain-hunting for. But he didn't feel like spending a fortune, either.

God Bless America, shouted another sign.

Was it God, Bless America? Like an order? Like a command? That didn't seem wise, ordering God around like that. And didn't that suggest that God hadn't blessed America? That America was unblessed? If He had blessed us, we wouldn't need another blessing, would we? Or was it God Bless, America. Like, See you later, America. Like, you're fucked. Like, find an attic. Fast.

A salesman quickly approached him.

Just looking, Kugel said to the salesman.

No problem, no problem, said the salesman. Just so you know, all sale items are marked with a yellow star.

Perfect, thought Kugel. I'm going to buy Anne Frank a Jewed-down deathbed with a yellow Star of David on it.

Spinoza.

What a jackass.

Of course, you don't buy a deathbed. There is no such thing. You buy a regular bed and croak on it. A Sleep Master or a Dreamweaver or a NightCloud, made with Advanced PolyCarbonate Progressive Coils, BioReactive TemperPads and GermResistant PermaSoft Memory Foam, the highest tech, the cuttingest edge; even the cheapest ones were hundreds of dollars, some were thousands. It made sense, Kugel thought as he looked at the prices, that an empire in decline should spend its finest scientific and intellectual capital on sleeping. On napping. On a snooze. Why didn't they sell deathbeds? he wondered. Specifically. A Serta PerfectDeath. A Sealy SwanSong. A Tempur-Pedic Ultra-Plotz with Advanced MortalCoil Technology. Something decent, something comfortable, but not something intended to last more than a few months, tops. These non-deathbeds had twenty-year warranties; why should he have to pay for nineteen and a half years of sleep he had no intention of using? He sure as hell wasn't going to use a bed after someone died on it. Maybe he could just return it after she died? Could you return a bed someone died on? How would they know?

Hitler was an optimist.

The more Kugel thought about Spinoza, the angrier he became. It's not like the guy was an idiot. What hope was there for the rest of us if a mind like that can still, when it comes to his emotions, be such a fool? And not merely a fool, but a stark, raving basket case. If the clearest logic the human mind is capable of is still woefully insufficient, why even bother? What hope is there?

Will you be checking any luggage today, Mr Spinoza?

Just the two bags. I'll be taking the deathbed as my carry-on.

Very good, sir.

Kugel made his way around the store. The selection was dizzying. Latex, foam, coil, twin, twin XL, queen, king. He hadn't even considered the size. What size would she need? Queen? The twins were the least expensive, maybe he should just get that and be done with it. She was small, what did she need with a queen?

Kugel lay down on one of the beds, rested his hands on his chest, and looked up at the ceiling.

There might be death throes.

Thrashing around or whatever.

At the moment.

Of her death.

Maybe go with a queen.

Stan Laurel, on his deathbed: I'd rather be skiing.

Do you ski, Mr Laurel? the nurse asked.

No, he said, but I'd rather be doing that than this.

The chaplain said to Chaplin: May the Lord have mercy on your soul?

Said Chaplin to the chaplain: Why not? It belongs to him.

Kugel closed his eyes. He didn't want Anne Frank falling off the side of her own deathbed.

I'm terribly sorry, Mr Spinoza, that deathbed isn't going to fit in the overhead compartment.

Soon Kugel fell asleep. He dreamed again of the elderly terminal patients in hospital gowns and bandages hobbling up his driveway. Again they walked past him, only this time he didn't try to stop them. He simply watched them shuffle and limp by, moaning and wheezing and bleating and farting, and he followed them, once again, out to the backyard, where they stepped, one by one, off the edge of the cliff. This time, though, Kugel pushed his way between them, made his way to the edge of the cliff, and peered over; he felt that he needed to know what became of them there, over the edge. At the base of the cliff, the dead were forming a mound of bloody, broken bodies, wooden canes, steel IV towers, bent walkers, cracked wheelchairs. Pools of blood formed around the base of the pile. Nobody made a sound, nobody struggled to get up. Kugel's knees grew weak as he was suddenly overcome with a fear of the cliff before him, and he tried to back away from the edge of the cliff, but he couldn't, there were too many of them now, pressing past him, nudging him closer to the cliff even as he pushed back against them.

Kugel woke to find the salesman nudging his shoulder.

That's a quality product, said the salesman. Serta Perfect Sleeper with Memory Foam Topper.

How much is it? asked Kugel.

It'll add years to your life, that one, said the salesman. One night and you'll feel ten years younger.

Kugel made a note not to get one for Mother.

How much? he asked.

In queen, said the salesman, you're looking at eight hundred, eight fifty or so, and we'll throw in the frame at no extra charge.

Eight hundred and fifty dollars? asked Kugel. What time is it?

Half ten, said the salesman.

Fuck, muttered Kugel.

We can get you wrapped up and out of here in five minutes, said the salesman.

How much is the futon? asked Kugel.

One fifty, said the salesman.

I'll take the futon, said Kugel.

By the time the salesman tied the futon to the

roof of Kugel's car, it was close to eleven o'clock. As Kugel pulled out of the parking lot he pictured Anne Frank dying. He pictured her lying on her back, in the gloomy evening half-light of his attic, peering into the middle distance, trying to speak, trying to say one last thing, but able at last only to draw one last breath, one last time, her miserable life coming to an end at last.

On a futon.

Would Spinoza have carried his mother's futon around?

Fear cannot be without hope, nor hope without fear; now give me a hand with this futon frame, it's heavy as fuck.

At the next traffic light, Kugel made a U-turn, drove back to the mattress store, and laid out over a thousand dollars for the Serta Perfect Sleeper with Memory Foam Topper.

Goddamn it, he thought.

He pulled into the office parking lot, a queen-size mattress and box spring tied to the roof of his car, at ten minutes past twelve. He was met in his office by his supervisor, a man from security, and a woman from the human resources department. There were a number of empty cardboard boxes on his desk.

We can no longer afford, said his supervisor, to look away.

Last words?

He would write those down.

CHAPTER 25

For almost a week, the fires had ceased. Kugel spent the evenings downstairs reading books about Anne Frank and the Holocaust, while Bree, upstairs, pored over the budget and bills. The police were said to have identified a suspect, though no details were being released, as the case was still under investigation and the suspect was still at large. Then, later that week, the arsonist struck again at the old farm on Sawmill Road, one of the grandest, most impressive farms in the region, setting fire to the horse stable and storage shed. Fortunately, it had been a long time since there were horses in the stable – the present owners were executives from the city who used only the main house – and the firemen arrived before too much damage could be done. Two days later, the arsonist struck the same farm, this time setting fire to the front and rear porches of the farmhouse itself. Again, the firefighters responded quickly; there were rumors of someone seen fleeing the scene, of someone being chased into the woods, of security cameras that had captured a photo of the arsonist even if the police had failed to capture him. The following day, the town was abuzz with the police department's public naming of a prime suspect: Wilbur Messerschmidt Jr.

The townspeople were shocked. None could believe it. Wilbur Junior was a volunteer fireman and a beloved member of the community. The family had lived in the area for almost two hundred years. Why would he do such a thing? Senior, Will's father, granted only one interview, with the local radio station, in which he tried to explain his son's actions, an interview Kugel listened to as he drove home with a mattress tied to his roof and a pink slip in his pocket.

The Messerschmidts, said Senior, had been farmers. For years, they successfully lived off the land, until industrial-scale agriculture, heavily subsidized by the government, made it impossible for them to compete. Lately, as they liked to say in the family, they lived on the land, but not off it. They began to lose their homes, one after another, defaulting on second mortgages, owing back taxes, watching as their history was sold off, piece by piece, to the young wealthy families that were beginning to leave the cities; what had once been family treasures where generations of Messerschmidts had been born and raised now sat empty all week, the owners coming up only on weekends, installing central air conditioning and in-ground pools and complaining about the slow hot-water heater. And so, said Senior, Wilbur Junior had decided that if the Messerschmidts couldn't have their farms, well, then, nobody could.

Wilbur Messerschmidt Jr, the interviewer noted, was still at large.

I can return it, Kugel said.

We're drowning, Bree said, tears of anger in her eyes.

We'll be okay.

Don't say that.

Okay.

It's not okay.

I'm sorry.

I don't care.

You don't care?

I don't care, said Bree. I care that we can't afford this house. I care that you chased away our only paying tenant. I care that you care more about them than you do about us.

That's not true.

It is true.

It isn't.

Kugel could understand her anger at the situation, but he couldn't understand her anger toward him. What options did he have? Even if he wanted to throw Anne Frank out, Mother would never let him. And Mother was almost dead herself, the doctors all but guaranteed it. It would all be over soon. What better indicator of that was there than a brand-new deathbed?

How much did it cost? she asked.

I can return it.

How much did it cost?

He told her.

She slapped his face, hard, and stormed away.

I can return it, he said.

The mattress and box spring stayed on the roof of Kugel's car overnight and into the next morning, when Pinkus agreed to come over and help bring them up to the attic; with his injuries, Kugel simply couldn't carry them alone. Mother, busy with her scrapbook, couldn't help, and Bree, furious, wouldn't. They left him alone there that morning, and for that he was glad – Bree took Jonah to day care, and Mother went along to do some shopping.

She should have some fresh bedding, said Mother.

Kugel waited on the front porch for Pinkus. The mattress, tied to the roof of the car, made him think of refugees. It made him think of fleeing. Where would they go if something happened?

If what happened?

He remembered reading something about papers, about needing papers – people in Holocaust books and movies were always worrying about their papers: getting them, not getting them, getting them when it was too late, getting them in the nick of time, forging them, hiding them, losing them. Did he even have papers? What were papers, anyway? Papers like what, like a passport? Papers like a birth certificate? So many people had trouble with these papers, it was the stories where people *had* their papers that always surprised Kugel.

Really, you have papers? How did you know you were supposed to have papers? Who gave you the papers? Did Bree have papers? Did Jonah have papers? Did they need papers?

iPod (headphones/charger)
EpiPens
Zyrtec
Papers (?)

He knew it, he hated to admit, from the very first time his mother showed him footage of the corpse piles at Dachau. That was his first thought: I wouldn't make it. He wasn't the survivor type. He was a succumber. A perisher. A plotzer. He never did get on that plane from LA. He had no idea how to get out of quicksand. Bree was a survivor. Bree was an overcomer. Bree would be out of the quicksand, showered, and changed before Kugel ever got a footing. Kugel hoped Jonah had some Bree in him. More Bree, less Kugel. He might make it then. But Kugel? Never. He wouldn't stand a chance. He would kill himself. He would lose his mind. He couldn't withstand a day of Auschwitz, not an hour, not a minute. And brother, Auschwitz happens.

Toodle-oo.

Canada.

He'd probably go to Canada, assuming that whatever it was that was going on here wasn't going on there. But that was what Otto Frank thought, wasn't it? That was Otto's plan. Northward Ho hadn't exactly worked out for him, had it?

Nowhere Ho, that's what Kugel wanted. Him, Bree, and Jonah, in his car, flat out, pedal to the metal on the Nowhere Highway, singing songs and stopping at drive-thrus.

Are we almost there, Dad?

Almost, buddy, almost.

He didn't even have roof racks, Kugel thought, looking at his car. Jesus Christ, what kind of an idiot in this world doesn't have roof racks? He remembered a legend he had been told in Hebrew school, of an angel that visits the baby inside the womb; the angel sits with the child and teaches him all the wisdom of the world, everything he will ever need to know to survive; then, just before birth, the angel presses his fingertip against the baby's upper lip, leaving behind a small indentation and removing everything he has been taught. Kugel could never understand the point of that, but now, he thought, he knew exactly what the angel must say to every child about to embark on a life on earth: Listen up, kid: roof racks.

You don't escape genocide in a sedan. You don't escape anything in a sedan. A sedan was just asking for trouble. He should trade it in for an SUV. Maybe a Jeep.

Military-like.

Prepared.

A list.

Listen up, kid: four-wheel drive.

And don't order the fish.

At last Pinkus arrived. It took the two of them the better part of an hour to drag the mattress, box spring, and metal frame up the stairs and squeeze them through the narrow stairwell of the attic. Pinkus left for work, and Kugel set about putting together the frame and setting up the bed.

When it was done, he lay down on it and looked at the roofing nails pointing down at him. He heard a slight shuffling behind the wall of boxes, and then that grim, creaky voice.

What the hell, asked Anne Frank, is that?

You're welcome, said Kugel.

I don't want it.

Don't mention it, said Kugel. It's a quality product.

Take it back.

It's not for you. It's for my mother.

Then put it in her room.

Silence.

Do you have any money? he asked.

More shuffling, then a heavy groan, as if she were lying back down on her pile of blankets.

The first Jewish homeowner in sixty years, Anne Frank said, and he wants to charge me rent. Perfect.

Kugel looked down at his right arm. He was beginning to get a rash of some kind. He scratched it with the cast on his left arm, then felt more itching around the base of his neck.

How's the book coming? he asked.

There was no answer.

How did you get out, he asked.

Silence again.

I asked you a question, he said.

Kugel sat up, swung his feet off the side of the bed, and pressed his clenched fist into his forehead.

Maybe he *should* kill her, after all.

Who would know?

He tried to control his anger.

Hitler was an optimist.

Monkeys are assholes.

Roof racks.

Father, I something something my something.

I've been reading, said Kugel. About you.

He'd ordered and read them all, looking for answers: all the testimonies of Anne Frank, the histories, the biographies, the martyrologies, the hagiographies. You might also like, said Amazon, *Rwanda: Portrait of a Genocide*, *Pol Pot's Bloody Reign*, and *The Starving of the Ukraine in Words and Pictures*.

Mazel tov, said Anne Frank. Reading is fundamental.

People saw you, said Kugel.

Fucking Spinoza.

In the camp, he continued. They saw you. You were sick. You were dying.

He stood and walked toward the wall of boxes.

People, he said. Numerous people. They saw you. Anne Frank.

Silence.

You were dead, Anne. Stone cold.

He stood at the wall, waiting, breathing through his nose, his hands on his hips.

Ach, said the old woman behind the wall. I'm sick of all that Holocaust shit.

Kugel kicked out with his good leg, sending a section of the wall crashing to the ground. The broken arm, the job, the rash, Bree, Jonah, the tenant, the finances – it all bubbled over. He shouted as he kicked over another section of the western wall, then another. Anne scurried through the shadows, hiding deep in the dark eaves as Kugel picked up a nearby broom in his good hand and began swinging it at the boxes on the two remaining walls, shouting and screaming and raising the broom overhead again and again as he smashed her boxes, her lamp, her table; everything was destroyed, the kitchen overturned, the bed quilts scattered; Anne Frank cowered in the eaves, her bony hand clenched in a feeble fist, and at last Kugel's rampage stopped, and he stood there, exhausted. He stayed like that for a few moments, threw the broom to the floor, turned, and went to the attic stairs.

I was dying, said Anne Frank.

I don't care, said Kugel.

Everyone was, said Anne Frank.

Finish your book, said Kugel, and get out.

Auschwitz was different, she continued. Auschwitz was a factory – a death factory, yes, but precise, orderly.

Kugel stopped at the stairs.

Belsen, though, Anne Frank continued, was a toilet. That was the idea of Belsen, you see, the whole concept. Filth and disease. Bodies lay everywhere, unburied. They were dying faster than they could get rid of them. I lay there on the wooden bed beside the door to our bunker, beside Margot, shivering despite the heat every time the door opened. She was dead, I don't know for how long, and I waited, hopefully, for death to come for me. But it never did. My fever broke. The blissful freedom of my delirium vanished and I was a prisoner again in my own sanity. I decided to remain with the dead. I didn't move, I don't know for how long. The other prisoners, thinking we were both dead, carried us outside the bunker and laid us down on the ground beside the other corpses. Again I didn't move. After some time there, I dared to let one eye creep open and realized that some of the other dead were not – that others there were doing the same thing as I, pretending to be dead; we spotted one another – a corpse who suddenly seemed to move, or whom you caught, for a moment, looking at you before quickly shutting her eye. At night, in the safety of the dark, some of the other non-dead would rise and move quietly about the yard, attempting to find some bread or water, and in the morning, before the dark lifted, they returned, bringing with them a piece of a turnip or crust of bread to the others they knew to be faking. A

Sisterhood of the Dead. The threat of the SS loomed as ever, but the greater threat was that of the starving prisoners who had taken to eating parts of the dead – cutting off a nose, a tongue, to stay alive one more hour, one more day. I watched such a thing happen to a woman who had brought me a turnip one morning – in the middle of the night, a starving figure approached, knelt over her body, and tore her ear off, shoving it desperately into its mouth. The woman, though, didn't move, didn't cry out; only when the figure scurried off did she roll to her side, the side of the bloody ear, because bleeding might give her away, and I heard her whimper softly. That much grief she allowed herself. In earlier days, it would only be an hour or so before they dragged a dead body to the mass graves; we had heard, though, in past weeks, that the war was coming to an end, that the Russians and British were already on German soil; we often heard such rumors before, but the SS were beginning to behave strangely, like frightened birds, neglecting their duties – even the sacred roll call was sometimes skipped – and it seemed perhaps that the rumors this time were true. Once the dead piled up, any fool could see that it would be safer to be among them; the SS officers were more concerned with their own escape than with burial or cremation. Many of the officers dressed in civilian clothes and simply left, walked away, and I began to think of escape. We had been warned when we arrived at Belsen that escape was impossible, that even if you got past the guards and dogs and electrified gates, the roads around the camp were laid with mines, but from where I lay, I could see that the trucks and cars outside the gate drove safely in and out without incident. I lay there next to my sister's corpse for two full days, and one night, as a transfer was taking place, I took my chance and stood, wobbling at first, for I hadn't stood or eaten in some time, and I ran as best I could for the gate, using an exiting supply truck to shield me from sight. My sister was dead, my mother was dead, I assumed my father was, too. I waited for the bullet to strike me in the back; I waited for the mine explosion to tear me in half; the grenade, the dogs. But they never came. I ran through the woods, with no idea where I was going or why. I don't remember how long I ran. At nights I pressed on, in the daytime I covered myself with leaves or hid beneath rocks and slept. One night, as I pressed through the woods, I came upon an old farmhouse. I hid among the bushes, not moving, watching, and when at last the sun rose, the man of the house came outside, got into his car, and drove off; soon after, his wife and young daughter did the same. I waited until I was certain they were gone, and I ransacked the place. I found a cloth laundry bag in the bathroom and filled it with everything I could: clothing, food, medicine. I thought, perhaps, I was dreaming, hallucinating. I washed myself in their sink, changed into some of the daughter's clothing – she was much younger than I, but I was very thin at the time, and they fit me. A new dress, it had been so long. I grabbed my sack of provisions and ran out the front door onto the front porch . . . and then I stopped. I froze. I didn't want to go out there again, Mr Kugel. The world seemed enormously cruel and dangerous. I had only vague memories of life before war; the only place I could ever remember feeling safe was the attic in Amsterdam, that tiny, stifling annex with Margot and Father and Mother. So I turned around, went back inside, climbed upstairs, and hid in their attic. It was a nice attic, not much different from this one. How happy I felt, how safe. The owners found me a few days later, and they brought me food and water and clothing. They hated themselves, you see, and so they took pity on me. Yes, yes, I know, pity is contempt; but you take what you can get. Years later, when they moved to America, they arranged for my own safe passage, too, through a number of admittedly illegal means. The husband died and soon after, the wife grew ill, and she arranged to move me to a new family, a new attic, and so I went, here and there, house to house, family to family – a Polish family first, for a short time, then an elderly Austrian couple – until finally I came here, thirty or forty years or so ago, where the Messerschmidts took over my care. I have been the blessed beneficiary of sixty years of humanity's guilt and remorse, Mr Kugel. Did you like the part about the cannibals and the ear? Or the part about the tiny dress that fit my emaciated body? These are true details, I assure you, but I know to emphasize them; I'm not a fool; I know of guilt myself, Mr Kugel. My sister died beside me. My mother died, my friends. I survived. That's not easy, either. Perhaps it's true that I am seeking to have it both ways; I want to be Anne Frank without the Holocaust, but I use the Holocaust to subsist, to get what I need: shelter, food, a place to work. To that I plead guilty. But would you have let me stay here if I hadn't told you who I am? I doubt it very much. I'm a survivor, Mr Kugel – not of this war or that, but as a type. I survive. I do what I have to. I survived death in my youth, and I've been surviving life ever since.

Kugel waited a moment and headed down the attic stairs.

Tell me, Mr Kugel, called Anne Frank. Have you really not read my diary?

No, he said.

Do you mind if I ask why not?

He got to the bottom of the stairs and turned around.

I'm sick of that Holocaust shit, he said.

Kugel folded the stairs and thought, as he closed the attic door, though it was certainly possible he was wrong, that he heard Anne Frank laughing.

CHAPTER 26

Bree took a job at Mother Earth's Bounty; the store needed some extra help for the upcoming July Fourth weekend, and a friend from her writers' group had put in a good word with the store manager (Think of this, she had said to Bree, as your main character's dark night of the soul, after which she emerges into a newer and brighter phase of life). The pay wouldn't cover the loss of Kugel's income, but they could continue their health insurance and keep from sinking too deep into debt if they could rent the two rooms, and maybe even the attic, without too much delay. Of equal importance was the employee discount that would help with their grocery bill; they were feeding themselves, Jonah, Mother, and Anne Frank on a salary that was barely enough to pay for just one of them.

Kugel felt terribly guilty about the situation, and wondered if it might be better if Bree left for a short while, and perhaps stayed in Mother's Williamsburg apartment, until he got back on his feet. Any free time she'd had for writing was, for the time being, gone, and for that Kugel felt the worst. The feeling of tension between them was great; Bree spoke infrequently to Kugel, only to keep up appearances before Jonah and to discuss their dwindling finances.

To complicate matters even more, there had been no way for Kugel to explain to Pinkus why he was moving a queen-size mattress and bed frame into the attic without telling him about Anne Frank. Pinkus, although expressing a fair degree of skepticism in the validity of the old woman's story, subsequently told Hannah. For Hannah, her own belief or doubt was irrelevant; if Mother believed it was Anne Frank – or that the lamp shade was her father or the soap her aunt – and if that belief had invigorated Mother and given her life, that was more than enough for Hannah. Whether she was or wasn't Anne Frank, said Hannah, was beside the point; she had made her way to this house for a reason, and that reason was to make Mother's last days vibrant and meaningful. For that alone she deserved their assistance. So Friday afternoon, Hannah moved into the vacated room next to Mother's, to both help her with the poor woman in the attic and to spend some time with her before she died. Pinkus joined Hannah, and at night, in their bedroom, they made loud, vulgar attempts at procreation, the sounds and dialogue of which drifted up through the heating ducts, emerging at Kugel's bedside, where he and Bree lay separated by piles of spreadsheets and mountains of Holocaust books, until at last, after what seemed like hours, with a loud cry, one or another of the never-to-be parents announced, with great fanfare, the completion of their latest, greatest attempt at making one more Kugel.

Mother, meanwhile, had been spending her time in the attic, fixing the damage Kugel had caused to Anne's walls – My own son, she said, attacking Anne Frank. You want Elie Wiesel's address? Maybe you could trash his bedroom, too? – and setting up the bed Anne Frank didn't want and refused to use. Mother dressed the bed with pink sheets and pillow-cases, and laid a white down comforter on top of them; she hung a pink ruffle sash around the bottom of the bed, on either side of which she placed two small white end tables, complete with turned legs and floral drawer pulls. Kugel noticed as well that, whereas initially Mother would go up to the attic without giving too much thought to her dress, she had begun of late dressing rather formally before ascending the attic stairs: dresses, blouses, shoes cleaned and shined. Soon she was covering her hair before going up, sometimes with just a simple white lace doily, sometimes with a fur felt hat and matching gloves, expressing displeasure with Kugel (though never in a raised voice; she only whispered when near the attic, or when ascending or descending the attic stairs) that he was dressing for his own visits in so common a manner.

Is that what you're wearing? To visit Anne Frank? Sweatpants? Dungarees? To visit Anne Frank, that's how you dress?

Sunday afternoon, Kugel took Jonah to the Stockton Independence Day parade; the police closed off the main street to through traffic, and the townspeople packed the sidewalks, waving flags and blowing into noisemakers as the elderly war veterans slowly walked by.

Sixty years earlier and a few thousand miles east, thought Kugel, and I'm in a whole different story. It's Hitler marching through town instead of the Stockton Old Timers' Band; it's swastikas instead of stars and stripes.

God Bless Germany.

Three cheers for the red, white, and black.

A black silhouette of the Battle of the Somme and the words Never Forget, in blood red.

Crowds worried Kugel. We're communal people, Pinkus had once said to him, we draw together as one; it is one of our most beautiful defining attributes.

So do monkeys, thought Kugel.

So do coyotes.

So do wolves.

Nowhere Ho.

Wilbur Senior was given the seat of honor in the mayor's parade car, right beside the mayor himself.

We love ya, Senior, the people called.

You're a good man, Senior.

Go get 'em, Senior.

Senior smiled through his grief and waved to the crowd. Even the various political protesters, stationed on corners along the parade route, cheered to see Senior. God, after all, had never said anything about the sins of the sons being passed to the fathers. As soon as he had passed by, though, they returned to their angry fist shaking and sign waving, calling attention to the plight of the Native Americans past and the victims of wars present. Protagonists, antagonists, nobody could decide. They were all agonists, though, that much they knew for certain.

According to John, Jesus' last words weren't Father, into thy hands I commend my spirit. According to John, Jesus' last words were this:

It is finished.

Or, Get me out of here.

Or, *Feh.*

Matthew and Mark didn't want to get involved in the whole Luke/John/Jesus last-words argument: both just agree that Jesus said, My God, my God, why have you forsaken me? at some point while on the cross, but not as last words, even though those would have been better last words than the last words that either Luke or John claimed (he ripped them off from David, of course, but there aren't that many good last words to go around).

A little fire.

A little rage.

Scream when you burn, said Bukowski.

Or when you're nailed to a cross.

Well, that's life for you, thought Kugel: You spend all your life thinking of the perfect last words to say, and nobody even bothers to write the damn thing down.

Monday morning, a Sergeant Frankel from the police department phoned. Sergeant Frankel informed Kugel that there was nothing to be concerned about, but that the arsonist had made a third attempt the previous night at burning down the farm on Sawmill Road; as a precaution, and only as a precaution, the sergeant was phoning the owners of the remaining half dozen or so Messerschmidt farms to make sure everything was okay, and to assure them that the full force of the Stockton Police Department was on the case.

Should I be worried? Kugel asked.

You should only worry, said Sergeant Frankel, about the things you can control.

If I could control them, said Kugel, they wouldn't worry me.

Exactly, said Sergeant Frankel.

Winston Churchill's last words were this: I'm so bored with it all.

No use, wrote Van Gogh in his suicide note, I shall never be rid of this depression.

Good-bye, wrote Sid Vicious.

Keep it short. To the point. Get in and get out. Less chance of typos that way. Kugel thought that might be his perfect ending: for he who had spent his life reading, surrounded by books and incapable of shaking his begrudging respect for the written word, he who had spent so much time and consideration trying to come up with the perfect final phrase, that set of words that said so much in so little, the best last thing anyone ever said, and then, in writing that perfect thought in his suicide note, to misspell it.

It is finushed.

Good-bye cruel werld.

Fuck all of you mothfuckers.

That night, Kugel and Bree sat in bed, trying to ignore the sounds of forced passion coming from Hannah's bedroom. Bree was crunching numbers, Kugel was reading about the liberation of Buchenwald. At last the sounds of sex came to an end, only to be replaced by the sounds of Mother, alive and suffering: *oy, ow, my back, ungh, feh, fart, belch, oy.*

Here she lies. Big surprise.

Bree sighed and shook her head at the numbers, and began to explain to Kugel exactly how much trouble they were in.

We owe another mortgage payment in two weeks, she said. We still haven't paid the last one.

Twenty full-page photographs inside, promised the cover of the Buchenwald book.

Now more ghastly.

Twenty percent more depressing.

Page seven of the promised twenty was the one of Smiling Man.

We can borrow the money from Jonah's college fund, said Bree, but that will only get us to September. The food costs are killing us.

Maybe he was religious, thought Kugel. Maybe

he was smiling because he believed in God, because he believed there was something after. Maybe he was thinking of his next life. Maybe he was hoping he would come back as candy.

Kugel's last conversation with Professor Jove concerned suicide. It wasn't that Kugel was considering it, but he was troubled by how much sense it seemed to make to him, why people didn't do it more, why they saw it as cowardice. It seemed like a reasonable idea.

I read, Professor Jove told Kugel, of an interesting experiment that had been conducted by a small government agency. It had been determined, by various studies, that the deterrent capability of capital punishment had weakened over time, due to overuse, and that perhaps it could be strengthened once again if there were a way, for those who committed certain crimes – pedophilia, murder, treason of course – to be killed twice. To be put to death, or something close to it, and then, in a sense, brought back, only to be killed again. A large sum of money was granted for research and development, and soon enough, a method was devised, using certain chemicals injected at precise moments into the condemned's arms, neck, and chest, to put him to death, and then, after a time, to bring him back. A prison was chosen – notorious was it for the brutality of its prisoners and, consequently, its guards – and on a certain day, a criminal, previously sentenced to death, was selected, and strapped into this machine. As the nature of the punishment was not just punitive but preventative, the prison officials also gathered together many of the other inmates to witness the proceedings, in order, of course, to dissuade them from committing this or any crime ever again. The warden informed the prisoners, moreover, that certain crimes might be punishable not by two deaths, but by three deaths, or four deaths, or more; there was no limit to the agony they were about to witness. With that he flipped a switch, and the hideous machine whirred to life, and a moment later the prisoner seized, arched his back, and collapsed, dead. His body twitched; silence filled the room as the prisoners realized this had not been an idle threat. The warden smiled to see their fear, knowing as he did that it was the key to discipline and control. The machine ticked off the prescribed amount of time, whirred again, and the prisoner jolted, his back arched, and he snapped forward again, and, dazed, a moment later, he opened his eyes, which were filled with terror and agony. The warden readied the switch to put the poor man to death again; he hesitated though, for effect, wanting the other prisoners to appreciate just how terrified this once-terrifying man had become. And it is here that the experiment went terribly wrong, for this prisoner, whose life can only be described as nasty and brutish and not nearly short enough, turned to the warden and began to cry, begging not, as the warden expected, to be allowed to live, but rather to be sent back, pleading to be put once more, for a final time, to death. It was so beautiful, he cried. So peaceful, so light, so free, free of this, of you, of me. And the prisoner began to beg: Please, Mr Warden, sir, please send me back, take my life, if you have an ounce of compassion left, kill me now without hesitation. The other prisoners, seeing this, and having always known only respect for this prisoner, began to beg for the same – for death. The warden grew furious and flipped the switch, instantly putting the man to death. Get them the hell out of here, he grumbled to the guards. The prisoners were led back to their cells, and in the following days, many killed themselves in whatever manner they could – hanging themselves in their cells, overdosing on whatever contraband they could find, flinging themselves onto the electrified fence that surrounded the prison yard. The program was decried an absolute failure and the warden's stature was greatly diminished.

Wouldn't that show, asked Kugel, that hope is a positive thing?

I can't imagine, said the professor, that anything that inspires men to take their lives can be said to be positive. We also don't know what that prisoner was actually experiencing. Was it true death? Was it the afterlife, or just some stray electrical pulses – that's all we are, after all – bouncing around his brain in the moments before they ceased completely? The story, however, doesn't end there. The warden, you see, being somewhat crafty in the field of punishment and human suffering, did eventually find an effective use for the machine. It was some time later, and a new prisoner arose, more feared than even the last and who knew no fear himself, who was a never-ending source of trouble for the warden and his staff, and upon whom no amount of punishment could elicit change. The warden then remembered the machine and had an idea: He ordered a room built to his exact specifications in the center of the prison – the walls and floors were covered in soft padding, the ceiling constructed from an iron mesh screen – and as soon as it was completed, he ordered the prisoner strapped into the machine and put to death. Once again, the prisoners were gathered around, once again the machine whirred to life, and once again, the prisoner, dead, then revived, began to beg, as the other had, to go back, to be put to death again. At this point, the warden stood, faced the assembled prisoners, and said, in a clear and loud voice: Let this be a lesson to you all. With that the prisoner was removed from the machine and dragged, kicking and screaming, into the padded room at the center of the prison, where there was no possible way for him to kill himself and where his screams of agony traveled freely through the screen ceiling, sending dread and horror down the spine of every man who heard them. By giving him hope for something after death, the warden had, in effect, sentenced this poor man to life.

Kugel looked down at Smiling Man. Maybe he hoped. Maybe he knew his life sentence was nearing an end. Kugel thought of the fawn. He thought of Jonah. He thought that if you're lucky enough to live in the eye of the storm, maybe you should just live it up. Maybe the people who had lived in the storm would be pissed off to learn that you hadn't, would be disgusted that you wasted your whole damned eye worrying about the storm to come.

Kugel got out of bed and looked out the window.

Are you even listening to me? Bree asked.

Was Wilbur out there? Kugel wondered.

He held up his middle finger, just in case he was.

Fuck you, motherfucker, said Kugel.

Excuse me? said Bree.

And then Jonah screamed, a piercing, terrified scream, a nightmare scream of panic and fear.

Kugel looked at Bree, too stunned to immediately move. Jonah never screamed like that. He screamed again, and that tore them from their shock. Kugel raced out the door, Bree right behind him, into the darkened hall.

If she's laid one finger on him, he thought, I'll fucking kill her.

CHAPTER 27

Jonah was shaking violently as Bree held him in her arms. His body heaved with every sob.

I heard a monster, he wept.

When Kugel was young, Mother told him that the way to survive a gas chamber is by urinating on a handkerchief and holding it over your mouth and nose when the gas starts coming out. Kugel had no idea if that was true. If it was, and you didn't do it because you didn't want to piss on a rag and hold it against your face for no reason, you'd die for a pretty stupid reason. If it wasn't true, and you tried it and it didn't work, that would actually make the death even worse, if that can be imagined, because now you didn't just die in a gas chamber, you died in a gas chamber with a piss-soaked rag in your face.

Should he tell Jonah that trick?

How could he?

How could he not?

What if it worked?

What if it didn't?

Bree gently rocked Jonah in her arms. There is a point at which anger cools and becomes

315

acceptance, and at that point, it is no longer even necessary to express one's rage; it is simply no longer worth the effort. This was the point, it seemed to Kugel, that Bree had now reached, as she didn't even glare at him, didn't grit her teeth or move away; she just rubbed Jonah's back, her eyes closed, whispering, *Shh, shh, it's okay.*

Which is exactly, Kugel thought, what he'd told the fawn.

Kugel tried to rub Jonah's back – the boy was wearing his favorite SpongeBob SquarePants pajamas, and SpongeBob's joy seemed, to Kugel, entirely out of place – but the boy moved away from him. Children notice everything, and Kugel's heart broke to think that Jonah understood in general what was happening, if not in the specifics: that his father was fucking up. SpongeBob's father had done a good job. SpongeBob was happy, confident, secure. It was hard to say what kind of job Patrick's father had done – perhaps he had mercifully dropped him on his head – but it was clear that Squidward's father was a failure. Squidward was bitter, angry, jealous. He didn't want to be Mr Squidward.

There's no such thing as monsters, Kugel said.

Yes, there is! Jonah shouted. I heard it!

Okay, said Kugel. Okay.

Mother hurried into the bedroom, tying her robe.

I heard a scream, she said.

It's okay, said Kugel with a nod to the ceiling. Jonah heard a monster.

Mother kissed Jonah on the head, rubbed his arm, and said, That's not a very nice thing to say, is it?

Mother, said Kugel.

At that moment, a sound filled the room that did indeed sound like that of a monster – a loud roar, a retch – and everyone jumped. It came again, and Kugel looked up.

It was Anne Frank, he knew. And it sounded, God help him, like she was vomiting into the vents.

Jonah began to scream. Bree held him tightly, grabbed his blanket, and hurried out of the room.

Goddamn it, muttered Kugel.

He turned to go up to Anne.

It isn't her fault, Mother begged, grabbing Kugel's shirtsleeve. She's old, she's not well. My God, what that woman . . .

Kugel tore himself free and stormed into the hall, pulled down the attic stairs, and stamped heavily up them.

It was hot in there again, humid; the air felt heavy, and the attic stank of vomit and shit; Kugel gasped as he entered, nearly getting sick himself. Was this what he had allowed his home to become? He didn't see her at first, all he saw was that she had removed the protective grate from the vent; vomit splattered the floor around it and coated the walls of the duct inside.

He pulled his shirt over his nose, and found her behind the western wall, curled in the fetal position on her mound of tattered blankets, eyes closed, a second and even larger pool of vomit beside her bed.

Anne, he said softly.

She didn't move.

Should I call someone? he asked.

She opened her eyes for a moment but made no answer before closing them once again.

Should I call? he asked again. Who should I call? Anne, I don't . . . who should I call?

He pulled the blanket from the bed and covered her with it, thinking perhaps that she was cold. Should he call a doctor? How? Where? He uncovered her, thinking that perhaps she was too warm. He stood there a while, stupidly, and then she retched again, and Kugel jumped backward.

I'll get a bucket, he said. I'll get some tea.

He hurried down the stairs, his leg aching, and he passed Bree in the hallway.

He's asleep, said Bree.

She's dying, he said.

He brought her up a cup of tea and a flask filled with hot water. He placed them beside her and opened one of the windows to let in some fresh air. He went back downstairs, got a bucket, some rolls of paper towels, and some cleaner. Mother paced nervously in the hallway.

Should I go to her? she asked.

Give her some space, he said.

Is she okay?

She'll be fine.

Maybe I can just go to her.

Mother, said Kugel. Please.

It took Kugel some time to clean the vomit out of the vent and ducts. To clean beside her bed, he needed to move aside all the boxes from the western wall – using just his one good hand – and then, kneeling beside her sleeping form, mop it up as best he could. He left the bucket beside her, along with the roll of paper towels. He made a note to get another board and nail it down, too, over the vent. Afterward, he slid the boxes back into place, and switched on the small lamp beside the unused bed.

Tap if you need anything, he said. Anne? Tap if you do.

He climbed back down from the attic, but left the attic stairs down, just in case.

Just in case of what?

Just in case.

It was two o'clock in the morning.

And Bree and Jonah were gone.

CHAPTER 28

In the morning, Kugel went outside to Mother's garden with a bag full of fruits and vegetables, though he could hardly afford them now. He had been as consistent as possible in leaving produce out for her every morning – there was something in the ritual, any ritual, in which he had begun to take some comfort – but he had been less so with regard to gathering it back up each evening. Now the meats, vegetables, and fruits from the previous week were rotting and turning brown; many were covered with ants and maggots. Kugel didn't bother to kick the old aside; he simply covered the old with the new, and moved on.

Bree, Hannah had informed him, had taken Jonah and gone down to Mother's apartment in Brooklyn.

Maybe they'll see a show, he thought. Maybe she'll do a little writing. Maybe she'll run into a famous writer, who could make all her dreams come true.

He hoped that she would.

Back in his bedroom, Kugel noticed that his rash

was spreading farther up his arms; the sun seemed to have made the itching worse.

He should get some calamine lotion. Or aloe. Aloe's good for a lot of things.

He took out his Last Words notebook, turned to the last page, and added to his list:

iPod (headphones/charger)
EpiPens
Zyrtec
Papers (?)
Aloe/calamine

Kugel could hear Anne Frank coughing. It was a deep, whooping cough, and it worried him. She was dying.

We have you in a double suite, Mr Spinoza, but I see you've brought your own bed. Shall we check it for you? Donald here will help you with your bags.

Kugel pitied the dying, but he envied the dead. Whenever he looked at photos – of JFK, of Elvis, of Smiling Man – he thought, Well, at least you got it over with. At least you can cross that off your list. He imagined the scene at the gates of heaven to be not unlike that at the finish line of a long and grueling marathon: everyone high-fiving, hugging, collapsing, elated that it's over, yes, it's finally over, pouring cups of water over one another's heads and saying, Holy shit, dude, that was fucking brutal. I am *never* doing that again.

The house, aside from Anne Frank's coughing

and vomiting, was miserably silent. Kugel went downstairs, desperate for company. As he was entering the kitchen, Mother was leaving.

I'm sorry, Mother said to him. I'm sure she'll come back. She'll like it in Brooklyn.

Kugel nodded.

Do you think she'll phone the police? Mother asked. She wouldn't do that, would she? Turn in Anne Frank just to get back at you?

Mother, due to Anne Frank's impending death, moved about that day with a desperate, mournful solemnity; she wore a long black dress, her silvery hair pulled back into a tight bun; she sighed loudly, bit her fingernails, and when Kugel returned to the living room, she had hung black cloths over all the mirrors. She stood by the window, peeking through the blinds.

Have you noticed? she said to Kugel as he entered. The police, she continued without turning around. That's the fourth time they've driven by.

Kugel assured her they were only keeping an eye out for Wilbur Messerschmidt Jr, but he had taken note of them earlier, too, from his bedroom window, and, privately, had similar concerns. Had a neighbor reported them? The UPS man? Anne Frank was illegal; what was the punishment for harboring an illegal? Jonah had screamed the night before, too; maybe somebody heard, maybe somebody was concerned, maybe somebody thought something was going on? Maybe Mother was right, maybe Bree had turned him in? She could have phoned the police, said she was a neighbor, said something was going on in the attic. Four times in one morning seemed excessive, didn't it? Why would they be patrolling in the daytime if all the fires occurred at night?

He could hear Anne Frank coughing.

I think we should phone a doctor, said Kugel.

Mother turned to face him. It was clear from her expression that she disagreed.

She's very ill, Mother.

She's been ill before.

Mother, she needs to be seen.

And then what? asked Mother. Dragged from the attic, the only place she feels safe, the one place she wants to be? Do you know that a doctor who sees her is legally obligated to admit her to the hospital if that's what he determines is necessary?

If it gets worse, said Kugel, we'll have to call someone.

I've been charged with saving her, said Mother.

Even if it means letting her die?

Yes.

I'm going to the pharmacy.

But for what, he wondered, as he roamed the brightly lit aisles lined with brightly colored bottles. What did Anne Frank have? A flu? A cold? A virus? He was worried he would get the wrong thing, or the right thing with the wrong thing in it – a Something/Whatever with Added Who-Knows-What, when all she really needed was the

Whatever, the Something could be lethal for the elderly, and she was allergic to the Who-Knows-What. When he was a child, pharmacies filled Kugel with joy and excitement. There were endless promises, countless possibilities: bottles that gave you shiny hair, fresh breath, white teeth; tubes that gave you clearer skin, longer eyelashes, rosier cheeks. We were malleable, Kugel thought, changeable, our bodies infinitely under our own control. Now those same aisles and shelves just reminded him of all the things that could go wrong. Did she need an expectorant? A suppressant? A flu remedy? A cold remedy? A hot compress? A cold compress? A hot/cold compress? A caplet? A tablet? A gel tab? An ointment? A salve? A rub? An anti-diarrheal? An anti-inflammatory? A decongestant? A dehumidifier? An enema? Oh, God, what if she needed an enema? The aisles that once seemed to hold endless promise and power – immortality! – now seemed pathetically weak and ineffective. All these balms for minor scrapes and scratches. Where was the cancer cleanser, the Alzheimer's rub, the cardiomyopathy cream? He imagined turning a corner in the store to find an Auschwitz prisoner in prison garb and armband, carrying a shopping basket in one hand and tapping his lips with the other.

Do you know where they put the typhus gel? he inquires politely of Kugel. Have you seen the malnutrition bars? The rickets spray? Dr Beckett's Go On lotion, for people who just can't go on?

This is it, Jonah, my boy, my love, my heart, my soul, my dream. This is our best shot at holding back the tide of death and disease: cherry-flavored DayQuil. That's the best we can come up with, kid. If you're dying, and need something fast, here it is, this is what we can muster up after hundreds of years of science: Maalox.

Tums.

Ouchless Band-Aids.

He felt dizzy upon leaving, as if he were dying himself, as if he were suffering, already succumbing, to something for which there was no tablet or caplet or liquid gel, while inside the store they were having a two-for-one special on Imodium EZ Chews. Kugel loathed going to the auto store for the same reason; he spent the week after worrying that his jets were clogged, his valves were loose, his plugs were shot.

When he got home, the house was dark, though it was only mid-afternoon. He thought for a moment that they'd had a power outage, which would be odd for the summertime, but he realized, soon after entering, that Mother, while he was gone, had hung black fabric over all the windows.

It wasn't safe, said Hannah.

What wasn't safe? asked Kugel.

It's a small town, said Hannah. People talk.

Kugel could see Hannah had been crying.

Where's Mother?

Upstairs, said Hannah.

Kugel found the attic stairs down, and climbed them, slowly, fearing the worst, fearing that he'd been too late, that Anne Frank was beyond the powers of DayQuil and Theraflu.

He found Mother kneeling quietly in front of the western wall of boxes, sobbing gently as she placed a small yellow adhesive note on the wall. There were at least a dozen other notes already on the wall, some crammed into the tiny cracks between the boxes.

She turned to Kugel, her eyes red.

She won't respond, she said softly. She's too weak to talk. I didn't want to leave her alone.

We should call a doctor, said Kugel.

Mother shook her head.

It may be her only hope, said Kugel.

Our hands are tied, said Mother.

Kugel went to Mother and helped her stand. He told her not to worry, that Anne would be okay, that he'd brought her some medicine, that she just needed some rest. Mother nodded and went downstairs, and Kugel pulled the stairs up behind her.

The ghastly stench in the attic contrasted violently with the pastoral, angelic bedroom set that Mother had created in the center of the attic. Mother had dressed the bed as if Anne Frank were still a young girl, with a teddy bear propped up on the pillows, and a pair of child-size one-piece pajamas. She had placed a Hello Kitty alarm clock on the bedside table, and some children's books as well, kept in place by a box of matzoh. A childscape, thought

Kugel, a won't-let-it-go tableau. Kugel hadn't eaten all day, and so, intestines be damned, he took a small piece of matzoh from the box, lay down on the bed, and turned on the bedside lamp. Mother, he noticed, had replaced the pink lamp shade with Kugel's grandfather.

He closed his eyes.

He was desperate to sleep.

Is she gone? he heard Anne Frank say.

She's gone, said Kugel.

Anne Frank began coughing again, a violent cough that Kugel could feel through his body, his bones.

How's the book coming? he asked when she had ceased.

She won't leave me alone, said Anne Frank.

She's trying to help.

I'm trying to work.

Kugel took a bite of the matzoh.

How's the book coming? he asked.

I took your advice, she said. I gave it up.

Kugel closed his eyes and shook his head.

Okay, he said. Okay.

She coughed again, and Kugel stood and passed the bag of cold remedies and pain relievers over the wall.

Danke, said Anne Frank.

Kugel turned and sank to the floor, his back leaning against the western wall.

Anne Frank, said Anne Frank, is the most recognizable symbol of Jewish suffering and death.

Kugel heard a book drop heavily to the floor.

The diary of Anne Frank, read Anne Frank, is the best known, and she has become a symbol of all the children who died in that genocide.

A second book dropped to the floor with a thud.

I am, she said, become death.

Kugel said nothing, but reached back and pulled one of Mother's notes off the wall. It read: I've made some chicken soup.

Another read: Let me know if you want me to turn on the heat.

Helen Keller, said Anne Frank, was a socialist. Did you know that?

I didn't know that, said Kugel, pulling off another note. It read: I've made some mistakes.

Kugel got to his knees and turned to face the wall.

Nobody does, said Anne Frank. She was a suffragist. A pacifist. A radical. A woman of ideas, of passions.

The notes at the top of the wall seemed to be the earlier ones. They were mostly offers of food or some kind of help or provision. Toward the middle and bottom, they took on a more personal tone. One, from the very bottom of the wall, read: I'm dying, too.

They wanted her to be their blind girl, Anne Frank continued. Their deaf angel. Me, I'm the sufferer. I'm the dead girl. I'm Miss Holocaust, 1945. The prize is a crown of thorns and eternal victimhood. Jesus was a Jew, Mr Kugel, but I'm the Jewish Jesus.

Please answer me, read one note.

Kugel dug one of the notes from between the boxes. It read: I drove my husband away.

I did my best, read another.

Kugel began to replace the notes, delicately, using his fingers to feel for the sticky spot on the wall, trying to locate the exact spot where Mother had placed them.

I'm pro-choice, said Anne Frank, did you know that?

I didn't know that, said Kugel.

Nobody does, said Anne Frank. I love God and hate his followers. I think America is the greatest wasted opportunity in the history of man. I think the answer to peace in the Middle East is to bomb the hell out of it; kill no one, but destroy it all – every mosque, every synagogue, all history, all the past, leave no stone unburned, leaving nothing holy behind. I think never forgetting the Holocaust is not the same thing as never shutting up about it. I'd like to scratch Abraham Foxman's eyes out.

You're a woman of ideas, Kugel said as he worked. Of passions.

Shall I tell you what I think, Mr Kugel? I think that when people die and go to heaven and they throw themselves at the Almighty's feet and beg Him, their voices choked with tears, not to send them to whatever idea of hell they arrived with, to spare them that agony and pain and suffering, God laughs and shakes His head and says, Send you to hell? Buddy, you just came from there.

I've got a professor you'd love to meet, said Kugel.

Kugel placed the last note back where he found it, stood up, and headed for the stairs.

You should get some rest, he said.

Here, she said, and placed her manuscript on top of the wall.

I took your advice, she said, and wrote about myself. Feelings, opinions, attitudes. It's only a first draft.

Kugel picked it up.

They're going to hate it, said Anne Frank.

Kugel headed back down the stairs.

Keep your mother away from me, said Anne Frank.

She's trying to help.

I just want to be left alone.

Last words, thought Kugel.

Maybe a tombstone.

SOLOMON KUGEL
I Just Want to Be Left Alone.

That wasn't bad.

That wasn't bad at all.

He went downstairs and met Mother in the hallway. She was holding her pillow.

How is she?

We should get her a doctor, Mother.

We can't risk it. I'll spend the night with her.

Mother, she just wants some quiet.

What's that? she asked, pointing to the manuscript.

330

It's something she asked me to read.

Mother looked hurt, though Kugel could not tell whether that was a result of Anne Frank's wanting space, or of Anne Frank's giving her writing to Kugel and not to her.

I'll just go check on her, said Mother.

I just did. Give her some space, Mother.

Fine.

Good.

Mother went back downstairs. Kugel went to his bedroom and called Professor Jove.

Jove wasn't in.

Kugel left a message.

CHAPTER 29

Kugel lay in bed that night, holding his pillow over his head trying to shut out the sounds filling his room – Hannah and Pinkus having sex; Mother moaning; Anne Frank coughing, shuffling, typing.

Her manuscript lay untouched on his nightstand.

After some time, Hannah and Pinkus finished, Mother stopped moaning, and the medicine had quieted Anne Frank's cough.

Silence.

At last.

Kugel's stomach grumbled. The matzoh, that toxic symbol of freedom from that holiday of unforgetting, began to do its work on the lining of his intestines. Kugel grabbed Anne Frank's manuscript and went to the bathroom, where he sat on the toilet and began to read.

He finished it, some time later, back in bed; his eyes were red, his cheeks streaked with tears.

She was right, he thought.

They were going to hate it.

He went back to the bathroom, his stomach still turning.

If Christ ever comes back, he'd heard it said, it will be the Christians who kill him this time. And they'll make the Romans, Kugel knew, look like pussies.

Christians? Christ will think at the moment of his second death. *That's how I die? Christians?*

Kugel heard a door slam and jumped.

Outside.

A barn door?

He hastily pulled his pants up – this is how they'll find me when the genocide comes, he thought; all my fantasies of resistance and gunfights will remain just that, as the reality of the situation creeps in: they're kicking in the doors, and I'm on the toilet with the worst case of shits in human history.

He hobbled to the bedroom, tossed the manuscript on his bedside table, and grabbed the cane and flashlight from beside the bed.

I should have gotten a dog.

I should have gotten a gun.

Something big.

He crept quietly down the stairs.

At no point, he wondered, maybe between Voorburg and The Hague, did Spinoza think, Hey, wait a minute – I'm carrying my mother's deathbed. This is fucked up. Not once? Did he sleep in it? Christ Almighty, did Benedictus de fucking

Spinoza sleep in his fucking mother's fucking deathbed?

He crept carefully through the foyer, the living room, and the kitchen. He paused beside the garden door and then yanked it open.

There was a full moon that night, and it cast an eerie glow across the yard. The doors of the garden shed flapped in the wind and crashed into their frames. He walked out to the shed, locking the doors tightly.

Maybe it was just nature, trying to scare him again.

Probably it was.

Probably not.

He peered into the darkness of the heavy woods. Nothing moved. Even the wind seemed to die down.

Will? whispered Kugel.

A match strike, a flash of flame, not more than two feet away. Kugel, blinded, stumbled back, his cast arm raised in defense.

Evening, Mr K, he heard Will say.

His vision began to return; Will stood before him, smoking a cigarette, as calmly as the day they had met at the grocery store.

How are you, Mr K, said Will.

He was wearing his usual overalls and plaid shirt, but his beard had grown in, and his hair was wild.

They stared at each other for a moment before Will nodded to the attic windows.

How's she doing? he asked.

Are you going to burn down my house? Kugel asked.

Will nodded.

Yep, he said. I am that.

Listen, Will, said Kugel. Listen. I love that house as much as you do. I know how you feel, really, it's a terrible thing losing your history, but I'll take good care of her.

Now, why, Mr K, asked Will, would I burn down something I loved?

Because you're upset, said Kugel. Because people are buying all your farms, your past is being sold off.

You've been listening to my old man, said Will.

Anne Frank began coughing; they could hear it clear through to the woods.

She's getting worse, said Will.

You're going to burn her down, too, Will? You're going to burn Anne Frank?

I'm burning it down, Mr K, because I hate it. I've got some history in that house, Mr K, I'll spare you the details, but you can well imagine. My old man didn't start drinking last week, I tell you what.

Then burn *his* house down, said Kugel.

This is his house, said Will. Truth be told, there wasn't a soul in the family that didn't know what he was up to, and nobody said a word. Keep the lie alive, because the neighbors won't like the truth.

My father, said Kugel, disappeared when I was six.

Well, that's a shame, Mr K. Or maybe it's a blessing, no real way to tell. Wish mine had, I tell you what, wish he'd gone right to hell. Maybe your tragedy was a blessing. My blessing of a father was a hell of a tragedy, I can tell you that. Swore when I was a child that I'd come back one day and burn the damn things down, all of them, every last damn Messerschmidt barn in the county.

Anne Frank coughed again.

What do you give her? asked Will. Day, two days?

Is that what you're waiting for?

Yep.

Why?

Now, how's that going to look, Mr K, said Will, a German burning down Anne Frank's house?

Not good, said Kugel.

Damn right, said Will. Besides, Mama died when I was a young one, so Anne's about the closest thing I ever had to a parent. That wasn't particularly close, mind you, but she never laid a hand on me, neither to hit me nor to hug me. I guess that's the best you can hope for sometimes, an even split. I'll come back when she's dead.

Do you want to say good-bye? asked Kugel.

Will shook his head.

Nah. She's probably trying to write or something, I suppose. That always came first. Could use a rewrite or two myself. You send her my best, Mr K.

And with that, Will turned and disappeared into the woods.

Kugel went back inside and sat on his bed.

He thought about calling the police, but Anne Frank was illegal, and, anyway, what would be the point? Will would be long gone. Besides, though he was shaken by their meeting, at least he now knew the rules. As long as Anne Frank was alive, he didn't have to worry about the house burning down.

There was comfort in that.

He could live peacefully, as long as Anne Frank did.

Maybe he would get her a microwave, after all. Maybe he would get her an e-reader. And he decided, too, that once the sun rose the following morning, he would phone a doctor. To hell with Mother and her paranoid fantasies. Redemption was at hand. After all he'd sacrificed for his mother, the one thing he could now do for his family – for his wife and child and their future – would be to keep their house intact. A roof, unburned, over their heads. They would catch Will soon, they always did; Kugel had only to keep Anne Frank alive until then. Soon after, no doubt, she would die, Mother would die, too, and the house would still be there, waiting to be filled with memories, laughter, life. The past would be gone. Maybe they'd have another child! Yes – a new last Kugel!

He laughed at the thought.

They'd call him Fin.

Fin Kugel.

Tomorrow, first thing in the morning, he would phone a doctor. He would take the black curtains off the mirrors, he would open the windows, let in the light, the fresh air.

He turned to shut off his bedside lamp, and noticed, without too much concern, that the manuscript he'd left on the bedside table was gone.

CHAPTER 30

As it turned out, the night Solomon Kugel discovered a fugitive arsonist hiding in the woods behind his house was the best night of sleep he'd had in weeks.

For once the sounds of Anne coughing and typing through the night were calming, as he knew that as long as she was alive, he was safe. His house would not burn down, his life would not be taken. He even managed to sleep late, as for once Mother had not woken up screaming. Perhaps helping Anne Frank had somehow assuaged her own guilt for not being a Holocaust survivor as well. Perhaps she was dead.

Don't get ahead of yourself, Kugel my man.

Kugel stood and stretched in the fine morning sunlight, and as he did, noticed out the bedroom window that the vegetables and fruit he'd left for Mother the other morning were gone. He'd forgotten last night to take them in, of that he was certain; had Mother really collected them? She hadn't done so in weeks.

Was that also a good sign?

Was her dementia accelerating?

Kugel, for the first time in ages, felt, well, happy. The begin-againer was beginning again.

He thought he would phone Bree, tell her the good news. No, Mother wasn't out yet and neither was Anne, but the family was safe from the fire, if they'd just keep her alive a little longer – Bree would have to admit, wouldn't she, that he was right to keep her in the attic! – and then, with Will caught and safely locked away, she would die, as she was terribly ill already.

He would wait for Bree to return, though – perhaps over a quiet candlelit dinner with a bottle of champagne – to tell her about Fin, and they would tumble after into bed, together again at last.

He considered for a moment calling Professor Jove to give him the good news. *Feh!* he thought. To hell with Professor Jove! He would just find a way to ruin Kugel's good mood, to find the cloudy lining to his silver whatever, and then send him a hefty bill. What did Professor Jove know, anyway, really know, about flesh and blood and life and death? Philosophy? The mind? The psyche? Luxuries. Like cleaning the windows, Kugel thought, on a condemned, crumbling house. He imagined the Professor sitting beside a dying Anne Frank somewhere in Bergen-Belsen:

I'm cold, Anne Frank would say.

Of course you are, Professor Jove would answer. You're dying.

But I want to live, Anne Frank would say, I'm just a child.

340

Knock knock, Professor Jove would answer.

What?

Knock knock.

Who's there, she would mumble feebly.

Death.

Death who?

Death, Anne. Death. You're dying.

I don't get it.

There's nothing to get. It's over. You're fucked.

No, he didn't need Professor Jove, not today, maybe not ever. Perhaps it was true that it was foolishly optimistic to believe that this was the best of all possible worlds. But then wasn't it equally foolishly optimistic to believe this was the *worst* of all possible worlds? To believe that there could be no place worse than this? Surely there could be, there must be – even if it was the same exact place as this, but lacking only, say, chocolate ice cream – a world exactly like ours lacking only chocolate ice cream would be a much worse place than this, and there would have to be a worse place, somewhere, still worse than that. A place with no Jonah, no Bree.

Maybe, at last, he would have the Big Talk with Jonah. Maybe he would introduce him to Anne Frank. It ain't the best world, kid, but it ain't the worst. Maybe Godot shows up in act three, my son; maybe the audience is just leaving too early.

Estragon: Where'd they all go?

Vladimir: They were just here.

Godot: Are they coming back?

341

They wait.
Curtain.

The last thing Lou Costello ever ate before his soul departed this world was a strawberry ice cream soda. Two scoops. His last words:

That was the best ice cream soda I ever tasted.

Lou wins, thought Kugel.

Smiling Man wins.

You get out laughing, you win.

Gogol's tombstone: And I shall laugh with a bitter laugh.

Mel Blanc's tombstone: That's all, folks.

SpongeBob SquarePants: I'm a goofy goober, yeah, you're a goofy goober, yeah, we're all goofy goobers.

Do not disturb any further.

Kugel dressed and went downstairs to the kitchen, where Mother was at the table, having a cup of tea.

I'm phoning a doctor, he said. I know you're opposed, Mother, but she is our responsibility, and my mind is made up. We cannot allow Anne Frank to perish on our watch.

Mother was silent for a moment, and then she said, in a low and angry voice: Get that fucking *whore* out of this house.

Kugel turned around.

What?

I said, Mother repeated, her voice rising, get that fucking WHORE out of this house.

She stood and held Anne Frank's manuscript in her hand.

Mother, said Kugel, just calm down.

Mother threw the manuscript at him, the pages fluttering wildly to the floor, and pointed to the ceiling.

I don't know who that bitch is, she said, but I know she isn't Anne Frank. Anne Frank would never write those things. Anne Frank would never *think* those things.

She put her hands to her face and paced back and forth, shaking with rage.

When I think of it, she said. Using the name of a poor murdered child to coddle favor, to get some free food, to sell some books. It sickens me, just sickens me.

She kicked at the pages of the manuscript on the floor.

Get her out of here, Solomon. Get that lying old whore out of here or I swear to God I'll drag her down the stairs by her hair and throw her out myself.

Mother, said Kugel. Calm down. Whoever she is, she's a survivor.

She's a liar, Solomon, she probably put those numbers on her arm by herself.

You're being ridiculous, said Kugel. We can't throw her out.

My God, Mother continued, the things I did for her, the things I told her, about myself, my most personal . . . and you! You call yourself a father?

You call yourself a husband? You let this woman come between you and your wife, you and your child – and still you defend her? This grifter, this phony, this, this . . . Nazi!

She turned to Kugel with hatred in her eyes.

Get her out of here, said Mother. Get her out of this house this instant.

Hannah came into the kitchen, and tried to calm Mother down.

What happened? she asked Kugel, helping Mother into a chair. Mother sat down heavily; her outburst over, she now seemed to have lost all her energy, all her will. She stared vacantly at the floor, muttering incoherently.

The last hurrah, said Kugel. The doctor said this would happen.

Let's get you to bed, Mother, said Hannah. Shall we go work on the scrapbook? Mother? Mother, would you like that, to work on your scrapbook?

Hannah helped Mother up and took her to the bedroom, where she stayed with her, cutting up newspapers and history books and gluing them to the pages of the scrapbook until Mother at last grew tired and fell asleep.

Kugel meanwhile had phoned a local doctor, who, after many objections, agreed to pay a house call later that evening.

Kugel hung up the phone and all but raised his hands in the air in victory. He was elated. No threat of arson, an almost-finished first draft, and

344

Mother, seemingly on her last breath. Could this day get any better?

Sol, he heard Hannah say.

He turned to her. She had Pinkus beside her.

I think it would be better, she said, if we moved out.

Unbelievable, said Kugel.

We're sorry, said Pinkus.

Un-be-*lievable*, Kugel said again.

Hannah apologized, too; but to stay, she felt, would be to validate the claims of the woman in the attic, which would only upset Mother further.

Kugel nodded.

At least, he said, let me help you pack.

Hannah hugged him, and he hugged her back. Pinkus offered to help Kugel take down the mattress from the attic, but Kugel assured him that wouldn't be necessary.

Mother rose only once the whole time they were packing, and that was to use the bathroom. She had definitely changed for the worse. She moved slowly again, and her whole posture seemed to have shifted, from upright and driven yesterday to hunched over today, the comforting old weight of whatever back on her stooping shoulders at last. Kugel watched and decided then and there that he would e-mail his supervisor the next morning to see if he couldn't come in for a little heart-to-heart talk; he would explain all that had transpired, accept all the blame, and request that he be given his old job back; they were a great team and had done great work together, and it would be a shame, wouldn't it, if all that were ruined over a few weeks of stress and anxiety. I've been here since the compost days, he would say. Did the supervisor know that moving into a new home was listed as one of the most stressful things a man could go through, short of a death in the family? Even more stressful than divorce? He would tell him, and who knows, stranger things have happened.

It was turning out to be quite a day. By the afternoon, even the remedies he'd bought for Anne seemed to be working; her coughing had ceased, he could hear her through the vents typing and muttering as usual. He helped Hannah and Pinkus out to their car, lifted the suitcases into the trunk, and closed it with a satisfying slam.

You'll thank Bree for us, said Hannah.

Of course, said Kugel, of course. She'll be back soon, tomorrow maybe. Hey, you know what? You guys should come over for a barbecue this Sunday, what do you say?

Well, said Hannah. Let's see how Mother's doing.

Of course, said Kugel, of course.

He waved to them as they turned out the driveway, and he smiled. He took out his cell phone and dialed Mother's old number in Brooklyn.

¿Sí? said a woman on the other end of the line.

Hello? said Kugel.

¿Sí?

Is Bree Kugel there? This is her husband calling.

346

No, no, said the woman, Miss Bree not here. I am here, with Jonah.

Oh, said Kugel.

She went to hear man reading, said the woman.

She went to a reading, said Kugel.

Yes, yes, a reading. A famous man.

Philip Roth?

I don't know.

It wasn't Philip Roth?

I don't know.

Kugel smiled. He was happy for her.

That's great, said Kugel, that's great. Will you tell her to phone me as soon as she returns?

Yes, *sí*.

And will you tell Jonah I'll see him soon?

Sí, sí.

Kugel closed his phone and took a deep breath. Whistling softly, he strolled around the side of the house to the back lawn. More seedlings were beginning to appear in the vegetable garden.

Will? he called.

He wanted to tell someone the good news.

Will?

Well, he'd tell him later.

It wasn't until Kugel got back to the front lawn of the house that he smelled the smoke.

Something was burning.

Was it the neighbor's stove? Was someone burning leaves? His mind raced, and then he saw the smoke creeping out from beneath the front door of the house.

347

Will! he shouted as he ran to the door. Will!

Had Anne died? It didn't make any sense; how would Wilbur know so quickly, even if she had?

Had Mother killed her?

Kugel threw the front door open. Smoke was already filling the downstairs hallway, and he could see flames licking angrily out of the bottom of Mother's bedroom door.

Mother! he called.

He ran to her door and tried to open it; the doorknob, hot from the flames behind it, singed his hand, and he began to kick at it with all his might; it wouldn't budge.

Mother! he called.

He ran back outside – the smoke now filled the entire downstairs – and raced around the house to the window of Mother's bedroom. The smoke was thick inside her room, but he could see Mother lying facedown on the floor beside the bed. He banged on the window, but she didn't move. The window was opened slightly, and he reached in and forced it the rest of the way up; the burst of oxygen fed the furious flames and lashed out at him, scorching the siding of the house. He waited a moment for them to subside, and climbed through.

Mother! he called once he was inside, but still she didn't move.

He ran to the bedroom door – she had, as usual, propped a chair up against the knob to keep it from being opened. He kicked the chair away, pulled his sleeve over his hand, and yanked the door open, trying to clear the air of smoke, but the flames simply roared again and poured like a wave of fury into the hallway. He stuck his head out of the doorway, coughing, trying to control his breath. Already the tenant's room was ablaze, and flames licked at the ceiling of the hall. Black smoke funneled toward the kitchen and up the stairs; the wooden rail of the stairs had caught fire, too.

He turned to Mother, who wasn't moving; all around her lay the burned and blackened pages of Anne Frank's manuscript. The rest of it sat on the grate of the sealed fireplace, where Mother had set it on fire.

Mother, he said softly, Mother, what have you done?

But she wasn't answering.

The pages were swirling around the room, spreading fire and ash. Nearby, the scrapbook and boxes of family photos had also caught fire and their ashes were also beginning to spread.

What have you done, Mother, what have you done?

With his one good arm he pulled her into a sitting position, bent her over his shoulder, and managed to stand. He limped out the bedroom door with her, down the fiery hallway to the living room. The ceiling above the front door had collapsed, and the only way out now was through the garden door in the kitchen.

The stairs were ablaze now, too; he had only a moment to decide. If he took Mother outside, he would never be able to save Anne Frank. If he saved Anne Frank, he would never be able to save Mother.

He knelt and rolled Mother off his shoulder onto the floor. Her legs were blackened, bloody and blistered, her clothing singed through in places, burning in others. Her neck was so badly burned, the skin had begun to bubble and bleed. Her breathing was shallow, and though her face was badly blistered and burned, and her lips cracked, Kugel could see that Mother was smiling. It had been so long since he'd seen it – had he ever? – that he thought it was a disfigurement caused by burns, but he leaned toward her and she smiled even more broadly. She was, in agony, happy at last.

Those sons of bitches, she said softly.

I know, said Kugel.

Ever since the war.

It's okay, Mother, said Kugel, kissing her on her forehead. It's okay.

Kugel turned from her and hurried up the stairs, pulling himself up with the banister in the places where the steps had already collapsed. He had no idea how he was going to get back down, but he would think of it later – perhaps by then the firemen would arrive and they could go out through one of the upstairs windows.

Did he hear sirens?

He thought he heard sirens.

They were probably sirens.

He pulled down the attic door, and black smoke billowed down from above. He climbed the stairs, calling for her, coughing, finding it harder and harder to breathe, to get any air into his lungs at all. The smoke was much heavier up there; he stopped, thought for a moment about going back down, but could not leave her there. He pressed himself up into the attic, trying to stay low to the floor, wasn't that what he was supposed to do, stay low to the floor, or was it the opposite, he was supposed to stay off the floor? He couldn't remember, but he remembered that the salesman had said that the Memory Foam Topper was somewhat flammable, and now he saw it burning brightly, a bed of fire, a bed of flames, as if it were more a bed of coals than anything else, a bed in hell, and he wondered if they would possibly take it back now, if he could get a refund, but he doubted it, and Bree would be upset, and he called for Anne again, and suddenly he saw the walls of boxes collapse, and he thought it was from fire, thought she must surely be dead, but through the smoke he saw the figure – was it? yes – of a man, a firefighter, he thought, no, the man had no helmet, no coat. Kugel couldn't quite make him out, the fire was so hot, the smoke burned his eyes, maybe it was a firefighter, maybe it was Will, was it Will? He didn't know, but somebody was standing upright, he was smaller than Will, and slight, but he was carrying Anne Frank in his arms, carrying her to the dormer window on the eastern side of the house, and Kugel heard her then, Anne Frank, and she was laughing at him.

You would have never made it, Mr Kugel! she called. You would never have lasted five minutes in Auschwitz! I'm a survivor, Mr Kugel!

Kugel crawled forward, trying to get to the window, trying to see who was there, maybe it was Professor Jove. Had Professor Jove come at last, or would he say that Kugel shouldn't even try to survive, that he should give up? What did the bartender say to the chicken? Why did the goat cross the farm? What do you get when you're on the cross? Ouch. Schmuck. *Feh*. Nowhere. Tell them I said something. Roof racks. Were those sirens? Did he hear sirens?

Kugel reached Anne's sleeping place, the old blankets and quilts burning, flaming, hot, and though she was already at the window and whoever was carrying her had nearly gotten her outside to the roof, Kugel grabbed her laptop and he reached out and he held it to her, and she laughed again.

No, thank you, Mr Kugel, she called, I'm sick of that Holocaust shit. I'm going back to my novel, Mr Kugel, I'm a writer, not some goddamned essayist! Thirty-two million copies, that's nothing to sneeze at . . .

. . . and as the man helped her through the window, Kugel caught a glimpse of him, just for a moment, in the sunlight, and he wondered,

Could it be, could it really be him, was it even possible, how could it be possible? Kugel strained to push himself up, just a bit, just the littlest bit, to get a better look, but he had no breath, no air, and pulled himself forward onto his knees with the last remaining strength in his burned and bloody body, and he saw him at last, yes, it was, my God, it was him, was it him? Could it be him? And he reached out to him, for help, for saving, but the man turned and left, and Kugel cried out to him, and the words that Solomon Kugel cried out then were the last two words Solomon Kugel ever spoke:

Alan, gasped Kugel. Dershowitz.

The flames roared around him, the world turned yellow and orange and black, and there was nothing but fire, and then darkness, and Kugel laid his head down and closed his eyes, for he was very, very tired and he desperately, desperately wanted to sleep.

Anne Frank? he thought.

It's funny.

EPILOGUE

Eve rolled down her window as she steered her car onto the gravel driveway leading up to the old Herschkopf property, letting the sound of her tires crunching on the loose stone driveway fill the car. She glanced in the rearview mirror at the Cohens – Nick and Sharon – holding hands, sitting close together in the backseat. Sharon turned to Nick and smiled.

I love that sound, Sharon whispered.

Nick smiled and kissed her.

Me, too, he said.

Here we are, Eve called out with a smile.

She pulled to a stop underneath the cool shade of the grand oak tree that stood in front of the stately old Victorian; Nick pointed to the tire swing that hung from its branches, and Sharon smiled again. Eve smiled at Sharon, who smiled at Nick, who smiled at Eve.

Eve had been out just yesterday to rehang the damn thing; it was the fourth tire swing she'd had to replace in as many months. Local kids had cut down the last one on Halloween night; she searched the woods nearby for almost an hour but couldn't find it, and wound up having to use the full-size spare from her trunk. It would cost her a hundred bucks to replace, but she wasn't taking any chances with Nick and Sharon; she had been working this sale for three months now, and wasn't about to lose it over a goddamned radial tire.

Eve had first met Nick and Sharon last June. The Herschkopf house was the first one she had shown them; it was the very same day, she recalled, that she had spoken for the last time with poor Mr Kugel, just weeks before that terrible fire took his life. She remembered, too, that Sharon had spoken with Mr Kugel that day, and as they drove out to the Herschkopf property, Sharon had been irate.

That man, Sharon had said to her, asked us if he could hide in our attic.

Your attic? Eve had asked.

In the event of a *holocaust*, Sharon had gasped. Can you believe that?

Well, Eve had said, he's going through a lot.

I lost family in the Holocaust, Sharon had said, crossing her arms over her chest. A *lot* of family.

Nick put his arm around her shoulders and held her close.

Sons of bitches, he had said.

Let's not talk about the past, Eve had said encouragingly. Let's talk about the future. *Your* future.

All told, this was now their fifth visit to the Herschkopf property. The house was in good condition, but not the condition Sharon and Nick wanted; they loved the exterior but hated the interior; Eve was dealing with a second couple who loved the interior but hated the exterior, and a third who loved the location but hated the house altogether (the idea that there was one single property that would satisfy every selfish, petty, nitpicking human being in the history of the world was enough, in Eve's opinion, to invalidate the notion of a heaven for all time). Unfortunately, though, the Herschkopf house had been designated historical by the Stockton Preservation Society, so Nick and Sharon were the only couple of the three who could actually do with it what they wanted. But while the Cohens had the financial resources to make the interior changes they wanted, they had heard some horror stories about the stresses of home renovations: couples once deeply in love, now separated or worse, their relationship methodically demolished as their home was painstakingly constructed, leaving behind a two-and-a-half-thousand-square-foot, million-dollar locket for a love that no longer existed.

Home sweet home, said Eve as she led them through the front doorway. I'll leave you be.

Eve waited in the living room as Nick and Sharon toured the house the very same way they had each time before: silently, almost solemnly checking out first the kitchen, then the dining room, nodding, shrugging, whispering before heading up the stairs, brows creased, where they checked the bedrooms, argued about the closet space, and took a cursory glance of the attic overhead before coming back downstairs, stopping to whisper on the landing – Do you . . . I don't think . . . But what if . . . It just doesn't make . . . – before joining Eve back in the living room, sighing heavily and shaking their heads.

We're just . . . said Sharon. We're just a little concerned.

About the renovations, said Nick.

About the stress, said Sharon.

A little concerned? asked Eve, lighting a cigarette and blowing the smoke out the corner of her mouth. You should be more than a little concerned. I am not a religious woman, Mrs Cohen, I assure you of that, but I have no doubt God created the world in six days – He's a heckuva builder, after all. The best. But I'll tell you this: if those six days are supposed to include working with architects, hammering out blueprints, bidding out the job to contractors, and wrestling with the local planning board, well, then, may God have mercy on my soul, but Genesis is nothing but a pile of horseshit. Construction is a bitch, and I should know, I've renovated more homes than I care to remember. Trust me – before you even get the final plans done you'll want to murder the architect, strangle each other, and bury the rotting bodies in the new foundation, and that's if the goddamned mason ever arrives. And I'll tell you why: blueprints.

Blueprints? asked Nick.

Architects, said Eve, are professional liars. It's nothing personal, that's their job. We pay them to lie to us, and if the lies aren't elaborate enough, we send them back to draw new ones, bigger ones, lies with infinity pools and soapstone kitchen islands and radiant heating. Blueprints are fiction, Mr Cohen. They're fakes. They're dreams and hopes and lies. That's why we like them so much – they're complete bullshit. The sunroom will go here, and we'll have the neighbors over for dinner here, and we'll put the Jacuzzi out back, and the kids' rooms upstairs, right next to ours, so they know that we're there, beside them, forever and always and more. So you shake hands, sign some checks, break ground, and that's when it all goes wrong. That, Mrs Cohen, is when all that wonderful fiction becomes horribly, terribly nonfiction. That's where the stress starts, when the fiction is revealed. That's why people love architects but hate builders; builders deal with the dreary muck of nonfiction; architects lie and builders have to call them on it. You see, it turns out there are drainage issues. The well's run dry. The foundation isn't level. The sunroom actually faces north, so there's not much sun in there to speak of, and you can forget about those parties because the neighbors are all assholes who refused your request for a variance; the Jacuzzi makes a racket and eats electricity, and you discover, when all is said and done and the work is finally completed and at long last the pickup trucks leave, that something is wrong with your genitals: your tubes are blocked, or his tubes are blocked, or his balls are too hot or your uterus is too cold, so those extra bedrooms you spent the line of credit on will now be nothing more than empty twelve-by-twenty reminders of the family you will never have. And so, faced with all this hideous, horrible nonfiction, we crack. We crumble. And we should. Reality is a nightmare. And so we shout, we shriek, we try to blame this nonfiction on each other. And you realize suddenly that you were better off before the fiction was ever written. But it's too late now, Adam, you can't go back; so sorry, Eve, you can't put that apple back on the tree.

So what's the answer? asked Sharon.

Eve stubbed out her cigarette on the top of the woodstove.

You can't go on renovating, she said with a sigh, you go on renovating. Because if you somehow muddle through, something amazing happens. A month, or two, or three down the road, the fiction returns. You find yourself sitting in front of the woodstove, watching the flames and sipping some wine and remembering your times in the house as better than they ever were. You rewrite it all: Remember the first time the electric came on? you'll say with a smile. Remember how exciting it was when they finished framing the bedrooms, remember how much fun we had painting the bathrooms, remember when the appliances arrived that evening and we cooked our first dinner in our new home and afterward we made love in the kitchen? Some people will rewrite the past as better than it was, some people will rewrite it as worse – the builder was an anti-Semite, the homosexual architect hated us because we were straight – but one way or the other, I promise you, fiction will return, if only because the nonfiction is too damned much to bear.

She raised up her hand and dangled the house keys between her thumb and index finger.

Do we have a deal? she asked.

Nick looked to Sharon, squeezed her hand and smiled.

Sharon smiled at Nick.

Nick smiled at Eve.

Eve smiled at Sharon.

Sharon inhaled deeply through her nose.

What about that smell? she asked.